ELSEWHERE

CREATED BY
JAY FAERBER & SUMEYYE KESGIN

IMAGE COMICS, INC.

Robert Kirkman—Chief Operating Officer
Erik Larsen—Chief Financial Officer
Todd McFarlane—President
Marc Silvestri—Chief Executive Officer
Jim Valentino—Vice President
Eric Stephenson—Publisher
Corey Hart—Director of Sales
Jeff Boison—Director of Publishing Planning & Book Trade Sales
Chris Ross—Director of Digital Sales
Jeff Stang—Director of Specialty Sales
Kat Salazar—Director of PR & Marketing
Drew Gill—Art Director
Heather Doornink—Production Director
Branwyn Bigglestone—Controller

www.imagecomics.com

ELSEWHERE, VOL. 1
ISBN: 978-1-5343-0469-7
First Printing. January 2018.

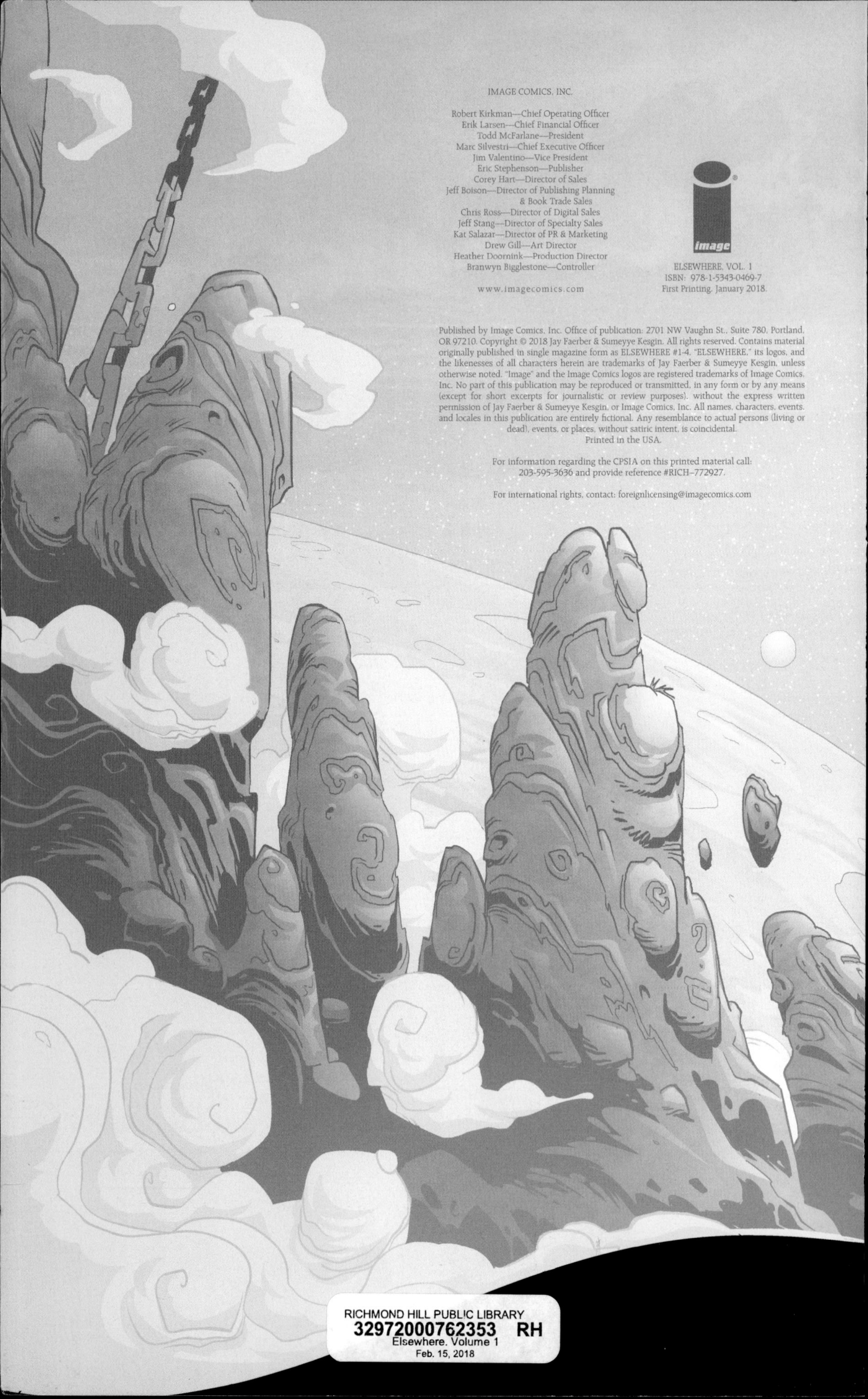

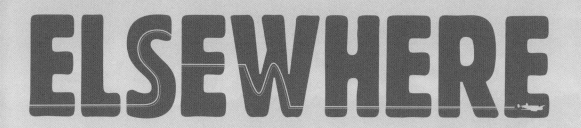

ELSEWHERE

WRITER
JAY FAERBER

ARTIST
SUMEYYE KESGIN

COLORIST
RON RILEY

LETTERER/DESIGNER
THOMAS MAUER

EDITOR
FRANK PITTARESE

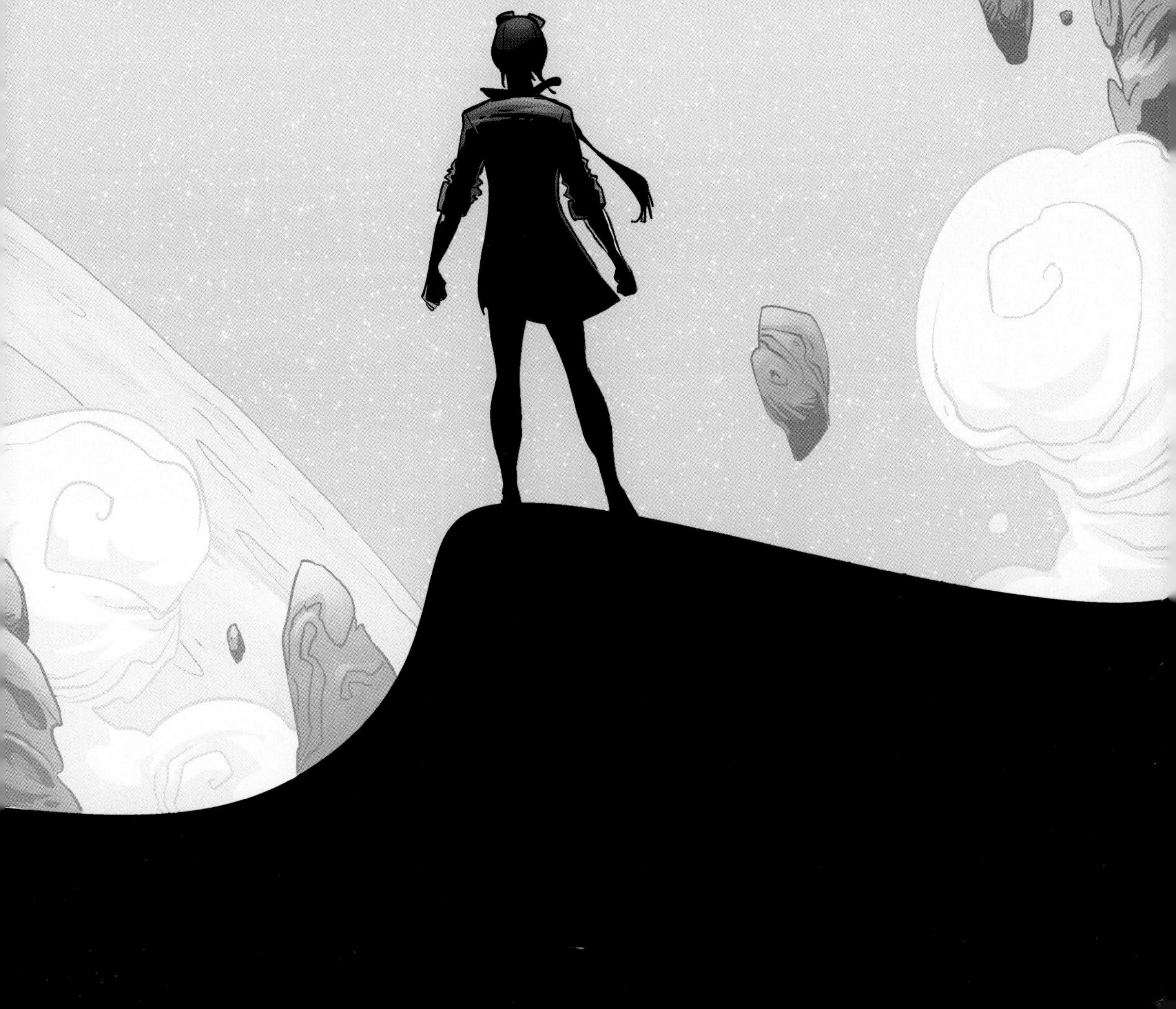

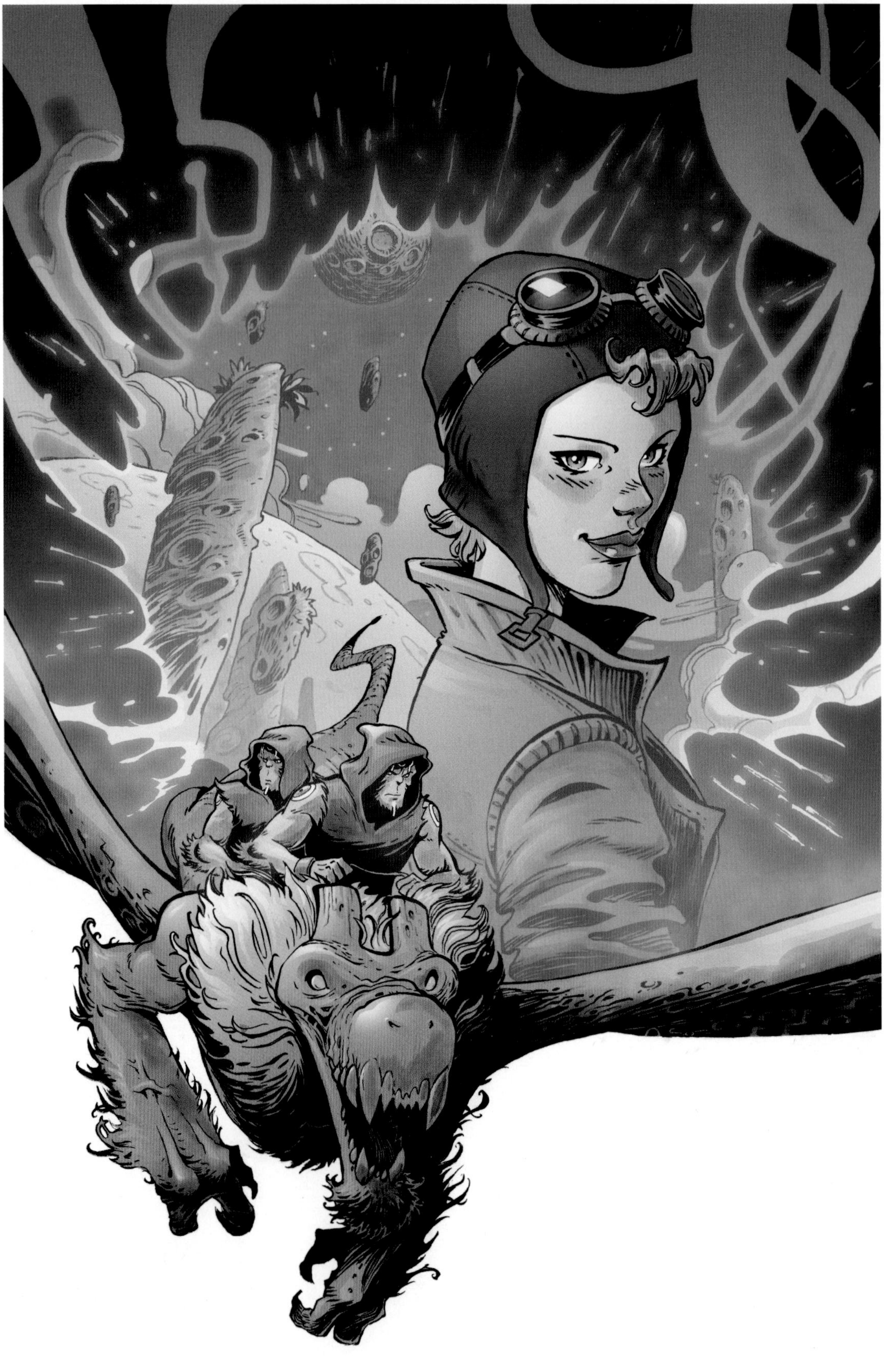

CHAPTER 1

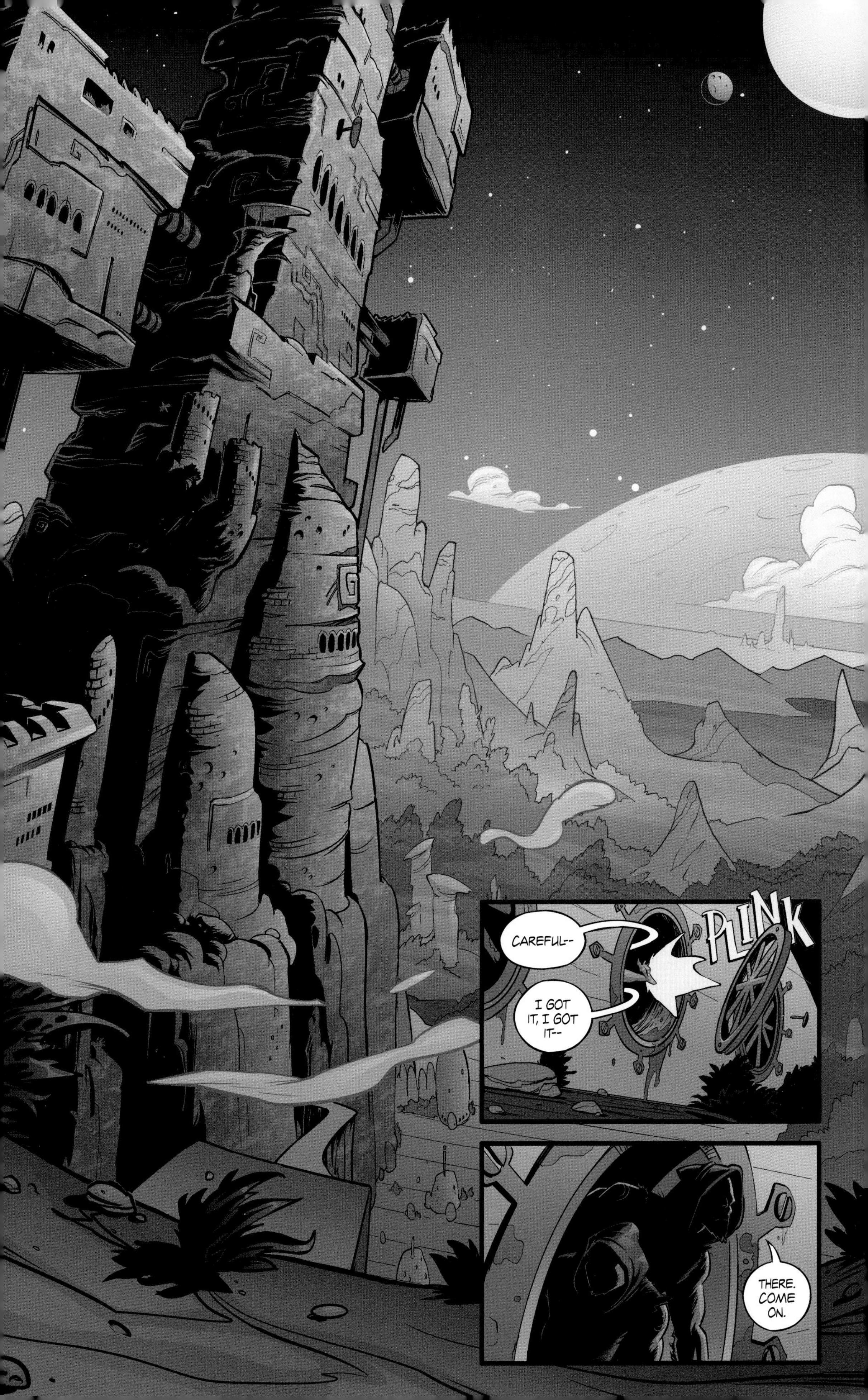
PLINK
CAREFUL--
I GOT IT, I GOT IT--
THERE. COME ON.

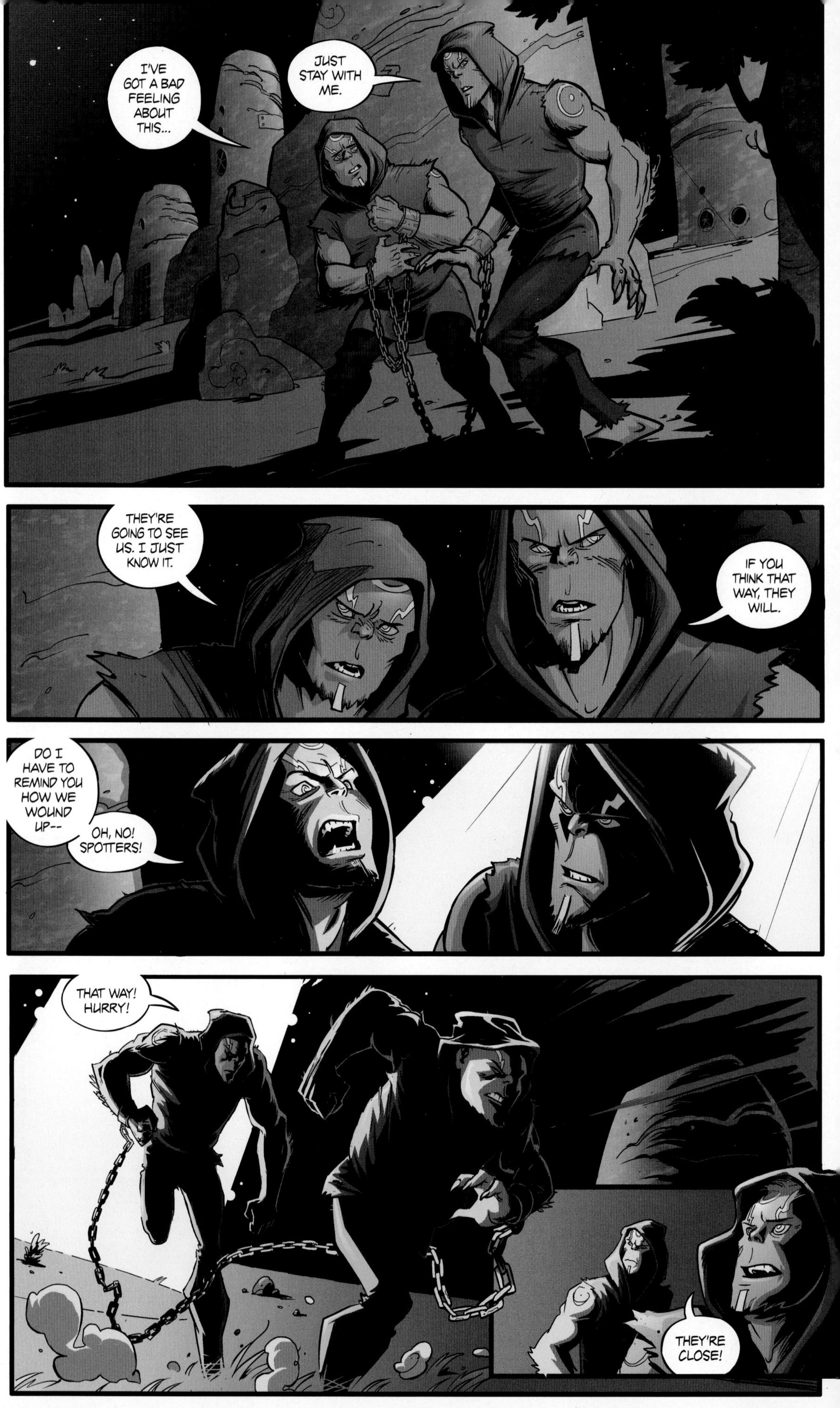
I'VE GOT A BAD FEELING ABOUT THIS...
JUST STAY WITH ME.
THEY'RE GOING TO SEE US. I JUST KNOW IT.
IF YOU THINK THAT WAY, THEY WILL.
DO I HAVE TO REMIND YOU HOW WE WOUND UP--
OH, NO! SPOTTERS!
THAT WAY! HURRY!
THEY'RE CLOSE!

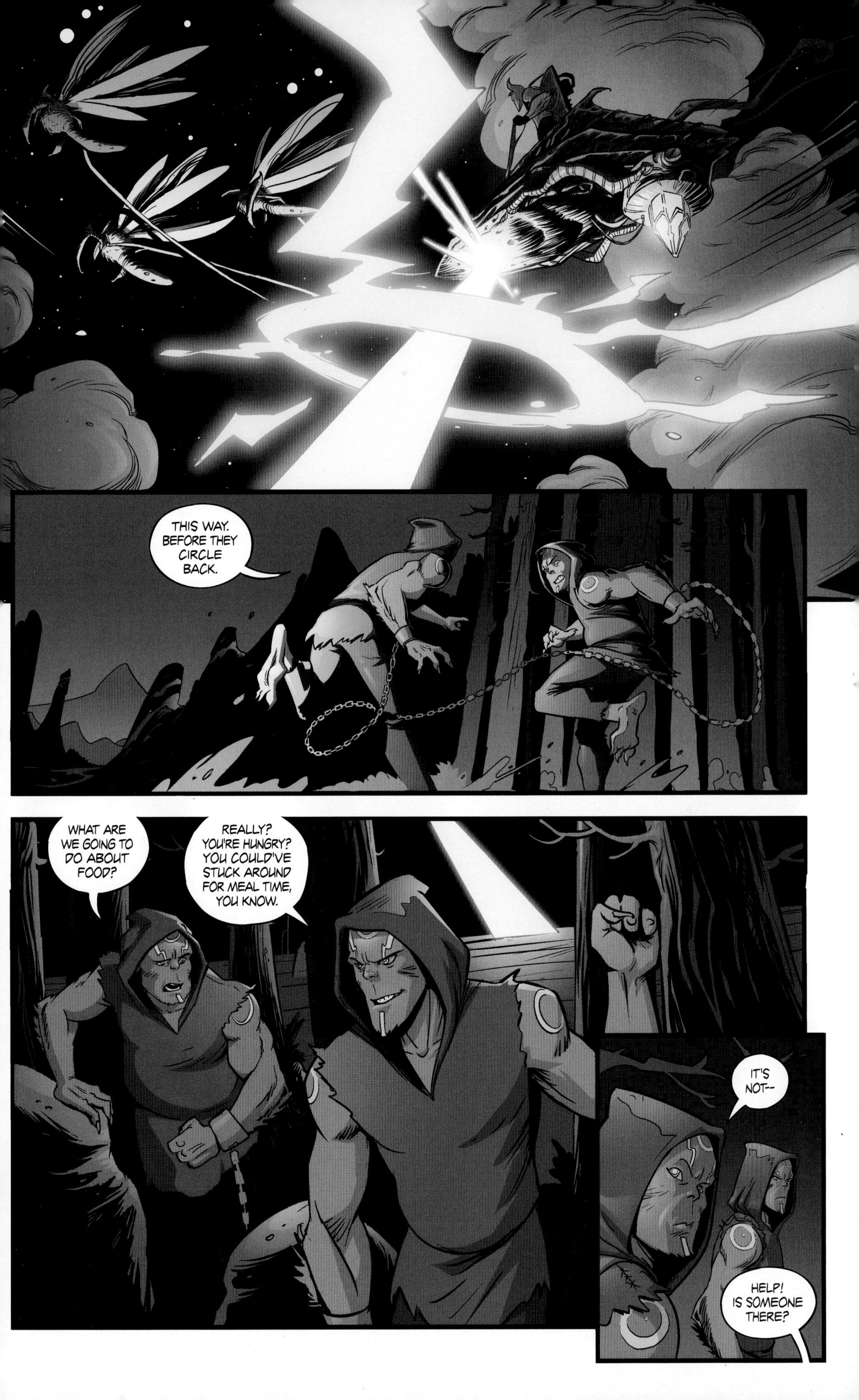
THIS WAY. BEFORE THEY CIRCLE BACK.
WHAT ARE WE GOING TO DO ABOUT FOOD?
REALLY? YOU'RE HUNGRY? YOU COULD'VE STUCK AROUND FOR MEAL TIME, YOU KNOW.
IT'S NOT--
HELP! IS SOMEONE THERE?

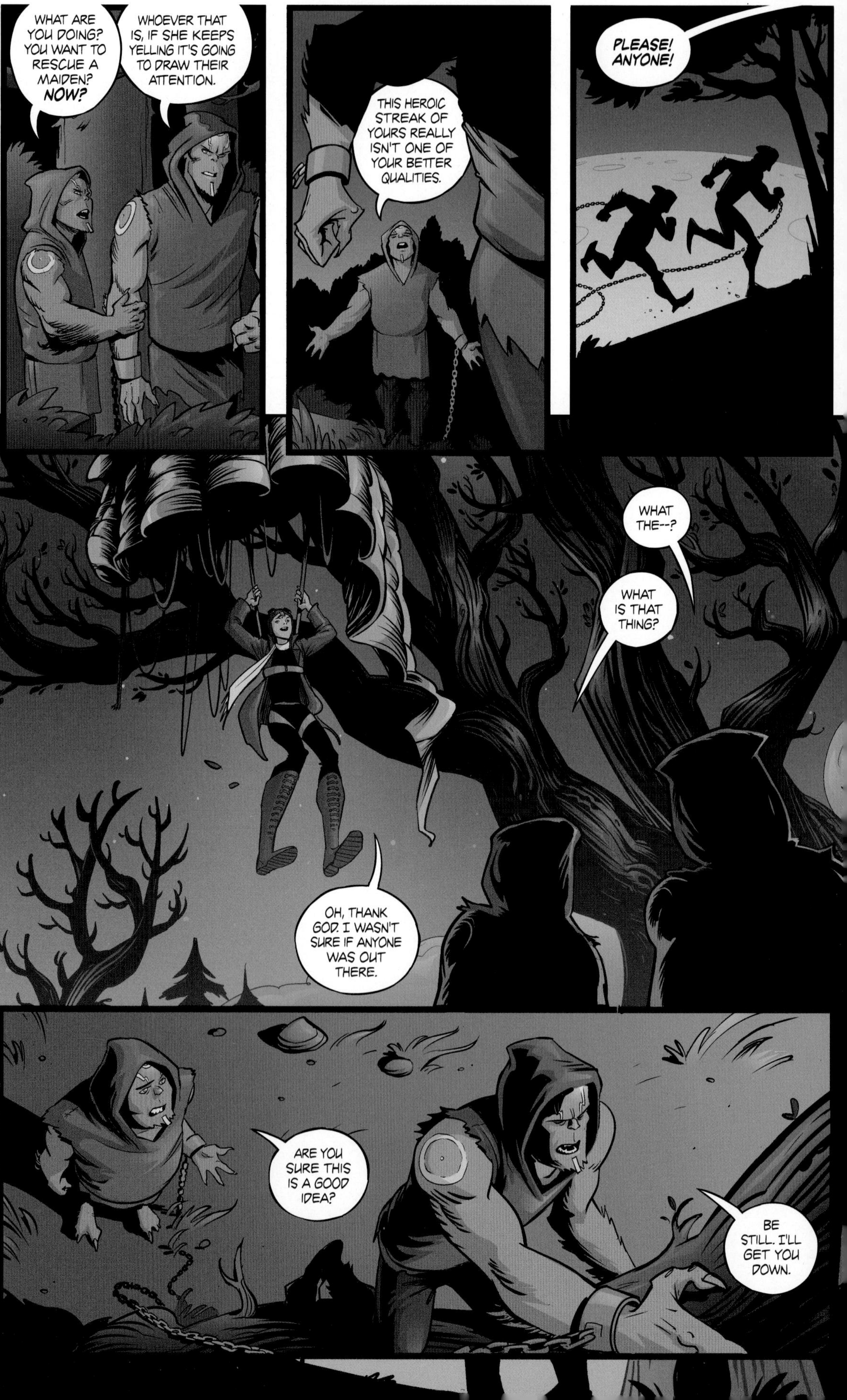
WHAT ARE YOU DOING? YOU WANT TO RESCUE A MAIDEN? NOW?
WHOEVER THAT IS, IF SHE KEEPS YELLING IT'S GOING TO DRAW THEIR ATTENTION.
THIS HEROIC STREAK OF YOURS REALLY ISN'T ONE OF YOUR BETTER QUALITIES.
PLEASE! ANYONE!
WHAT THE--?
WHAT IS THAT THING?
OH, THANK GOD. I WASN'T SURE IF ANYONE WAS OUT THERE.
ARE YOU SURE THIS IS A GOOD IDEA?
BE STILL. I'LL GET YOU DOWN.

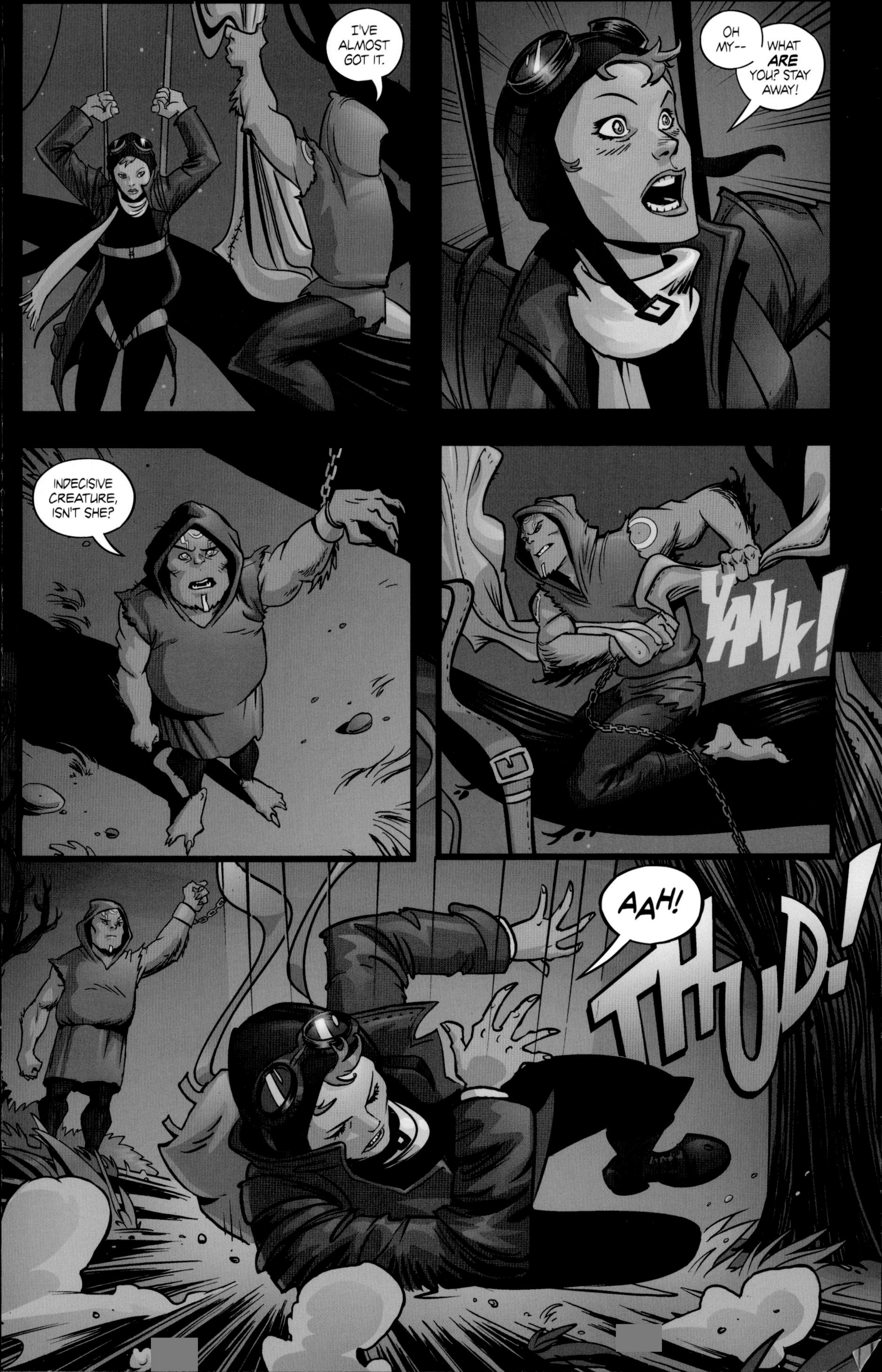
I'VE ALMOST GOT IT.
OH MY--
WHAT ARE YOU? STAY AWAY!
INDECISIVE CREATURE, ISN'T SHE?
YANK!
AAH!
THUD!

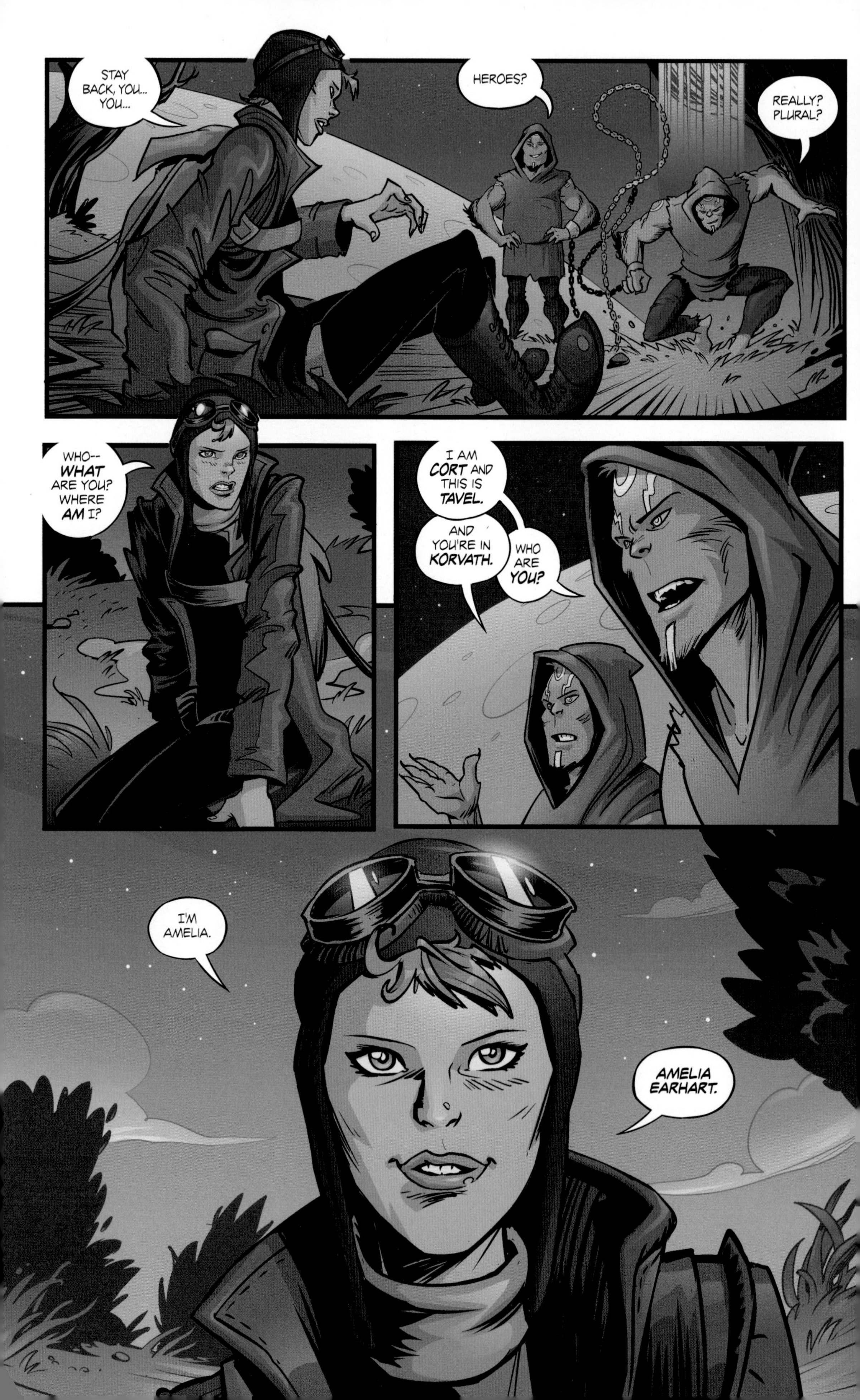
STAY BACK, YOU... YOU...
HEROES?
REALLY? PLURAL?
WHO-- WHAT ARE YOU? WHERE AM I?
I AM CORT AND THIS IS TAVEL.
AND YOU'RE IN KORVATH.
WHO ARE YOU?
I'M AMELIA.
AMELIA EARHART.

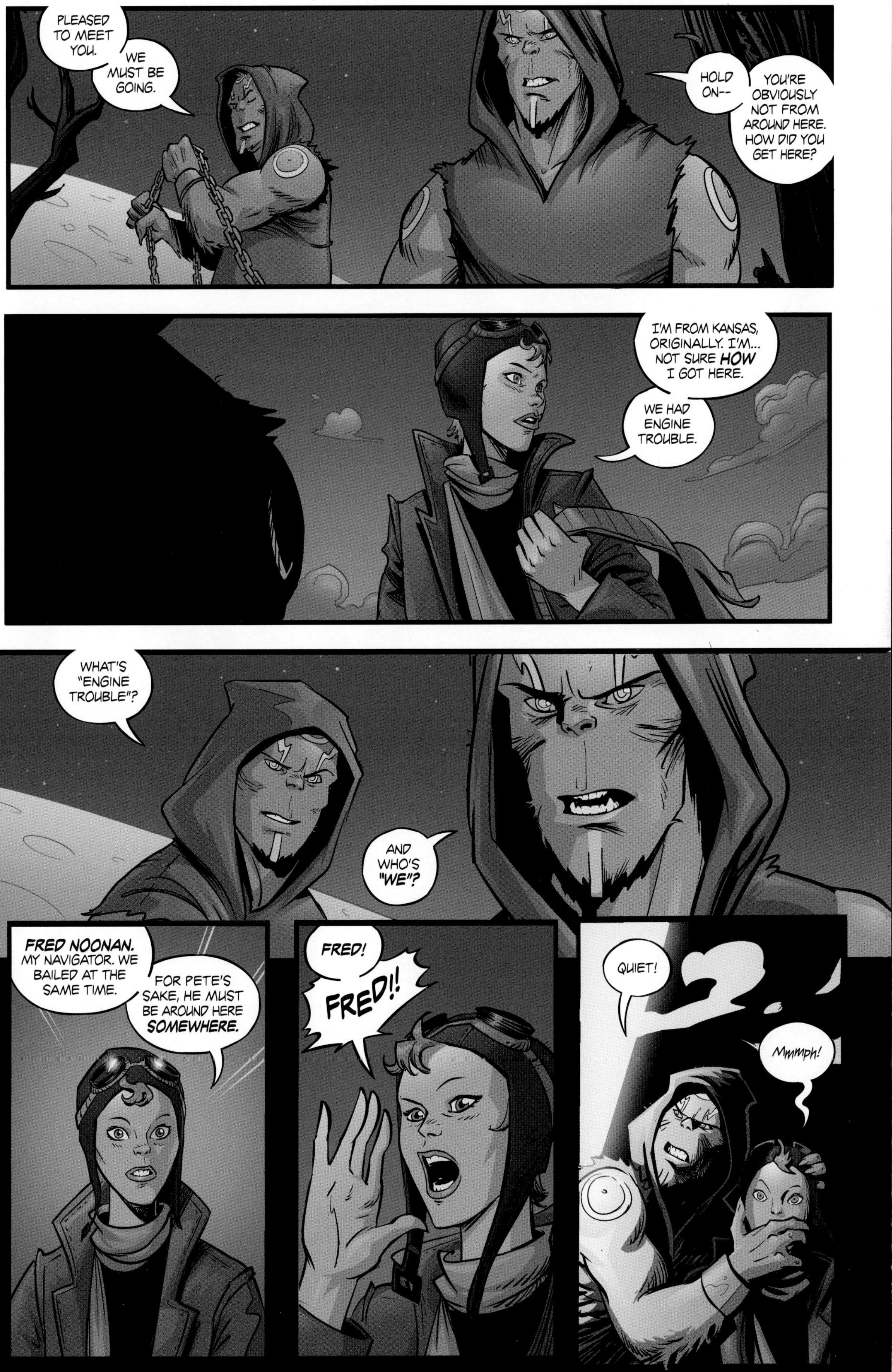
PLEASED TO MEET YOU.
WE MUST BE GOING.
HOLD ON--
YOU'RE OBVIOUSLY NOT FROM AROUND HERE. HOW DID YOU GET HERE?
I'M FROM KANSAS, ORIGINALLY. I'M... NOT SURE **HOW** I GOT HERE.
WE HAD ENGINE TROUBLE.
WHAT'S "ENGINE TROUBLE"?
AND WHO'S **"WE"**?
FRED NOONAN. MY NAVIGATOR. WE BAILED AT THE SAME TIME.
FOR PETE'S SAKE, HE MUST BE AROUND HERE **SOMEWHERE.**
FRED!
FRED!!
QUIET!
Mmmph!

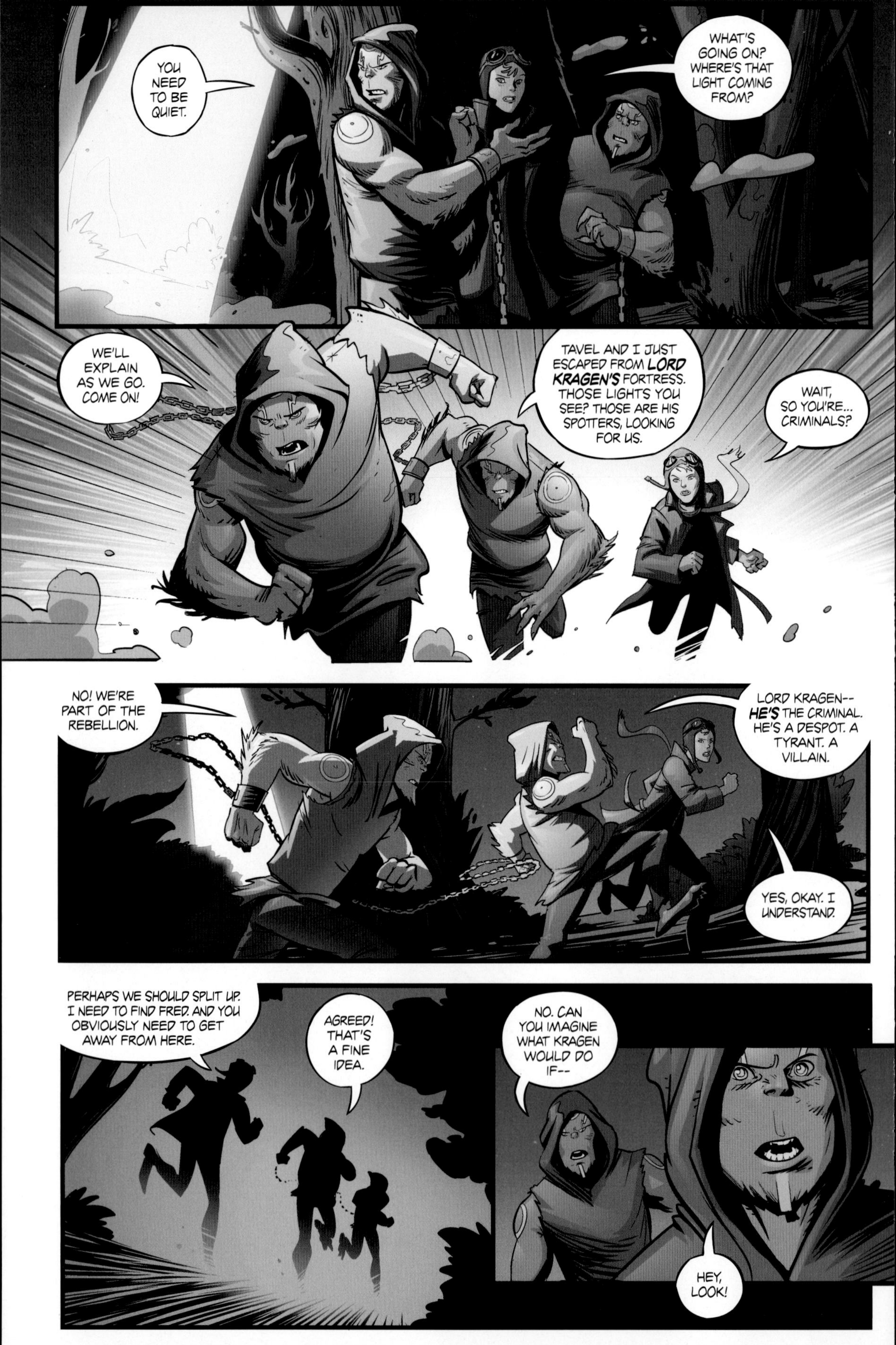
YOU NEED TO BE QUIET.
WHAT'S GOING ON? WHERE'S THAT LIGHT COMING FROM?
WE'LL EXPLAIN AS WE GO. COME ON!
TAVEL AND I JUST ESCAPED FROM LORD KRAGEN'S FORTRESS. THOSE LIGHTS YOU SEE? THOSE ARE HIS SPOTTERS, LOOKING FOR US.
WAIT, SO YOU'RE... CRIMINALS?
NO! WE'RE PART OF THE REBELLION.
LORD KRAGEN-- HE'S THE CRIMINAL. HE'S A DESPOT. A TYRANT. A VILLAIN.
YES, OKAY. I UNDERSTAND.
PERHAPS WE SHOULD SPLIT UP. I NEED TO FIND FRED. AND YOU OBVIOUSLY NEED TO GET AWAY FROM HERE.
AGREED! THAT'S A FINE IDEA.
NO. CAN YOU IMAGINE WHAT KRAGEN WOULD DO IF--
HEY, LOOK!

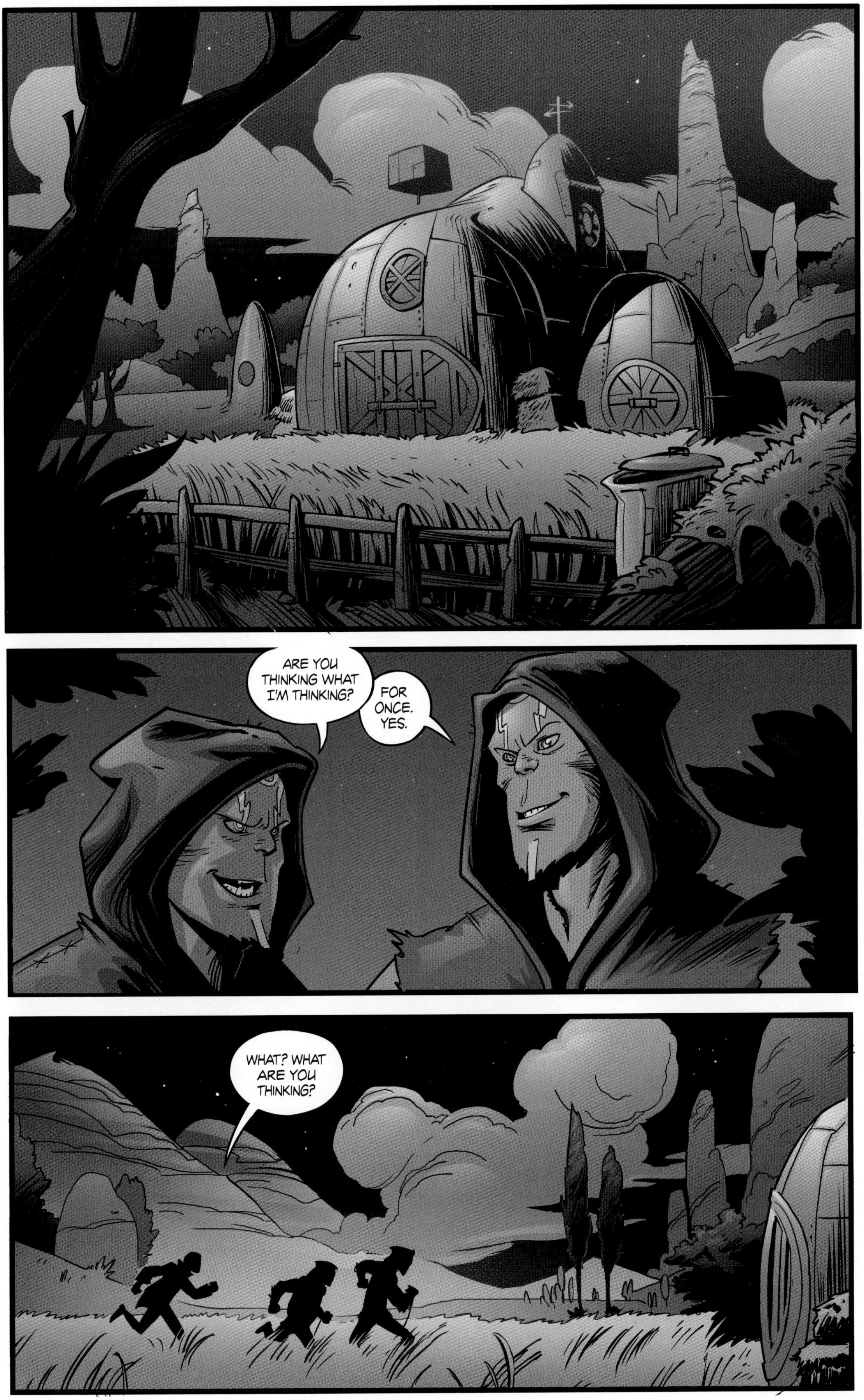
ARE YOU THINKING WHAT I'M THINKING?
FOR ONCE. YES.
WHAT? WHAT ARE YOU THINKING?

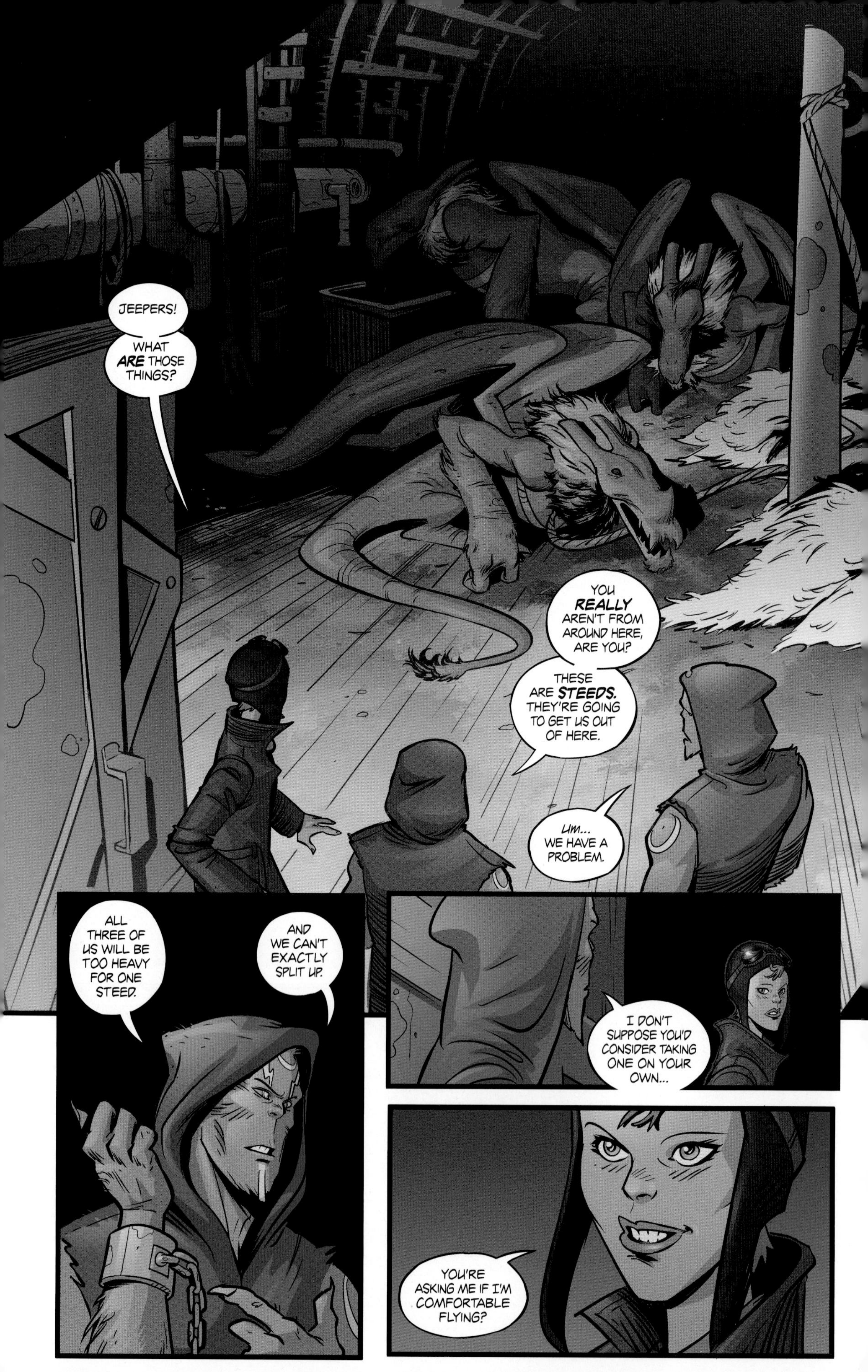
JEEPERS!
WHAT ARE THOSE THINGS?
YOU REALLY AREN'T FROM AROUND HERE, ARE YOU?
THESE ARE STEEDS. THEY'RE GOING TO GET US OUT OF HERE.
UM... WE HAVE A PROBLEM.
ALL THREE OF US WILL BE TOO HEAVY FOR ONE STEED.
AND WE CAN'T EXACTLY SPLIT UP.
I DON'T SUPPOSE YOU'D CONSIDER TAKING ONE ON YOUR OWN...
YOU'RE ASKING ME IF I'M COMFORTABLE FLYING?

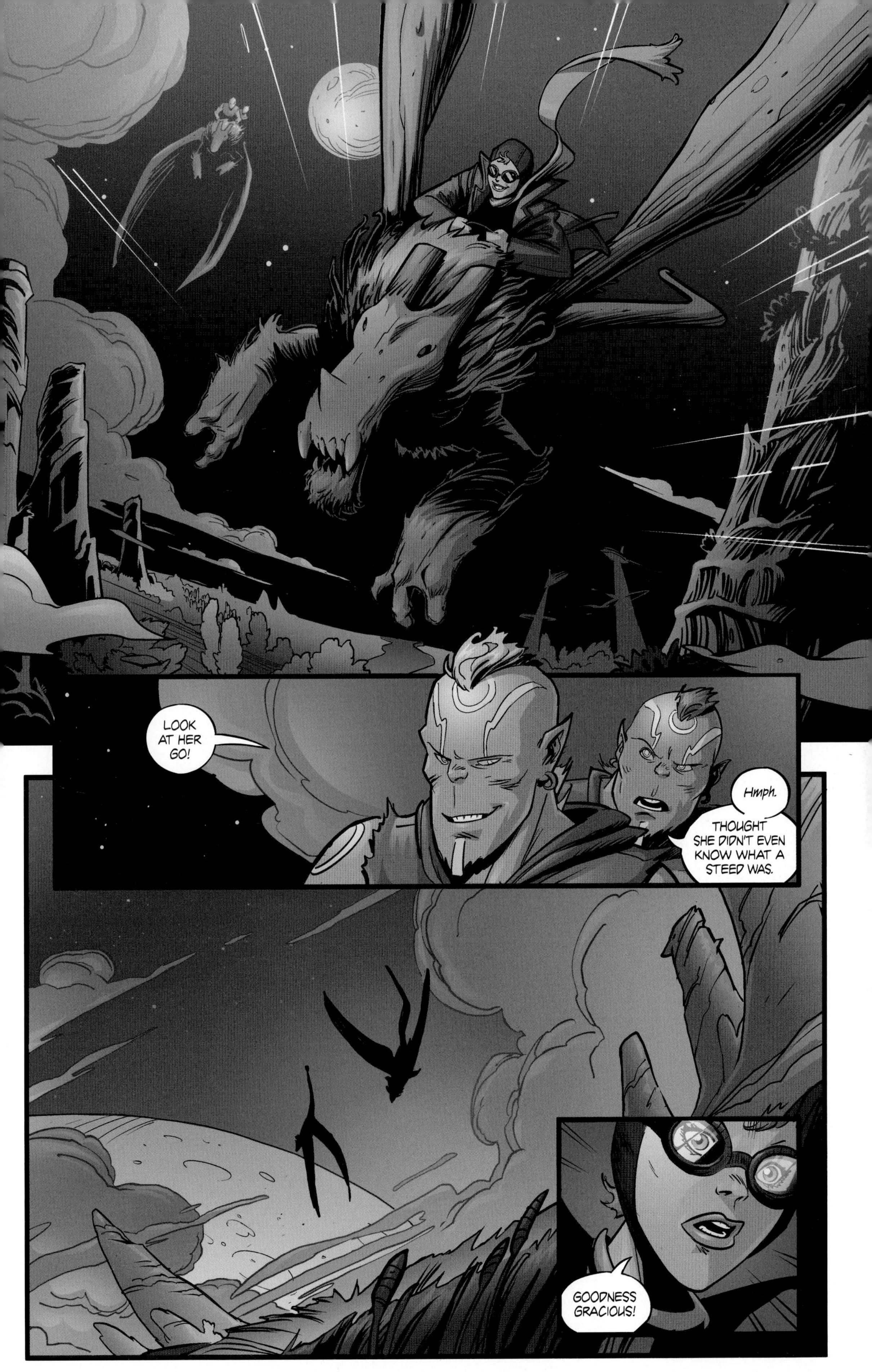
LOOK AT HER GO!
Hmph.
THOUGHT SHE DIDN'T EVEN KNOW WHAT A STEED WAS.
GOODNESS GRACIOUS!

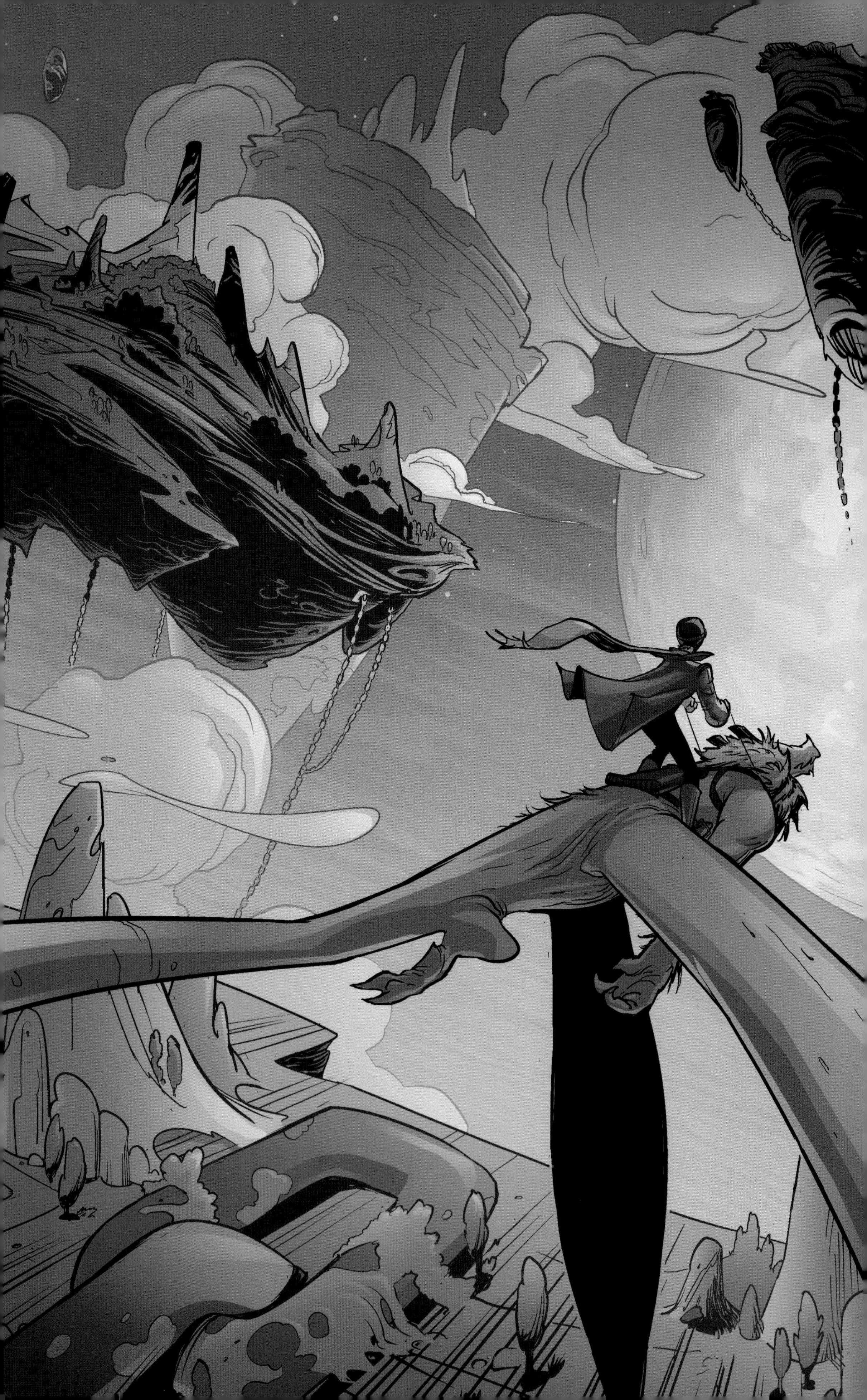

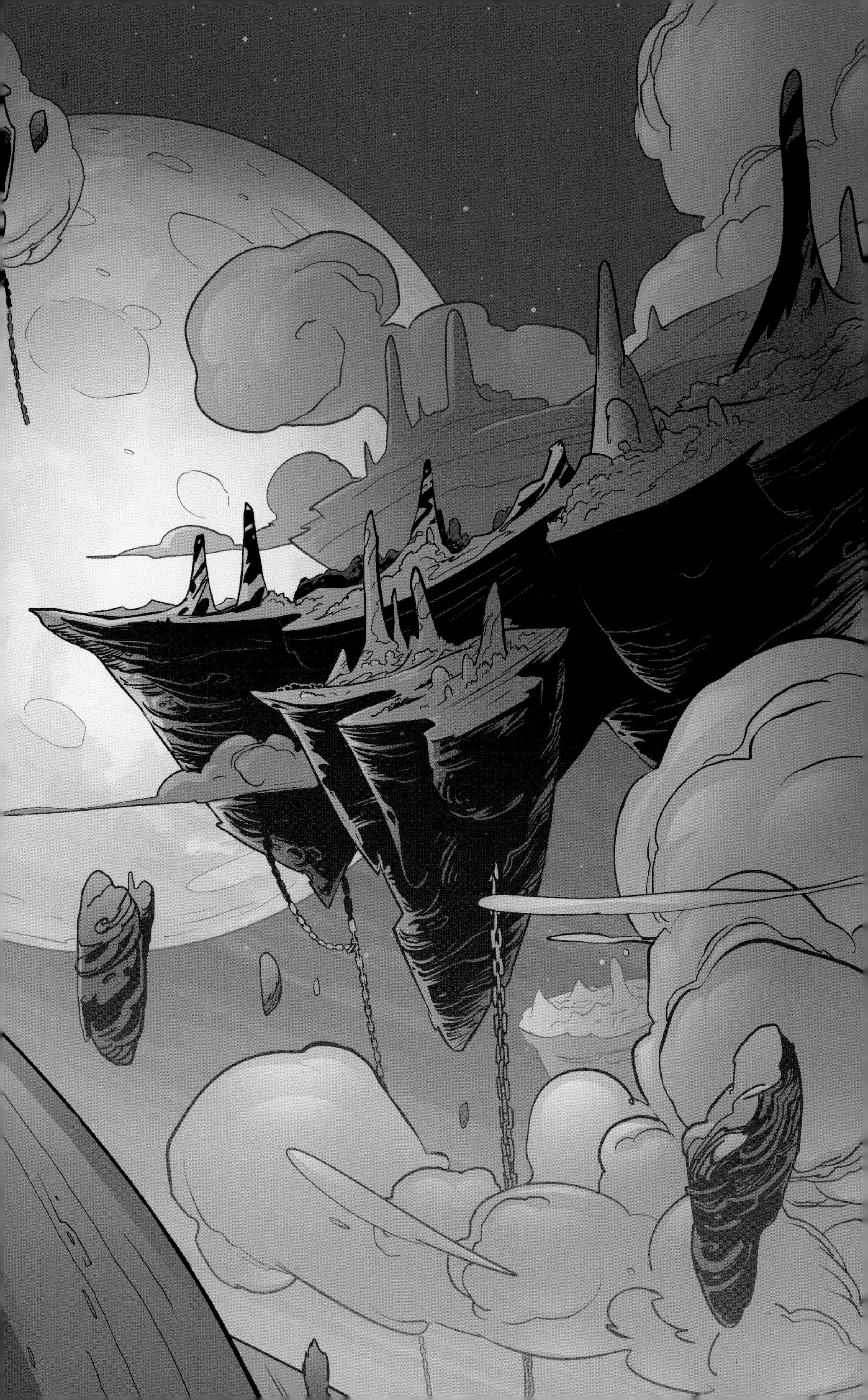

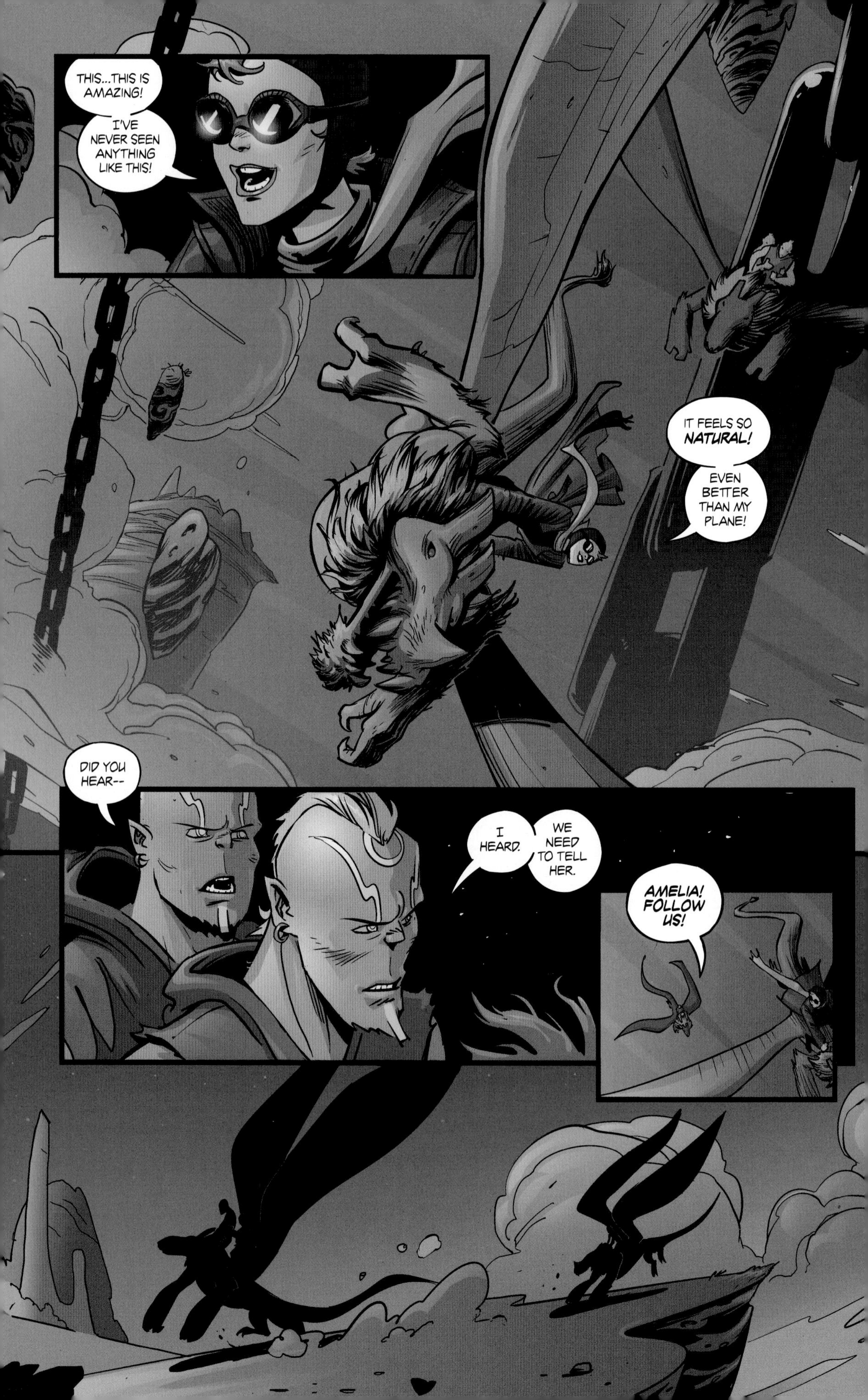
THIS...THIS IS AMAZING!
I'VE NEVER SEEN ANYTHING LIKE THIS!
IT FEELS SO NATURAL!
EVEN BETTER THAN MY PLANE!
DID YOU HEAR--
I HEARD.
WE NEED TO TELL HER.
AMELIA! FOLLOW US!

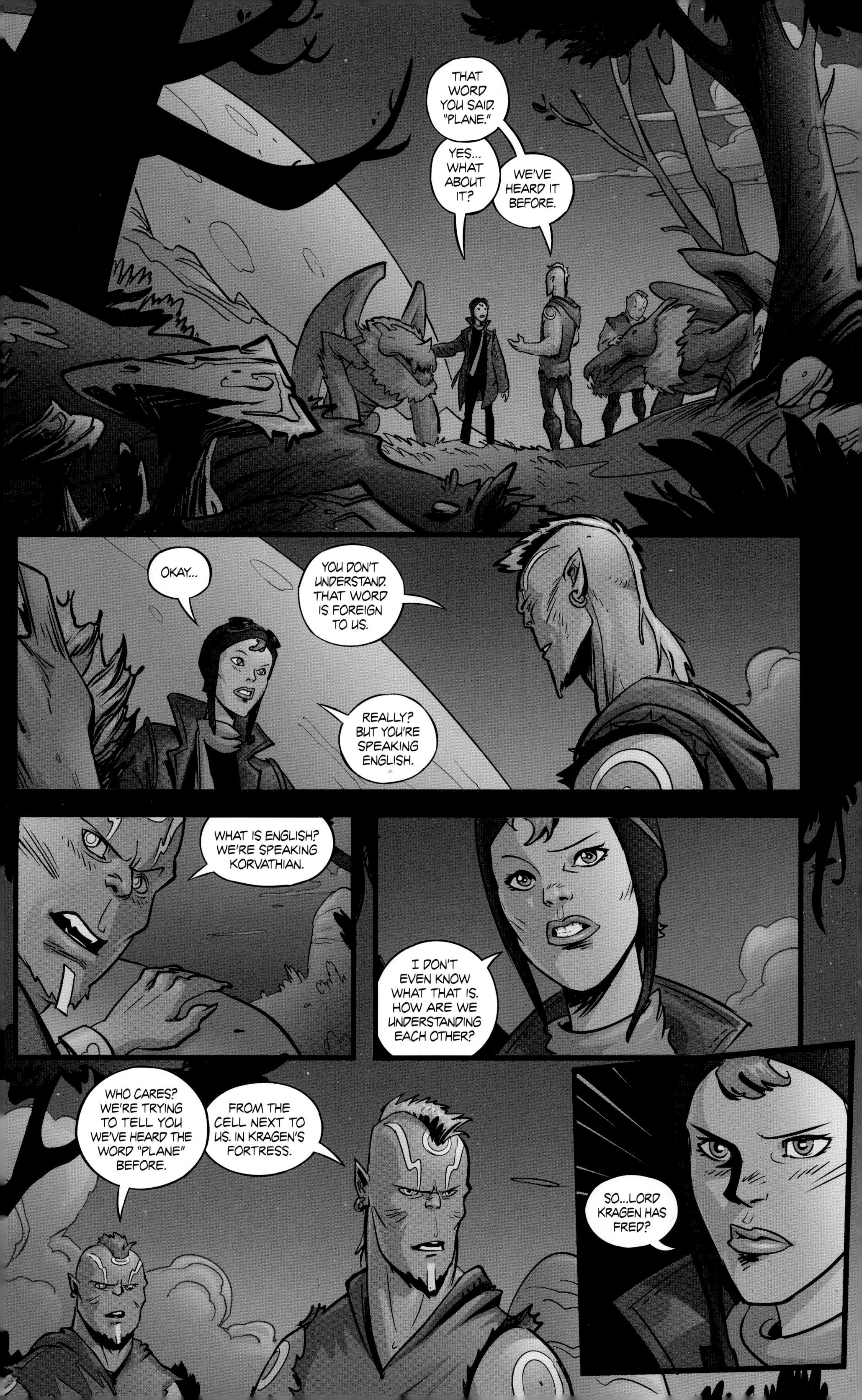
THAT WORD YOU SAID. "PLANE."
YES... WHAT ABOUT IT?
WE'VE HEARD IT BEFORE.
OKAY...
YOU DON'T UNDERSTAND. THAT WORD IS FOREIGN TO US.
REALLY? BUT YOU'RE SPEAKING ENGLISH.
WHAT IS ENGLISH? WE'RE SPEAKING KORVATHIAN.
I DON'T EVEN KNOW WHAT THAT IS. HOW ARE WE UNDERSTANDING EACH OTHER?
WHO CARES? WE'RE TRYING TO TELL YOU WE'VE HEARD THE WORD "PLANE" BEFORE.
FROM THE CELL NEXT TO US. IN KRAGEN'S FORTRESS.
SO...LORD KRAGEN HAS FRED?

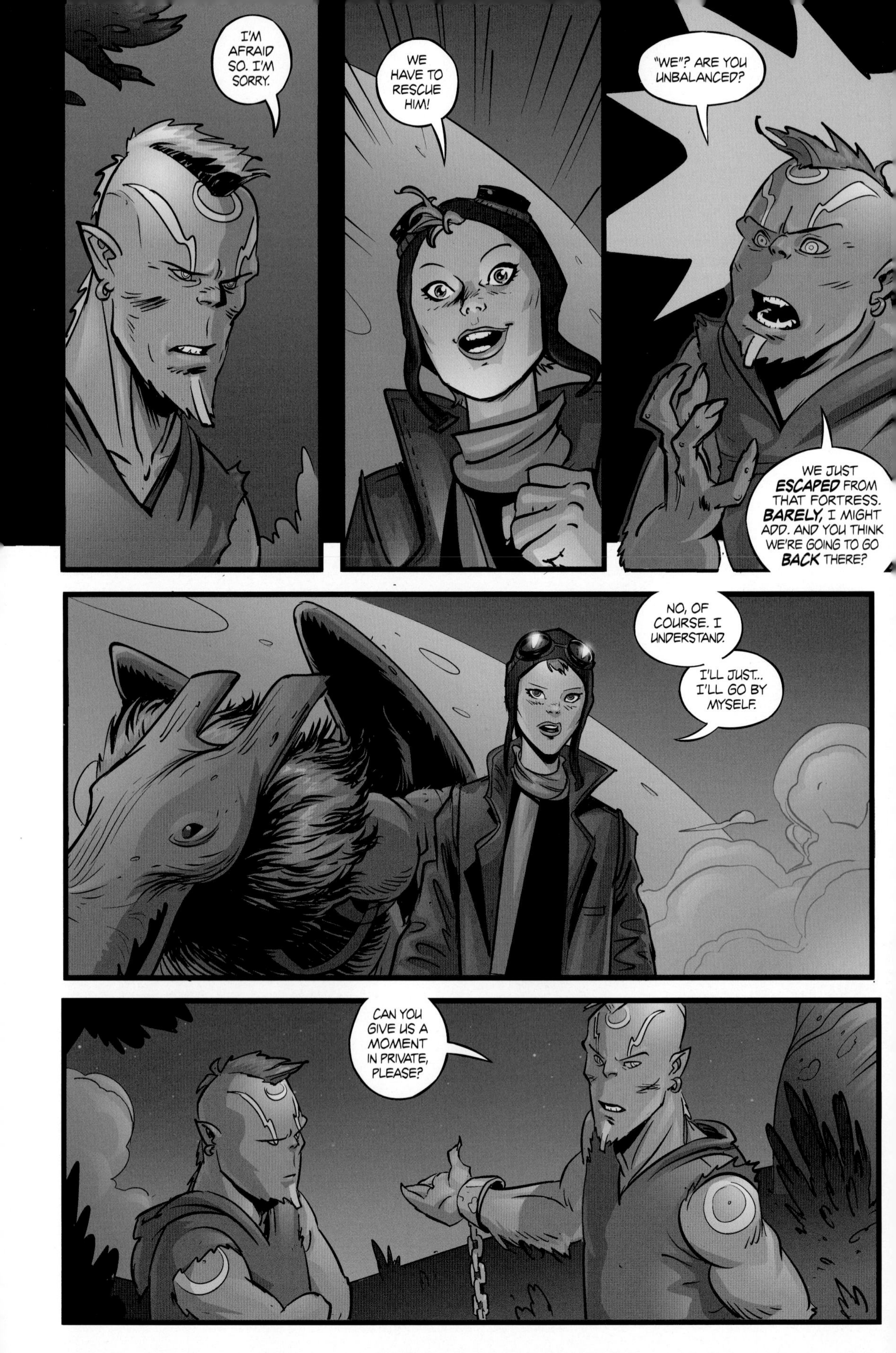
I'M AFRAID SO. I'M SORRY.
WE HAVE TO RESCUE HIM!
"WE"? ARE YOU UNBALANCED?
WE JUST ESCAPED FROM THAT FORTRESS. BARELY, I MIGHT ADD. AND YOU THINK WE'RE GOING TO GO BACK THERE?
NO, OF COURSE. I UNDERSTAND.
I'LL JUST... I'LL GO BY MYSELF.
CAN YOU GIVE US A MOMENT IN PRIVATE, PLEASE?

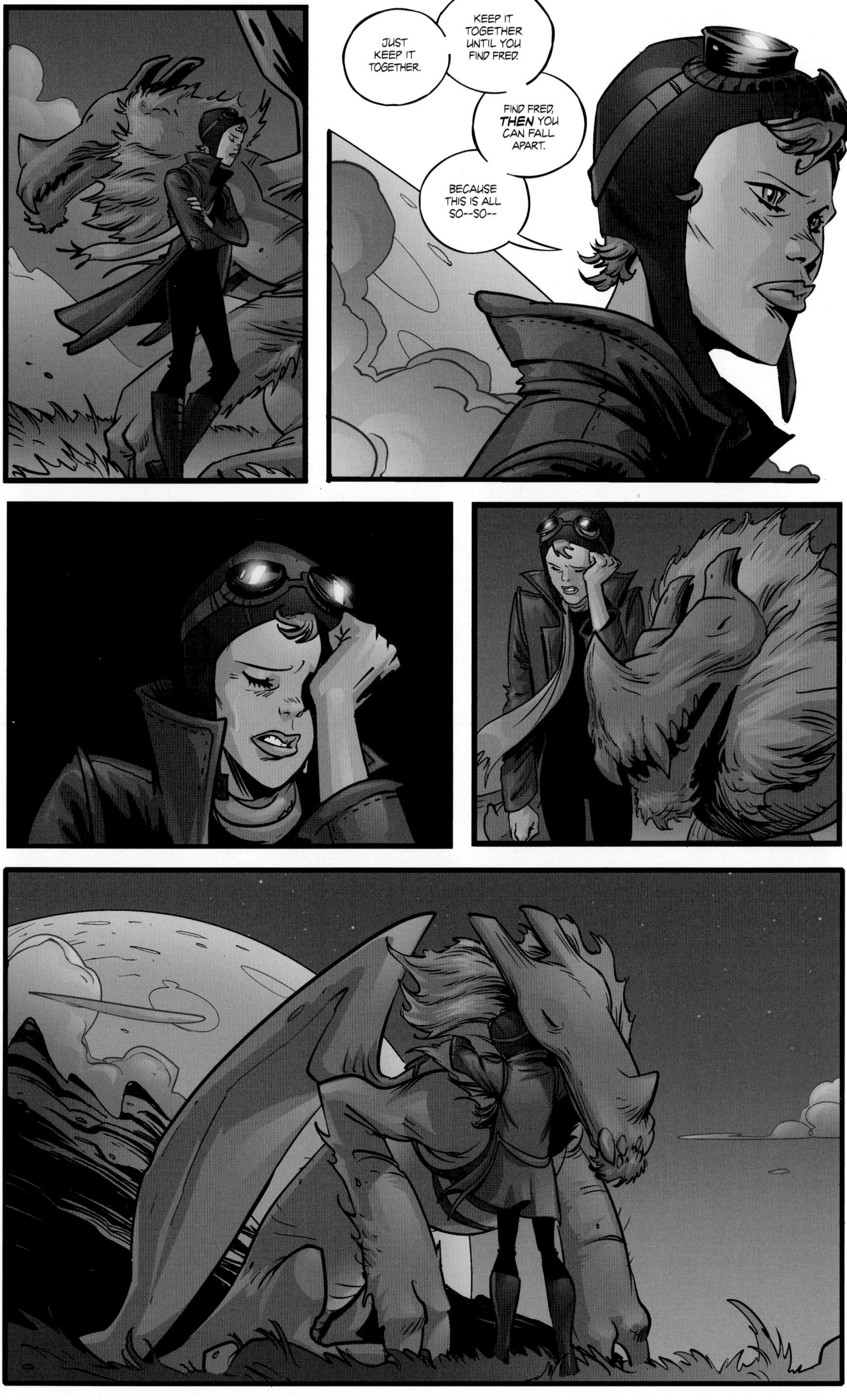
JUST KEEP IT TOGETHER.
KEEP IT TOGETHER UNTIL YOU FIND FRED.
FIND FRED, **THEN** YOU CAN FALL APART.
BECAUSE THIS IS ALL SO--SO--

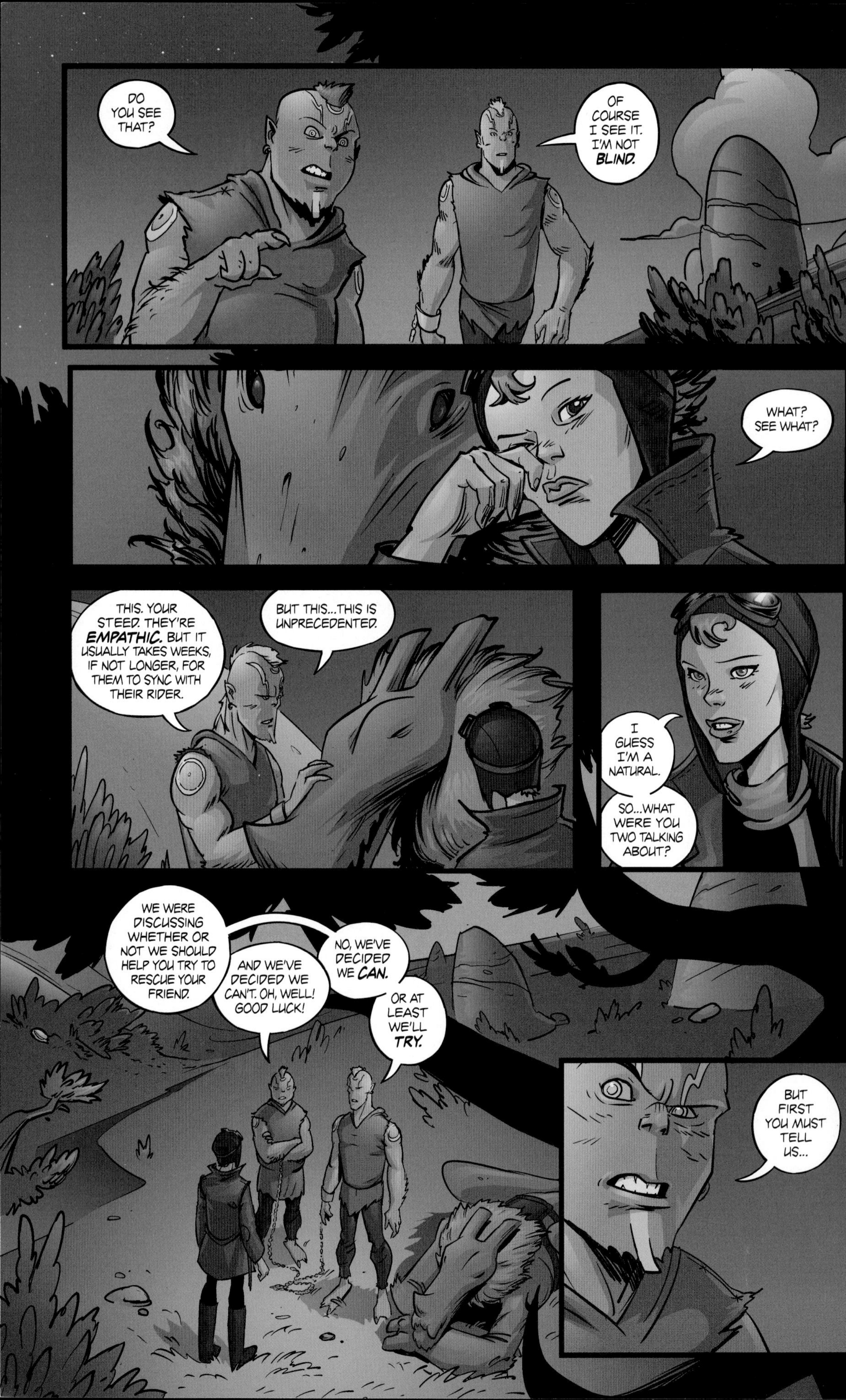
DO YOU SEE THAT?
OF COURSE I SEE IT. I'M NOT **BLIND.**
WHAT? SEE WHAT?
THIS. YOUR STEED. THEY'RE **EMPATHIC.** BUT IT USUALLY TAKES WEEKS, IF NOT LONGER, FOR THEM TO SYNC WITH THEIR RIDER.
BUT THIS...THIS IS UNPRECEDENTED.
I GUESS I'M A NATURAL.
SO...WHAT WERE YOU TWO TALKING ABOUT?
WE WERE DISCUSSING WHETHER OR NOT WE SHOULD HELP YOU TRY TO RESCUE YOUR FRIEND.
AND WE'VE DECIDED WE CAN'T. OH, WELL! GOOD LUCK!
NO, WE'VE DECIDED WE **CAN.**
OR AT LEAST WE'LL **TRY.**
BUT FIRST YOU MUST TELL US...

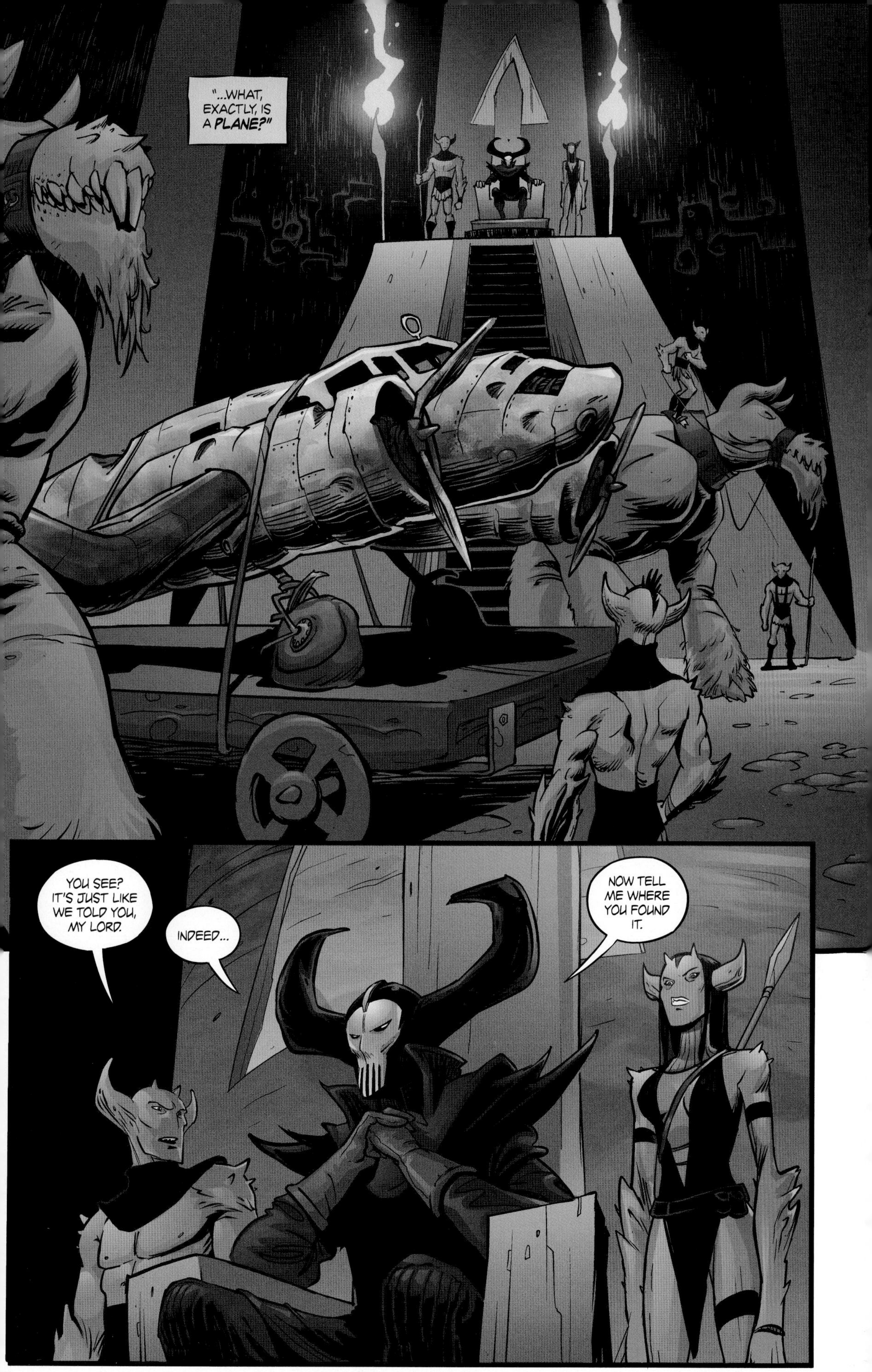
"...WHAT, EXACTLY, IS A *PLANE?*"
YOU SEE? IT'S JUST LIKE WE TOLD YOU, MY LORD.
INDEED...
NOW TELL ME WHERE YOU FOUND IT.

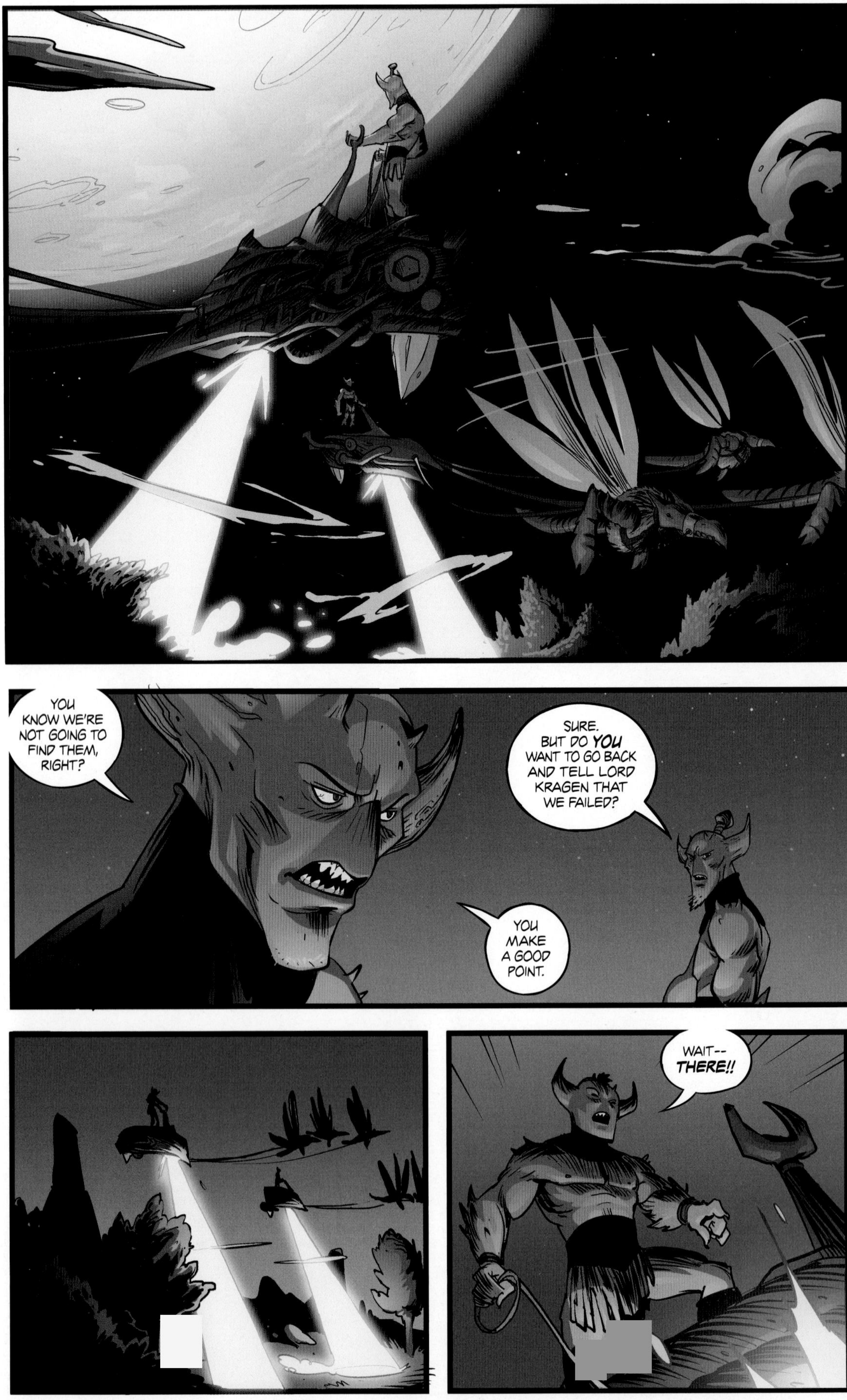
YOU KNOW WE'RE NOT GOING TO FIND THEM, RIGHT?
SURE. BUT DO **YOU** WANT TO GO BACK AND TELL LORD KRAGEN THAT WE FAILED?
YOU MAKE A GOOD POINT.
WAIT-- **THERE!!**

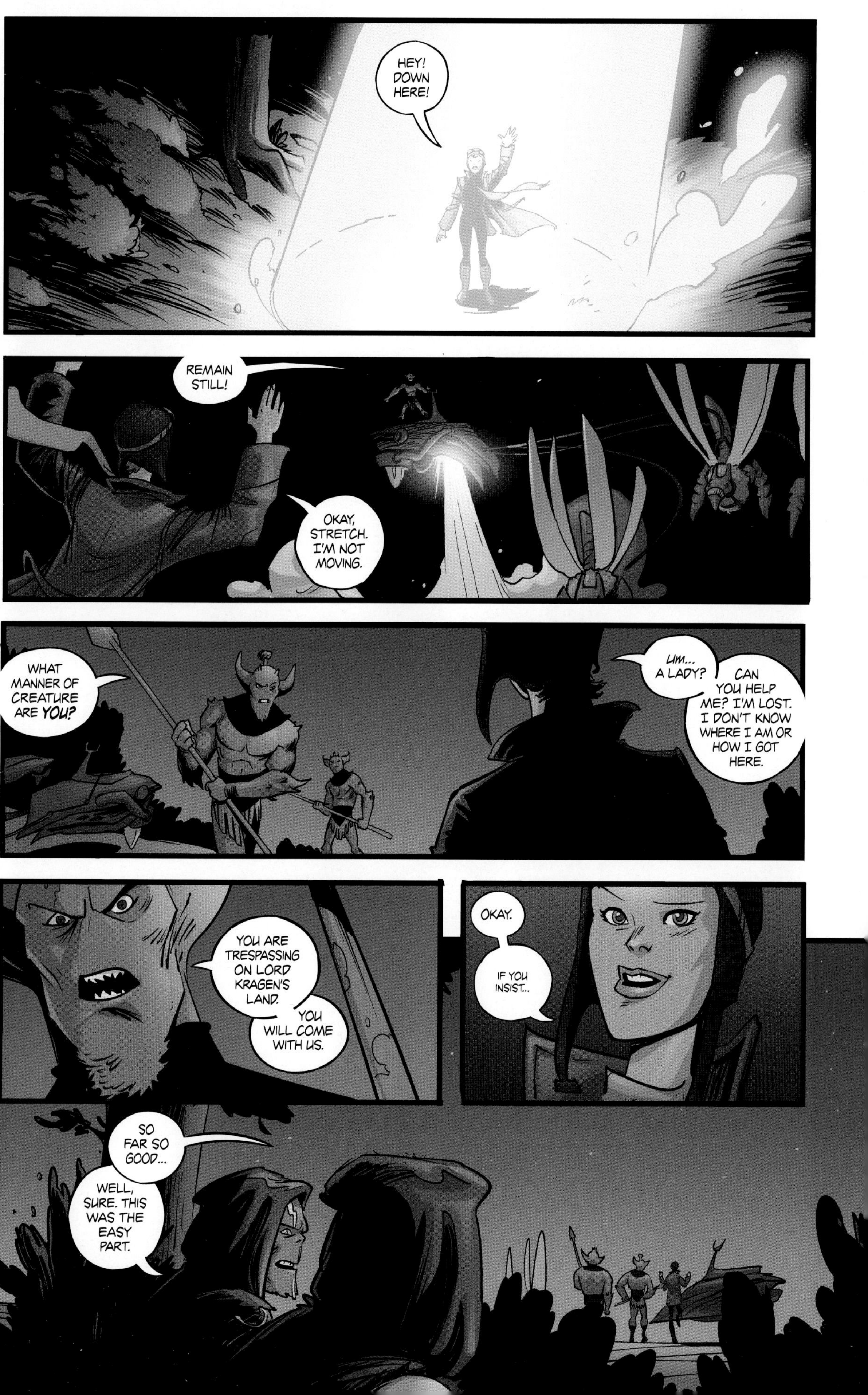
HEY! DOWN HERE!
REMAIN STILL!
OKAY, STRETCH. I'M NOT MOVING.
WHAT MANNER OF CREATURE ARE *YOU?*
UM... A LADY?
CAN YOU HELP ME? I'M LOST. I DON'T KNOW WHERE I AM OR HOW I GOT HERE.
YOU ARE TRESPASSING ON LORD KRAGEN'S LAND.
YOU WILL COME WITH US.
OKAY.
IF YOU INSIST...
SO FAR SO GOOD...
WELL, SURE. THIS WAS THE EASY PART.

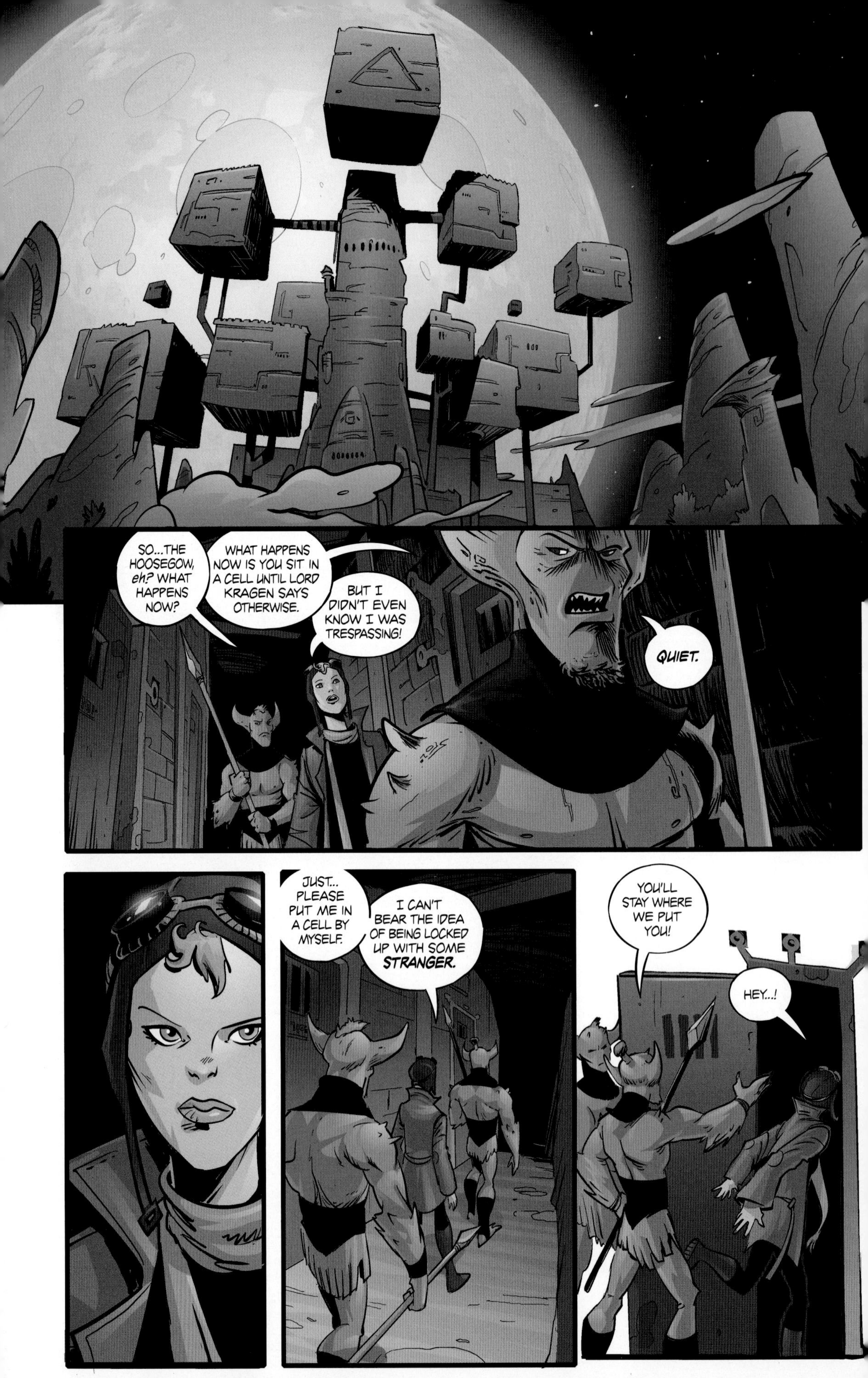
SO...THE HOOSEGOW, eh? WHAT HAPPENS NOW?
WHAT HAPPENS NOW IS YOU SIT IN A CELL UNTIL LORD KRAGEN SAYS OTHERWISE.
BUT I DIDN'T EVEN KNOW I WAS TRESPASSING!
QUIET.
JUST... PLEASE PUT ME IN A CELL BY MYSELF.
I CAN'T BEAR THE IDEA OF BEING LOCKED UP WITH SOME STRANGER.
YOU'LL STAY WHERE WE PUT YOU!
HEY...!

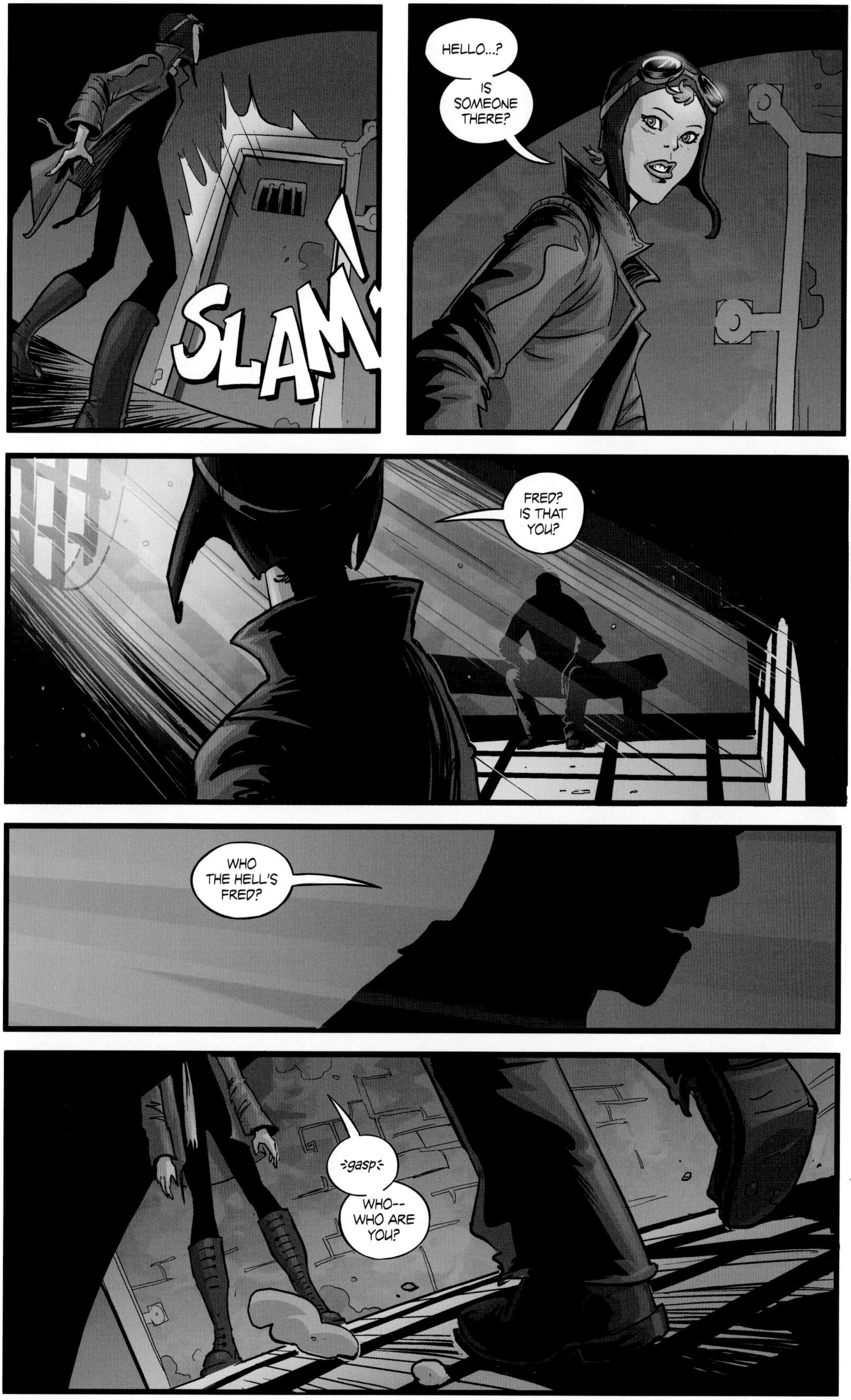
SLAM!
HELLO...?
IS SOMEONE THERE?
FRED? IS THAT YOU?
WHO THE HELL'S FRED?
gasp
WHO-- WHO ARE YOU?

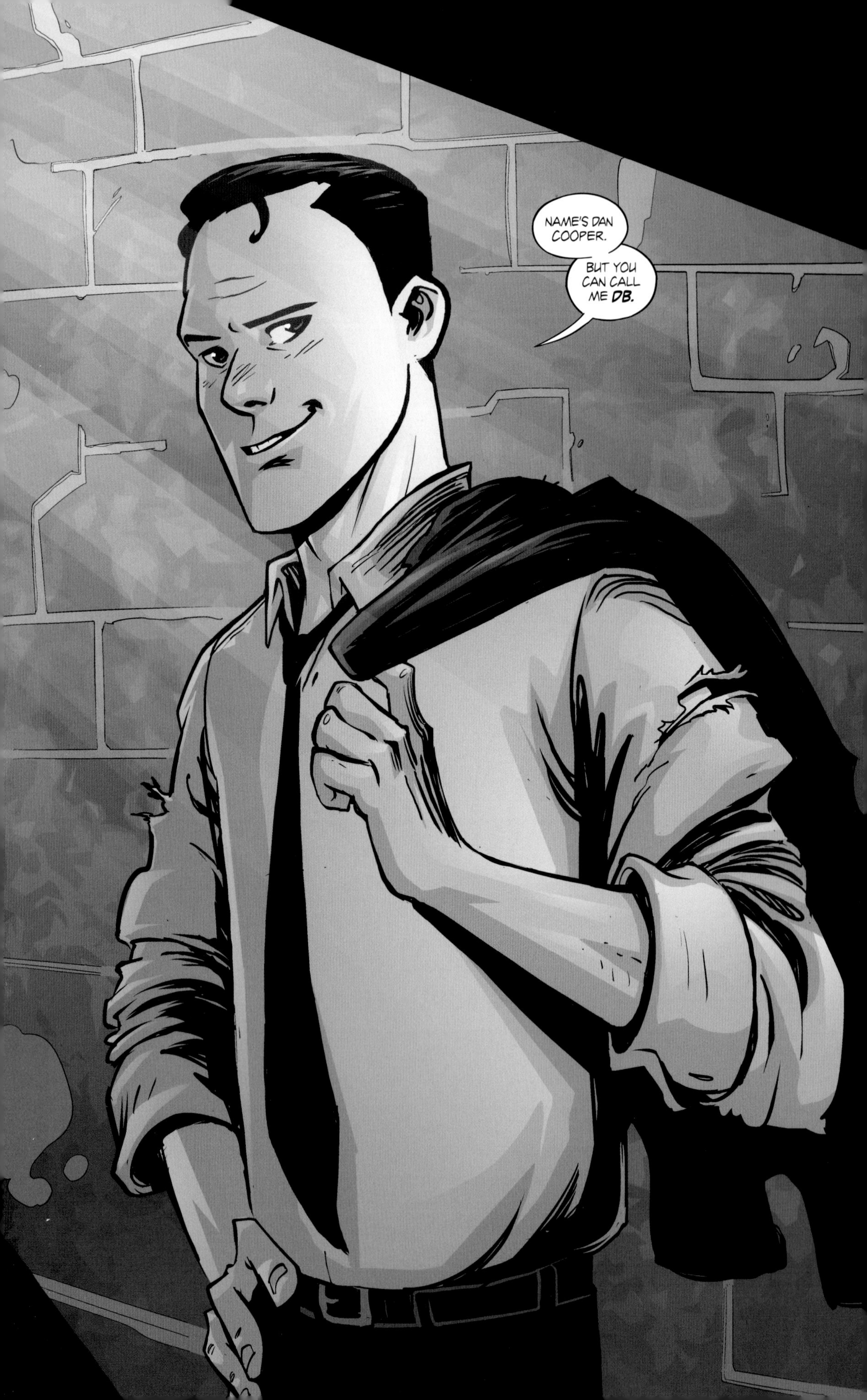
NAME'S DAN COOPER.
BUT YOU CAN CALL ME *DB.*

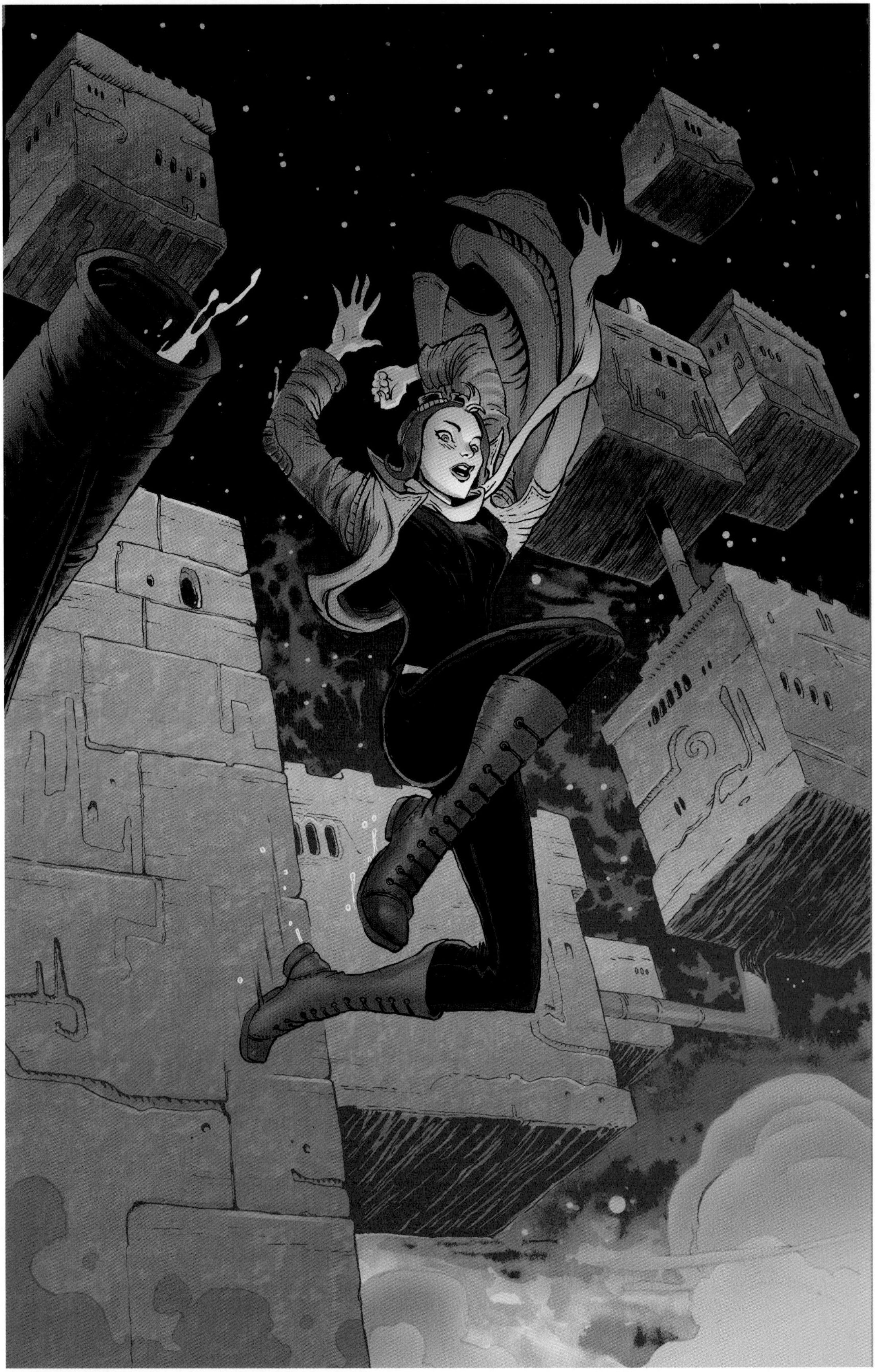

CHAPTER 2

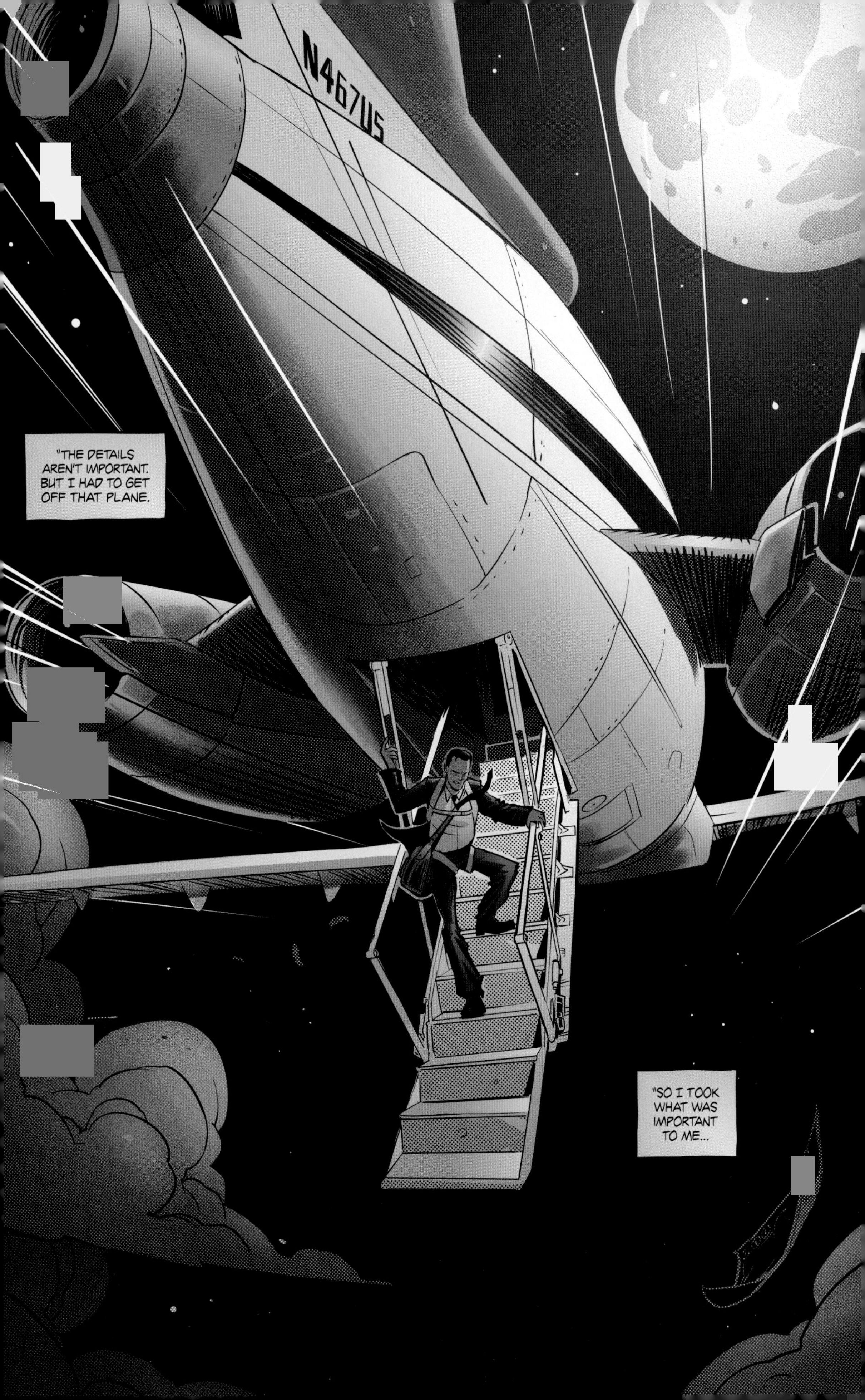
N467US
"THE DETAILS AREN'T IMPORTANT. BUT I HAD TO GET OFF THAT PLANE.
"SO I TOOK WHAT WAS IMPORTANT TO ME...

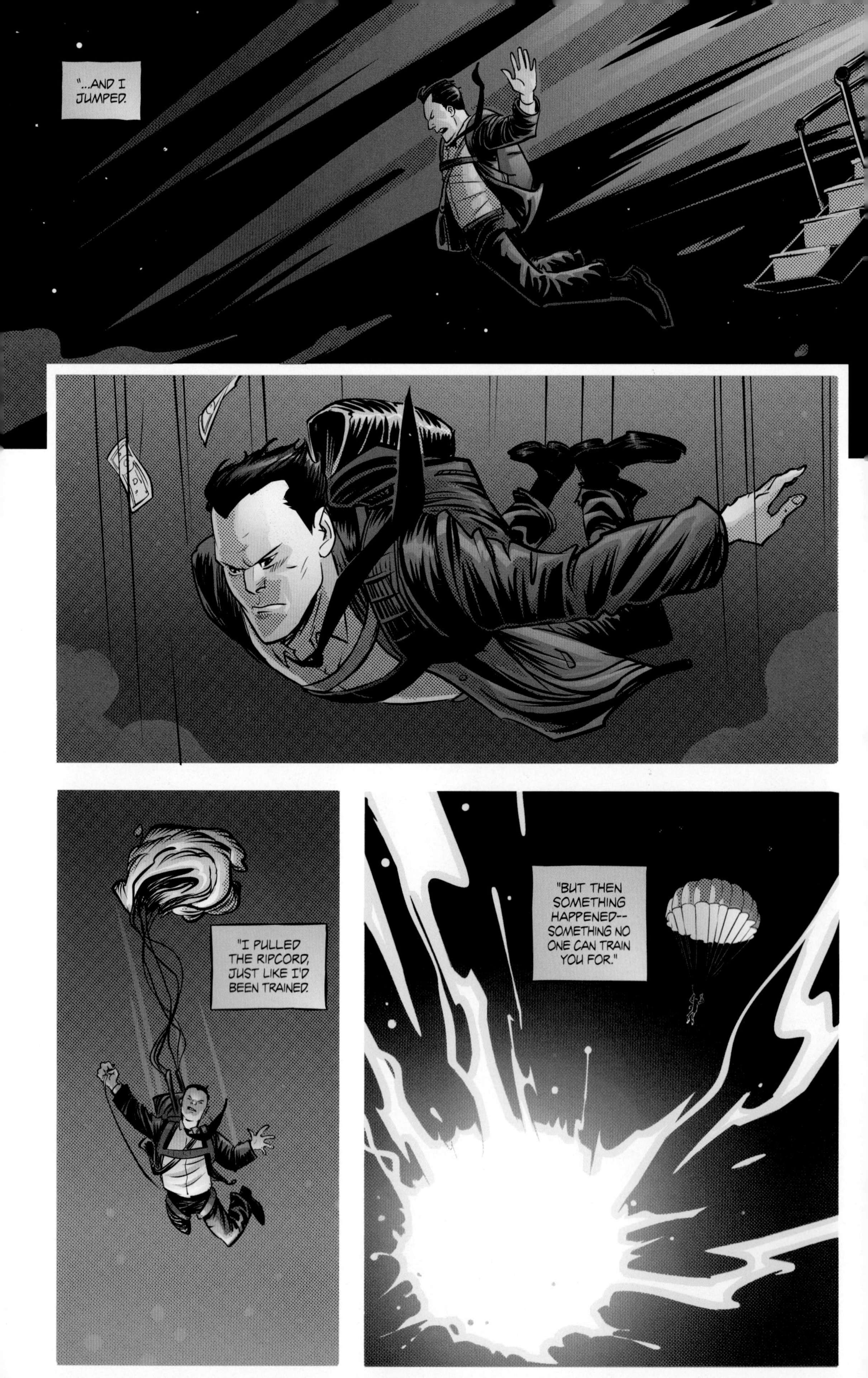
"...AND I JUMPED.
"I PULLED THE RIPCORD, JUST LIKE I'D BEEN TRAINED.
"BUT THEN SOMETHING HAPPENED-- SOMETHING NO ONE CAN TRAIN YOU FOR."

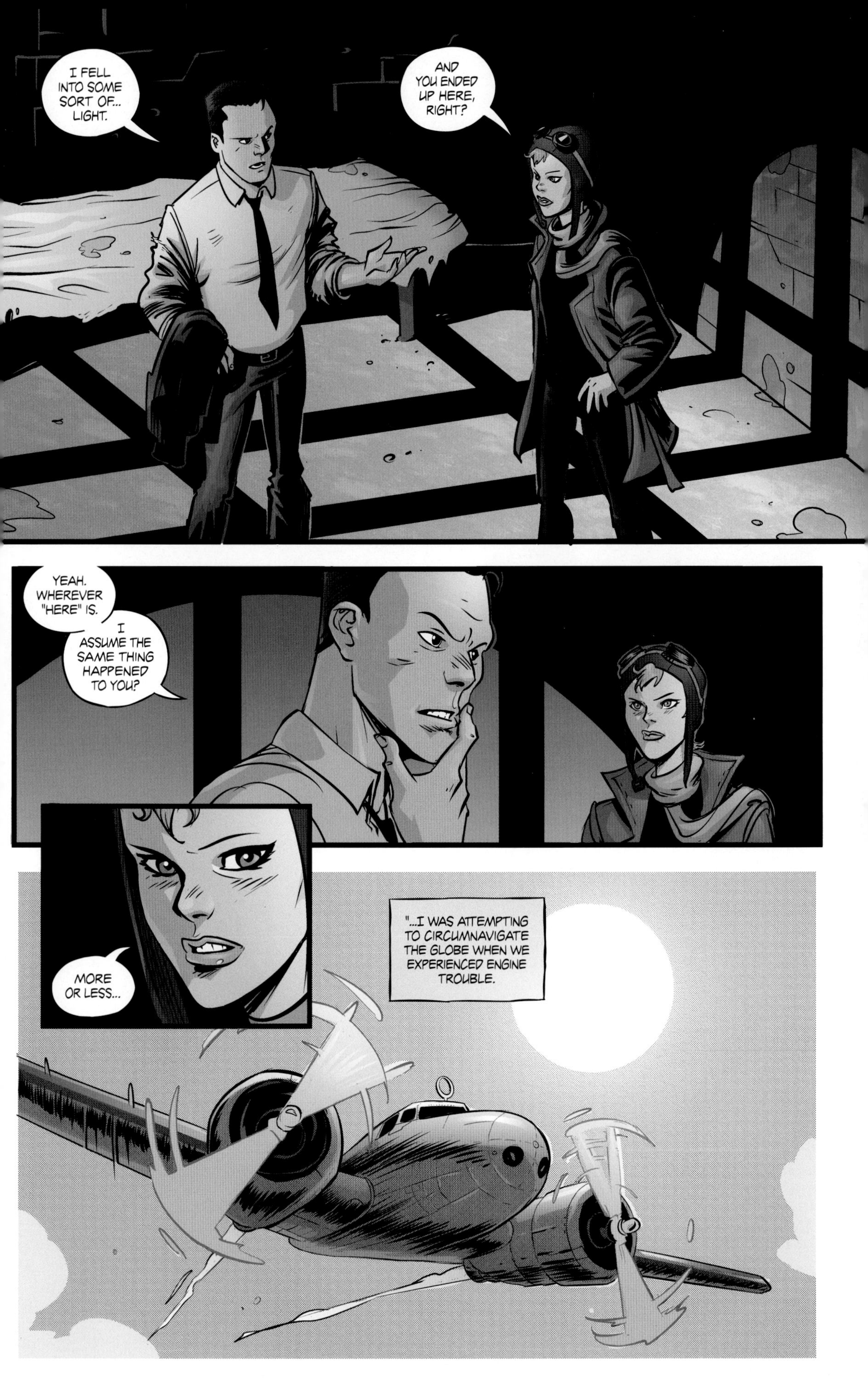

I FELL INTO SOME SORT OF... LIGHT.
AND YOU ENDED UP HERE, RIGHT?
YEAH. WHEREVER "HERE" IS.
I ASSUME THE SAME THING HAPPENED TO YOU?
MORE OR LESS...
"...I WAS ATTEMPTING TO CIRCUMNAVIGATE THE GLOBE WHEN WE EXPERIENCED ENGINE TROUBLE.

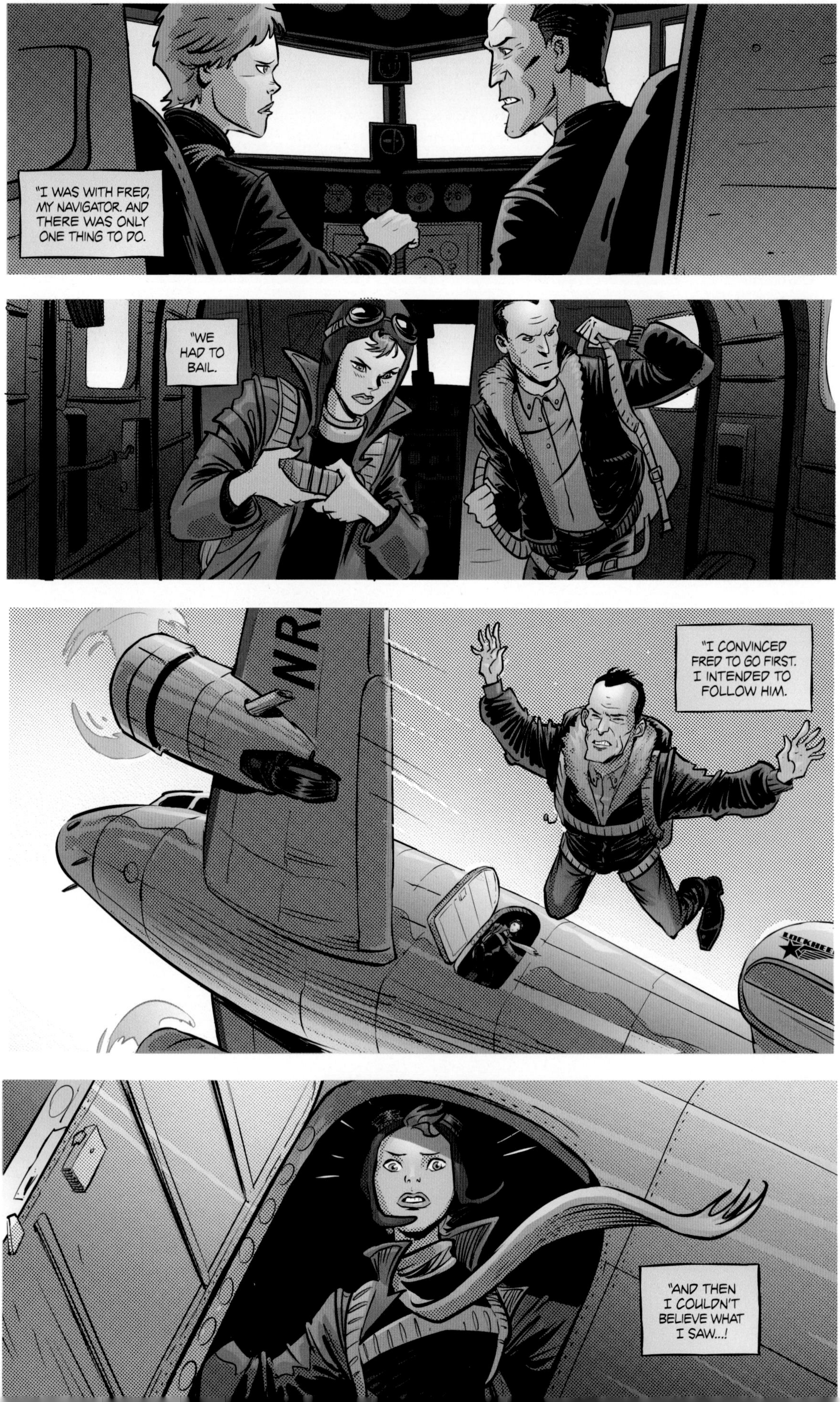
"I WAS WITH FRED, MY NAVIGATOR. AND THERE WAS ONLY ONE THING TO DO.
"WE HAD TO BAIL.
"I CONVINCED FRED TO GO FIRST. I INTENDED TO FOLLOW HIM.
"AND THEN I COULDN'T BELIEVE WHAT I SAW...!

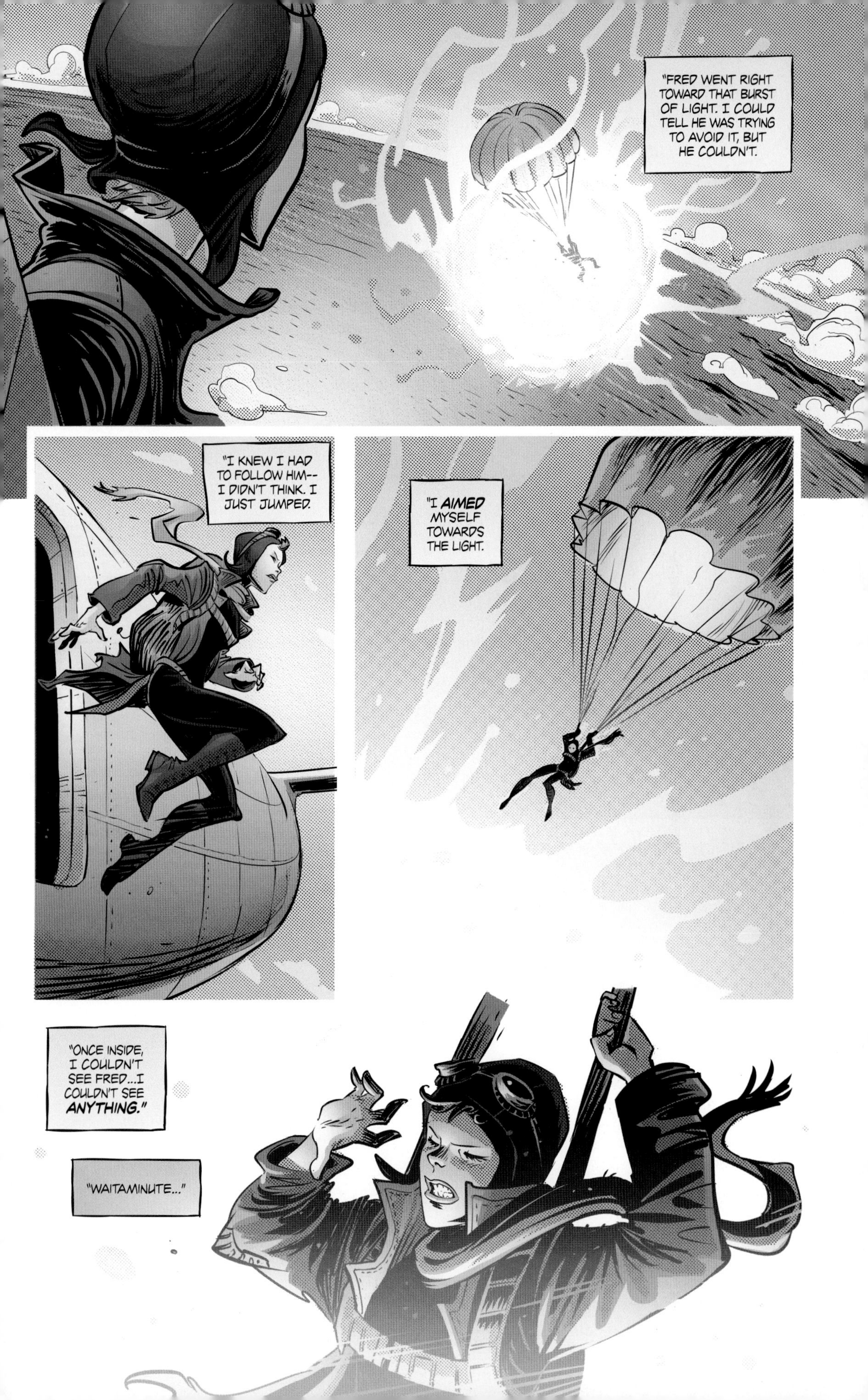
"FRED WENT RIGHT TOWARD THAT BURST OF LIGHT. I COULD TELL HE WAS TRYING TO AVOID IT, BUT HE COULDN'T.
"I KNEW I HAD TO FOLLOW HIM-- I DIDN'T THINK. I JUST JUMPED.
"I AIMED MYSELF TOWARDS THE LIGHT.
"ONCE INSIDE, I COULDN'T SEE FRED...I COULDN'T SEE ANYTHING."
"WAITAMINUTE..."

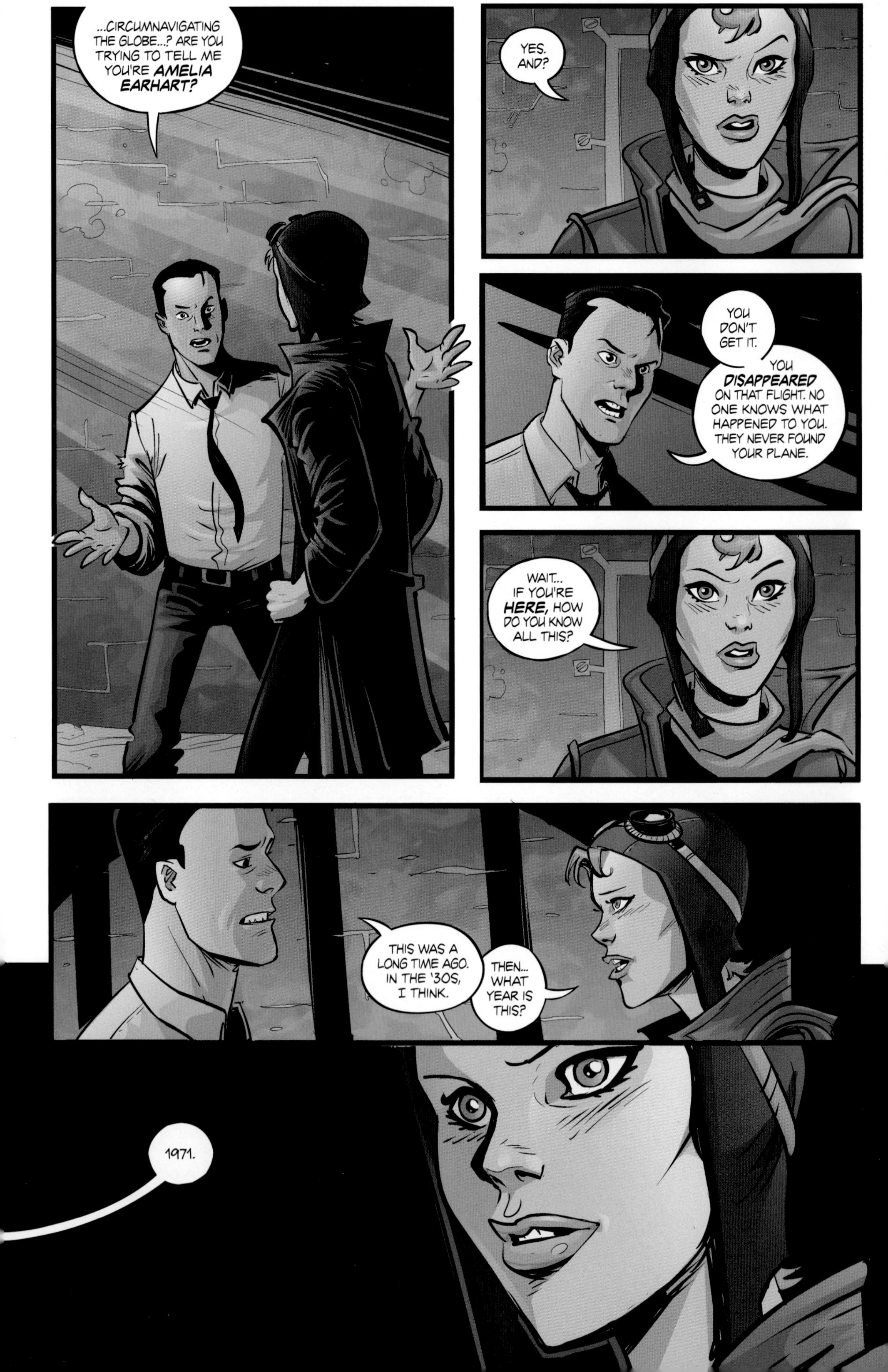
...CIRCUMNAVIGATING THE GLOBE...? ARE YOU TRYING TO TELL ME YOU'RE **AMELIA EARHART?**
YES. AND?
YOU DON'T GET IT.
YOU **DISAPPEARED** ON THAT FLIGHT. NO ONE KNOWS WHAT HAPPENED TO YOU. THEY NEVER FOUND YOUR PLANE.
WAIT... IF YOU'RE **HERE,** HOW DO YOU KNOW ALL THIS?
THIS WAS A LONG TIME AGO. IN THE '30S, I THINK.
THEN... WHAT YEAR IS THIS?
1971.

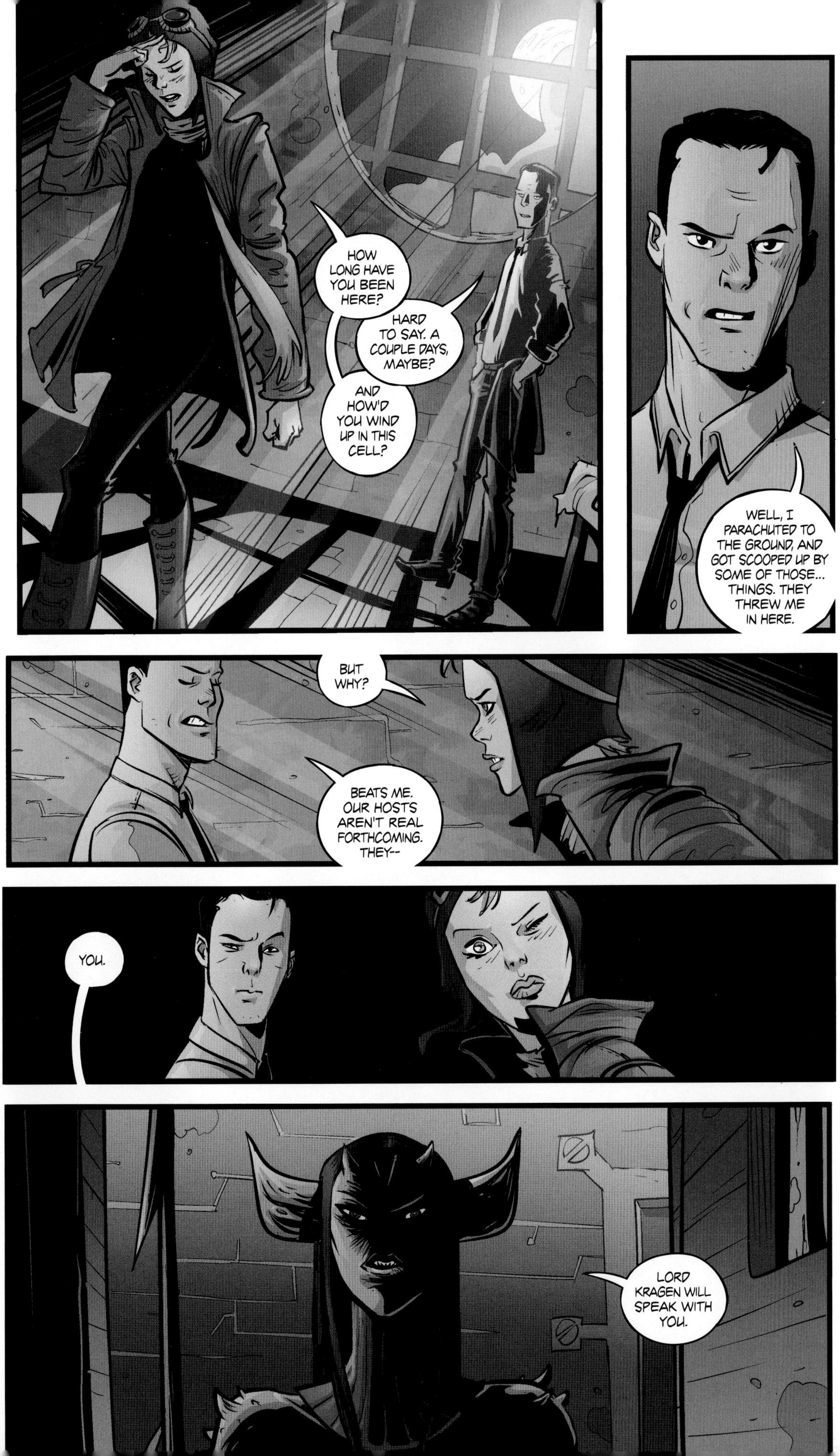
HOW LONG HAVE YOU BEEN HERE?
HARD TO SAY. A COUPLE DAYS, MAYBE?
AND HOW'D YOU WIND UP IN THIS CELL?
WELL, I PARACHUTED TO THE GROUND, AND GOT SCOOPED UP BY SOME OF THOSE... THINGS. THEY THREW ME IN HERE.
BUT WHY?
BEATS ME. OUR HOSTS AREN'T REAL FORTHCOMING. THEY--
YOU.
LORD KRAGEN WILL SPEAK WITH YOU.

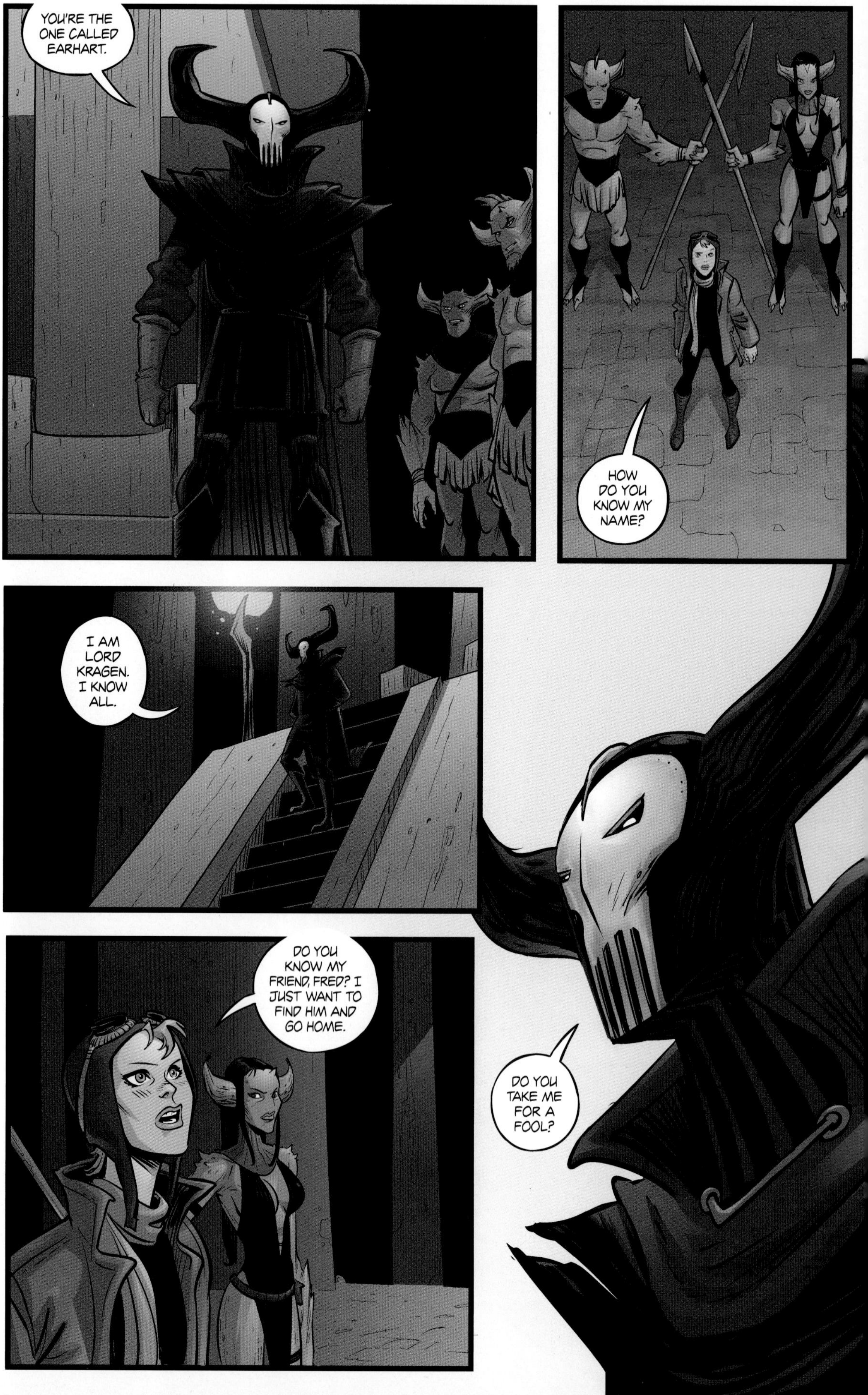
YOU'RE THE ONE CALLED EARHART.
HOW DO YOU KNOW MY NAME?
I AM LORD KRAGEN. I KNOW ALL.
DO YOU KNOW MY FRIEND, FRED? I JUST WANT TO FIND HIM AND GO HOME.
DO YOU TAKE ME FOR A FOOL?

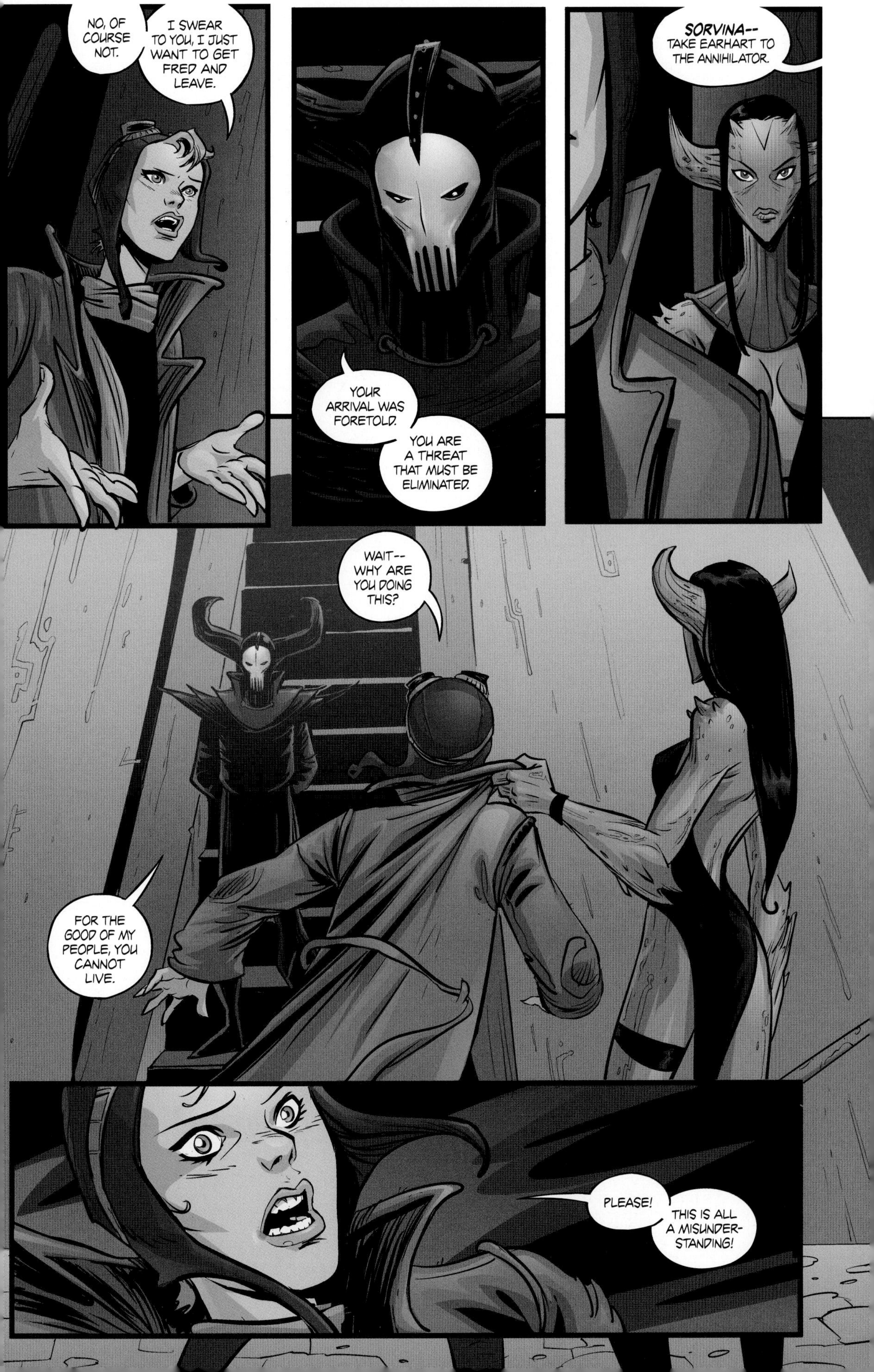
NO, OF COURSE NOT.
I SWEAR TO YOU, I JUST WANT TO GET FRED AND LEAVE.
YOUR ARRIVAL WAS FORETOLD.
YOU ARE A THREAT THAT MUST BE ELIMINATED.
SORVINA-- TAKE EARHART TO THE ANNIHILATOR.
WAIT-- WHY ARE YOU DOING THIS?
FOR THE GOOD OF MY PEOPLE, YOU CANNOT LIVE.
PLEASE!
THIS IS ALL A MISUNDER-STANDING!

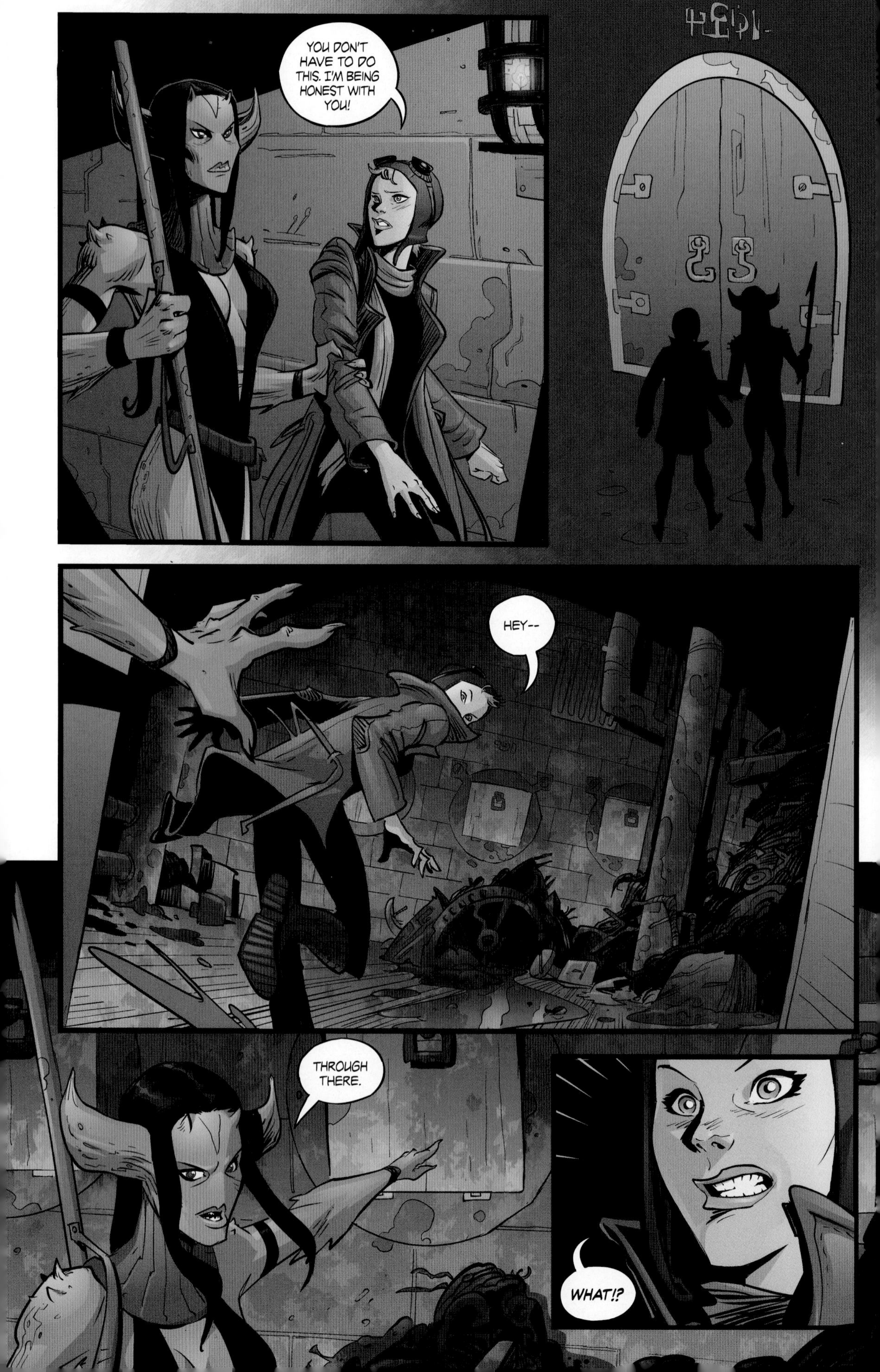
YOU DON'T HAVE TO DO THIS. I'M BEING HONEST WITH YOU!
HEY--
THROUGH THERE.
WHAT!?

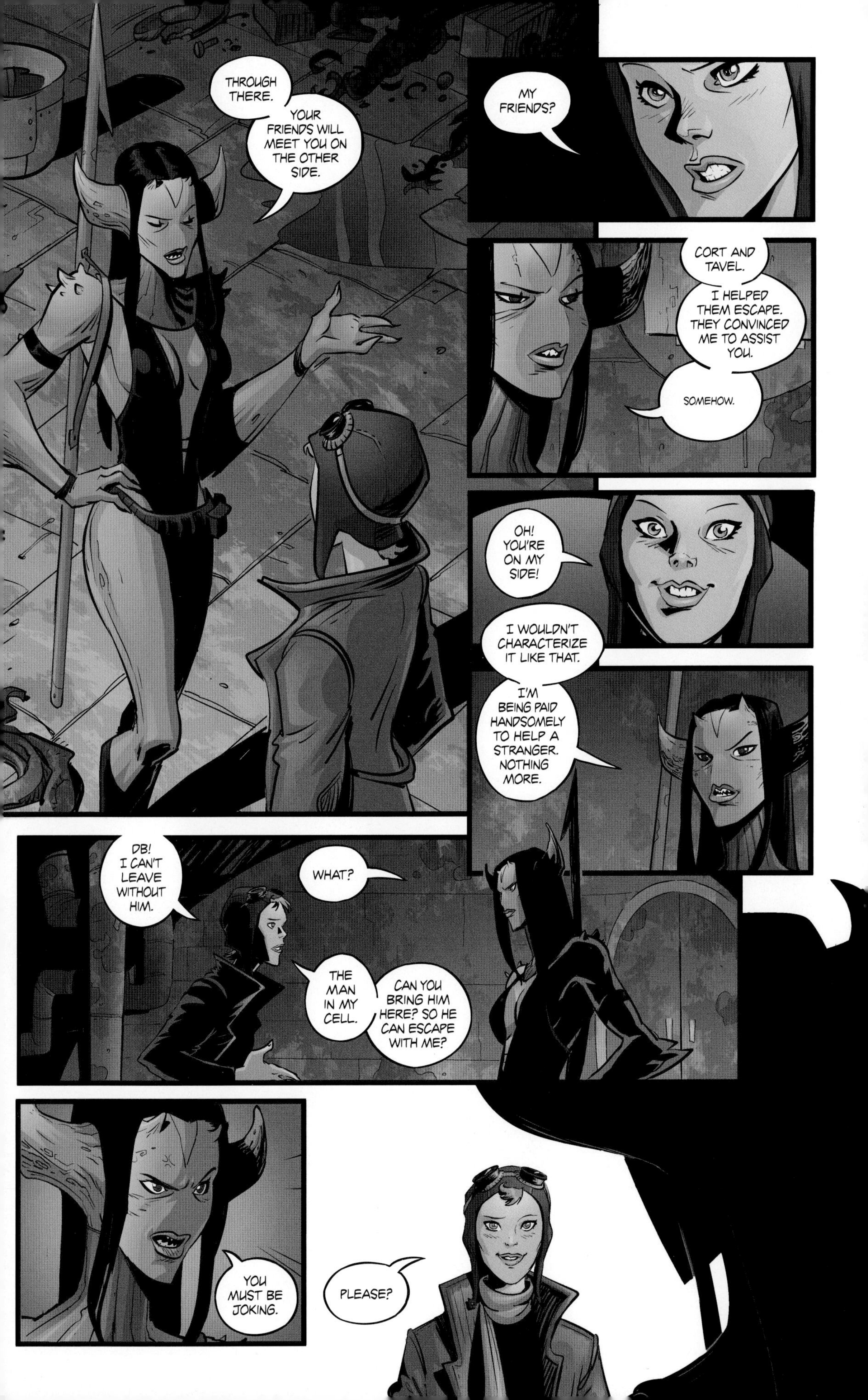
THROUGH THERE.
YOUR FRIENDS WILL MEET YOU ON THE OTHER SIDE.
MY FRIENDS?
CORT AND TAVEL.
I HELPED THEM ESCAPE. THEY CONVINCED ME TO ASSIST YOU.
SOMEHOW.
OH! YOU'RE ON MY SIDE!
I WOULDN'T CHARACTERIZE IT LIKE THAT.
I'M BEING PAID HANDSOMELY TO HELP A STRANGER. NOTHING MORE.
DB! I CAN'T LEAVE WITHOUT HIM.
WHAT?
THE MAN IN MY CELL.
CAN YOU BRING HIM HERE? SO HE CAN ESCAPE WITH ME?
YOU MUST BE JOKING.
PLEASE?

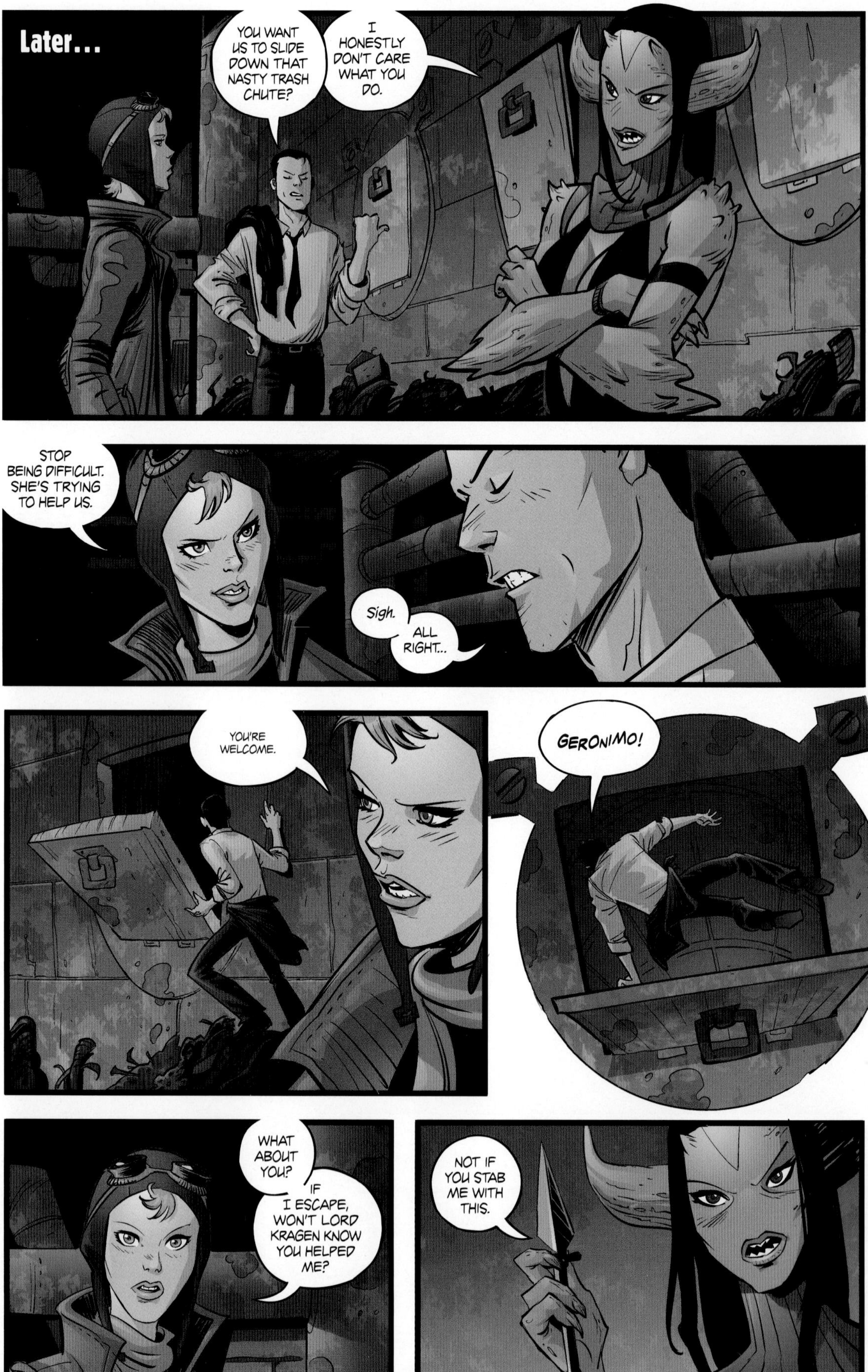
Later...
YOU WANT US TO SLIDE DOWN THAT NASTY TRASH CHUTE?
I HONESTLY DON'T CARE WHAT YOU DO.
STOP BEING DIFFICULT. SHE'S TRYING TO HELP US.
Sigh.
ALL RIGHT...
YOU'RE WELCOME.
GERONIMO!
WHAT ABOUT YOU?
IF I ESCAPE, WON'T LORD KRAGEN KNOW YOU HELPED ME?
NOT IF YOU STAB ME WITH THIS.

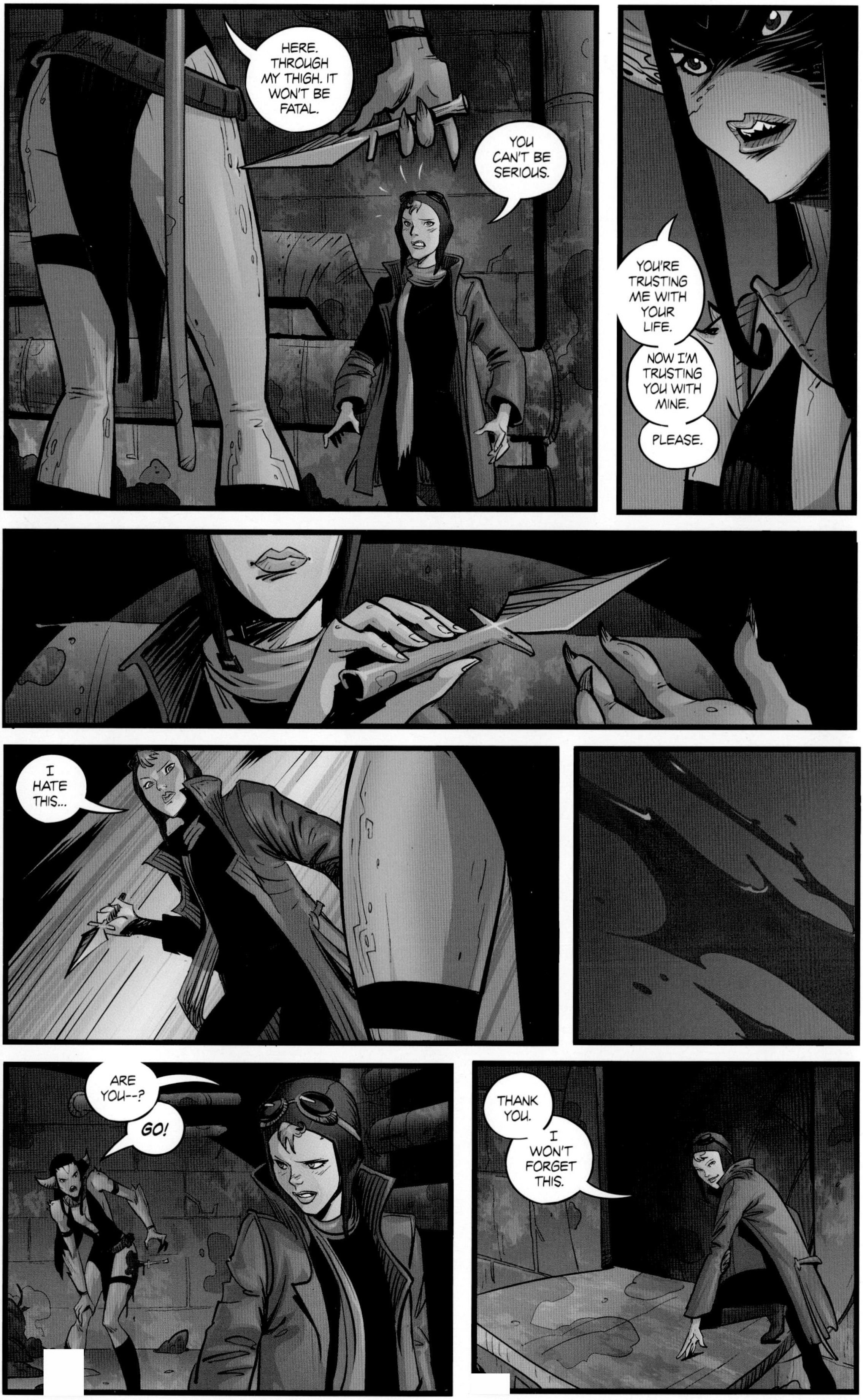
HERE. THROUGH MY THIGH. IT WON'T BE FATAL.
YOU CAN'T BE SERIOUS.
YOU'RE TRUSTING ME WITH YOUR LIFE.
NOW I'M TRUSTING YOU WITH MINE.
PLEASE.
I HATE THIS...
ARE YOU--?
GO!
THANK YOU.
I WON'T FORGET THIS.

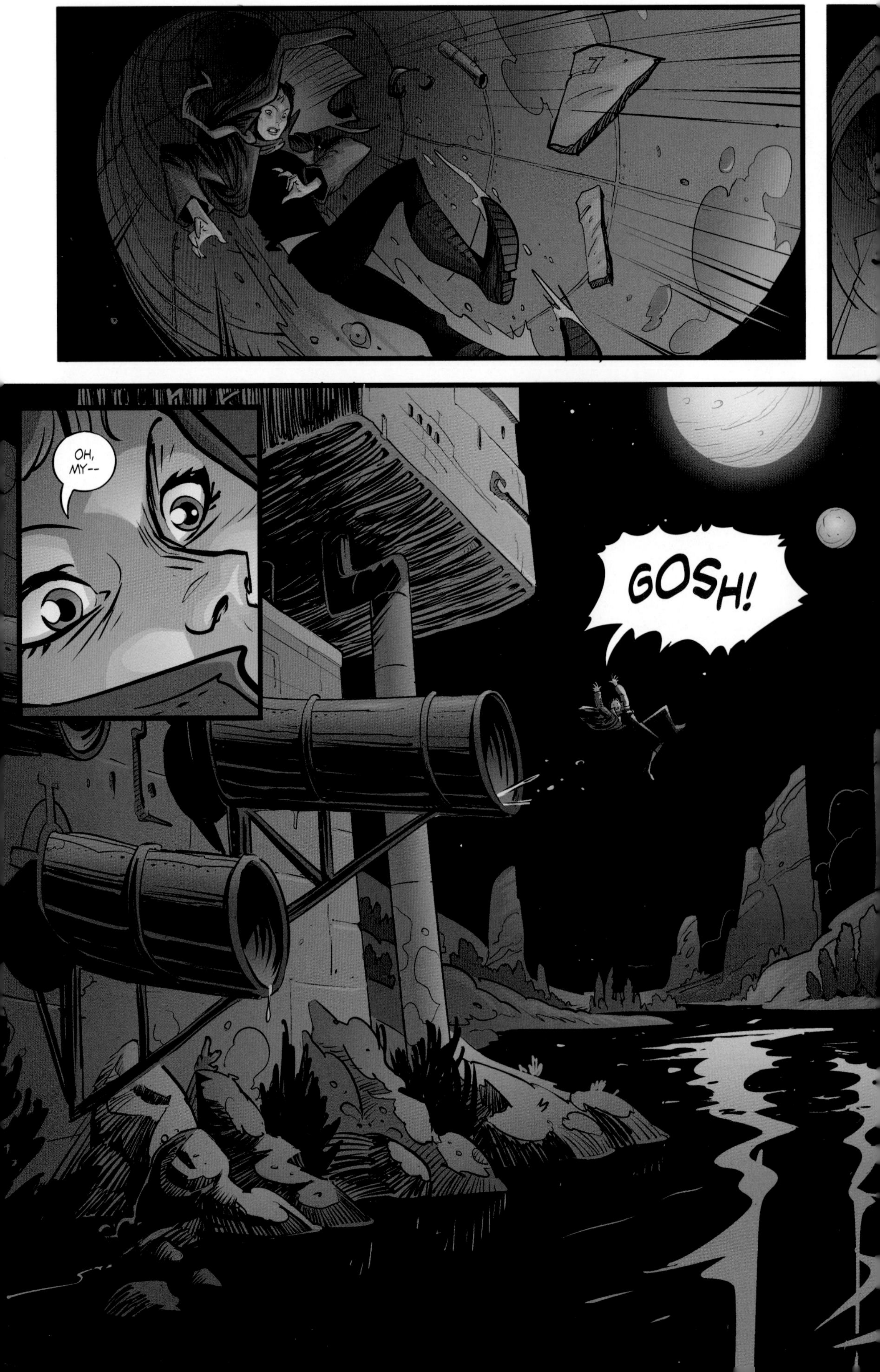
OH, MY--
GOSH!

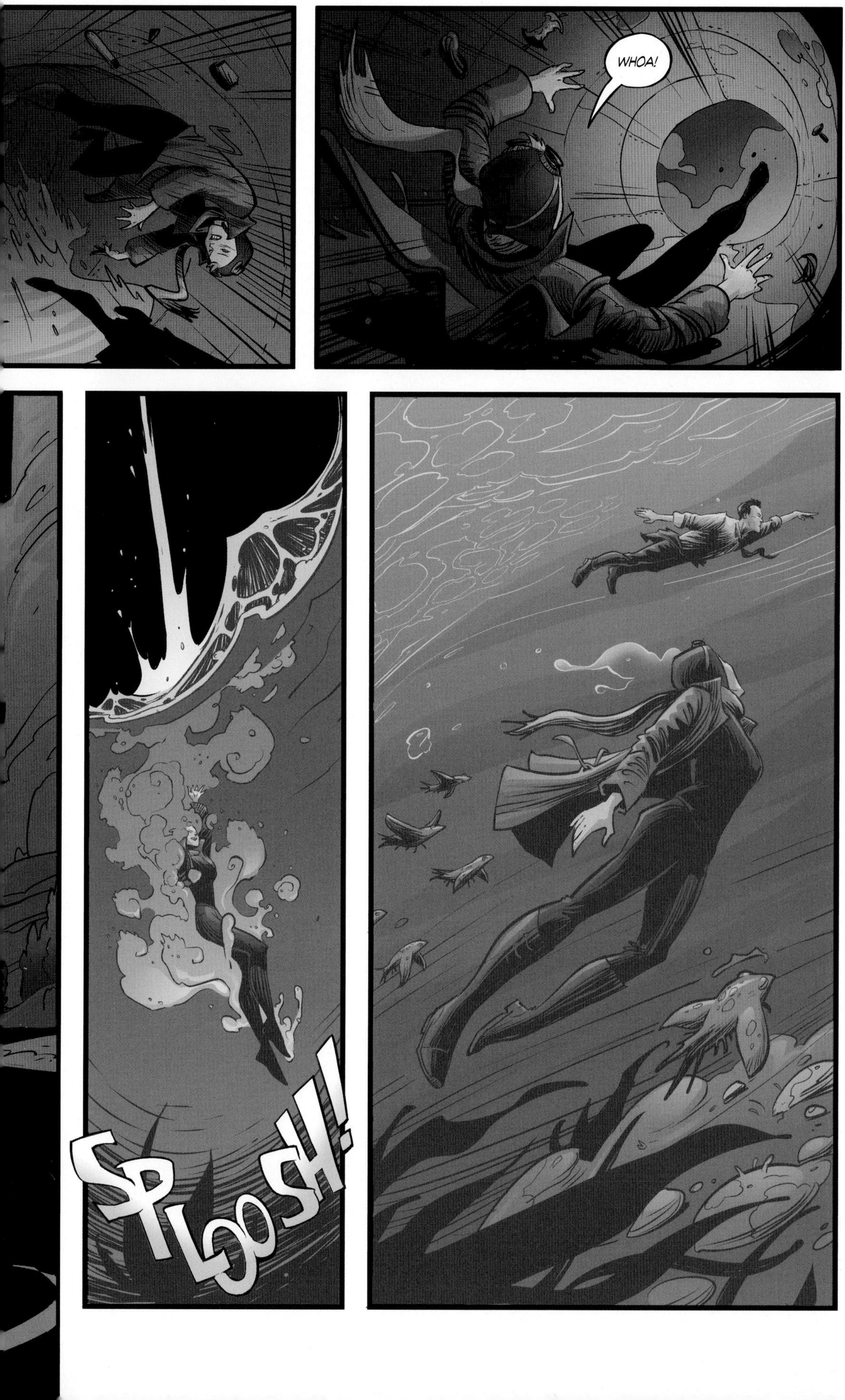
WHOA!
SPLOOSH!

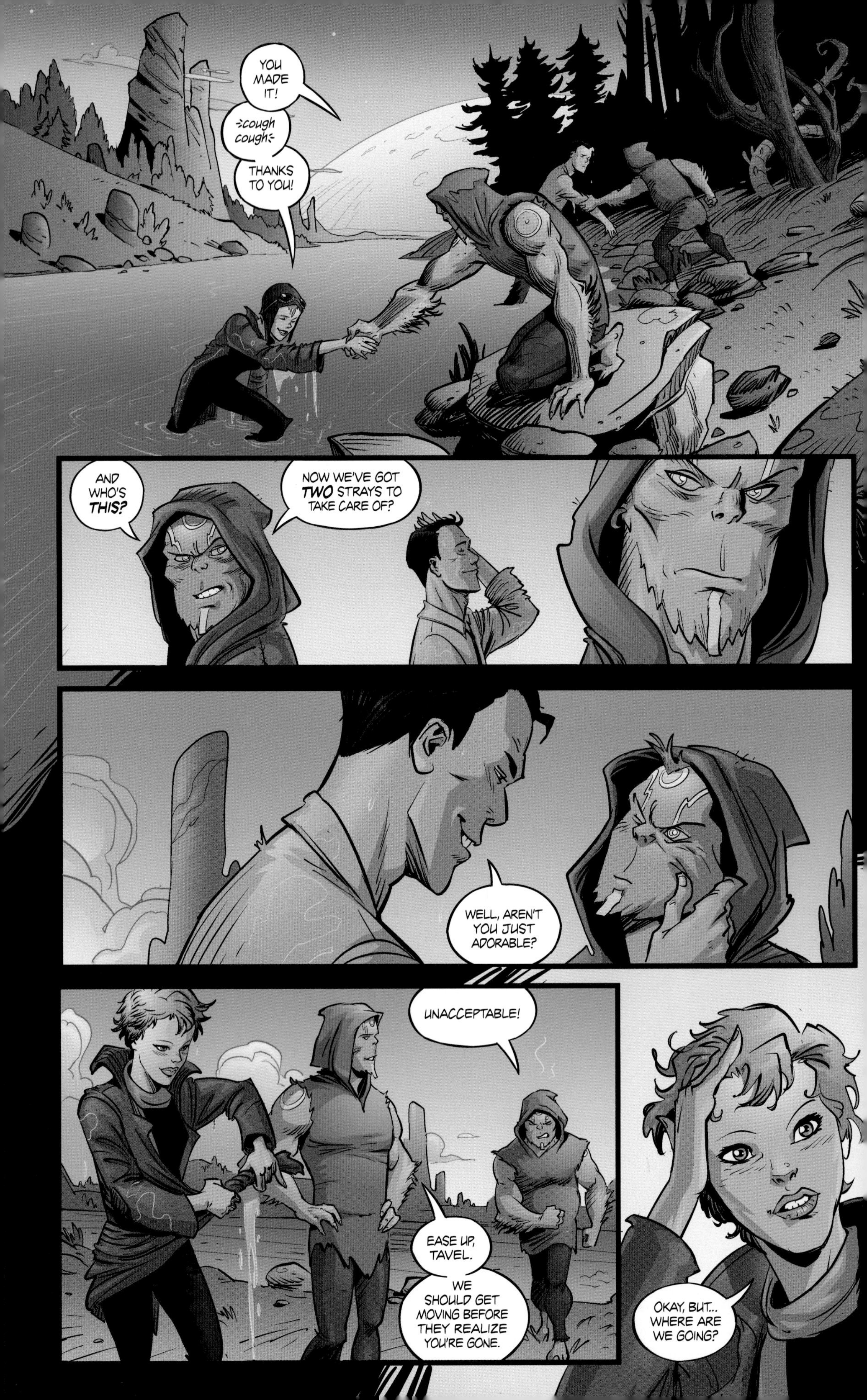
YOU MADE IT!
-cough cough-
THANKS TO YOU!
AND WHO'S THIS?
NOW WE'VE GOT TWO STRAYS TO TAKE CARE OF?
WELL, AREN'T YOU JUST ADORABLE?
UNACCEPTABLE!
EASE UP, TAVEL.
WE SHOULD GET MOVING BEFORE THEY REALIZE YOU'RE GONE.
OKAY, BUT... WHERE ARE WE GOING?

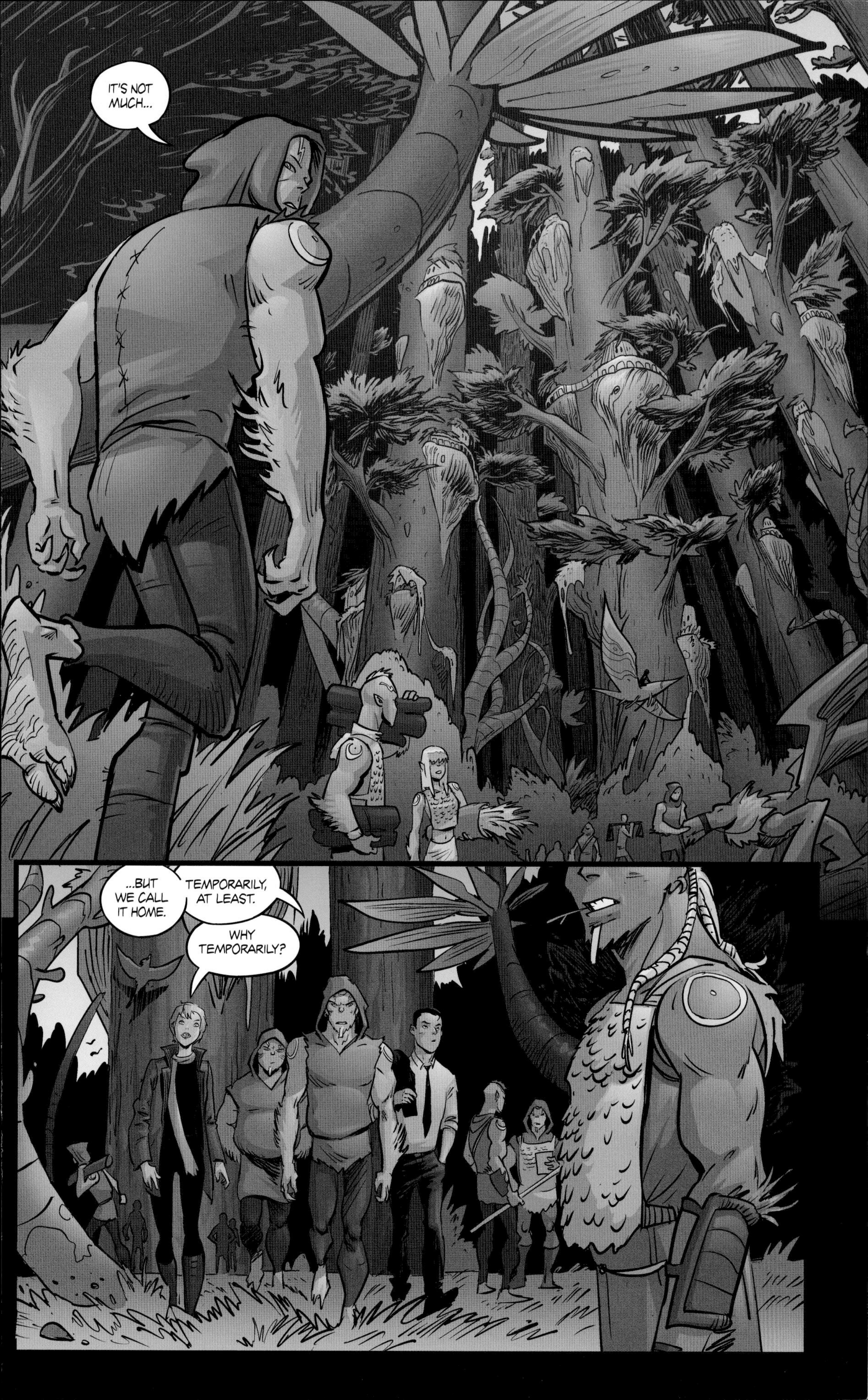
IT'S NOT MUCH...
...BUT WE CALL IT HOME.
TEMPORARILY, AT LEAST.
WHY TEMPORARILY?

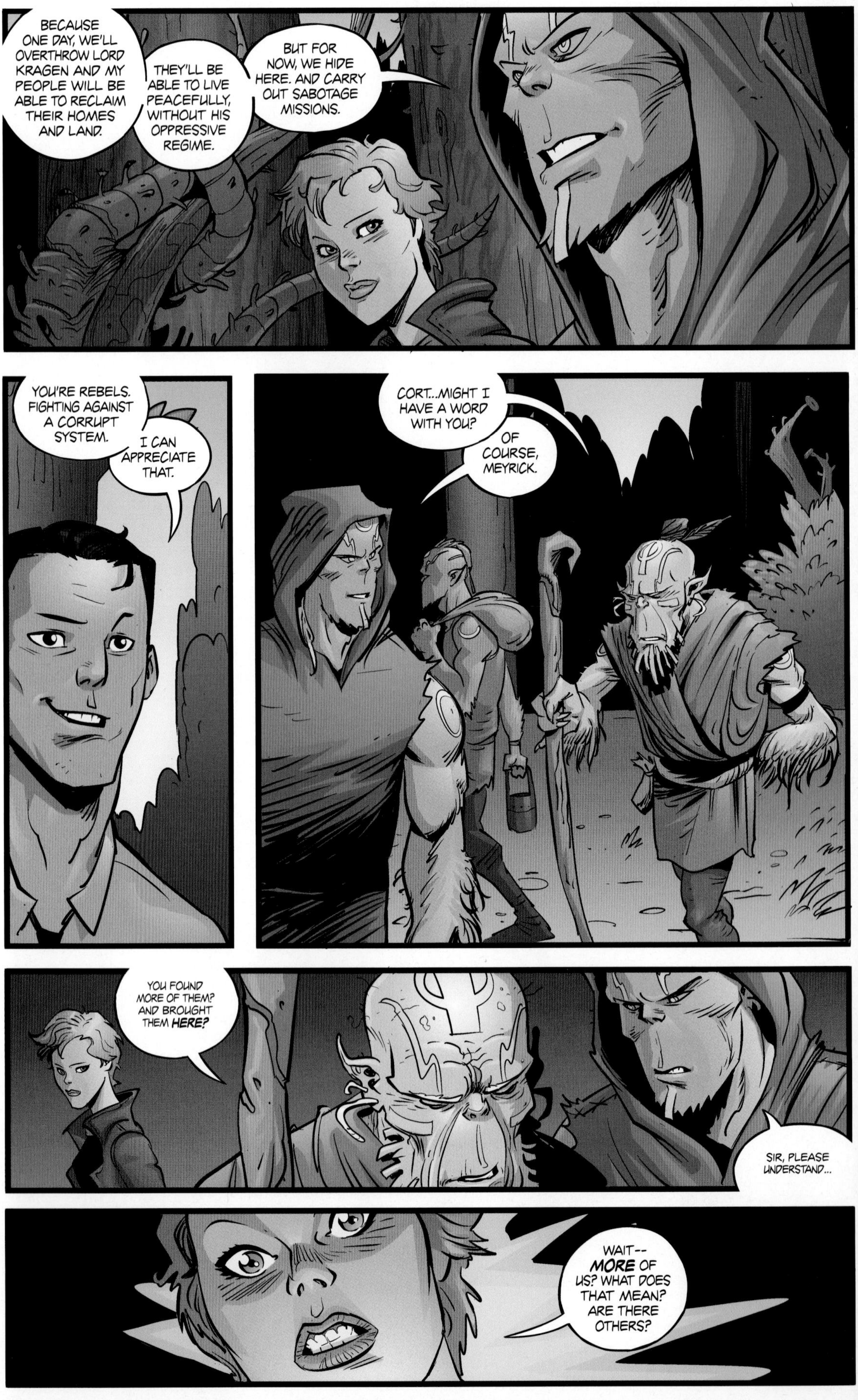
BECAUSE ONE DAY, WE'LL OVERTHROW LORD KRAGEN AND MY PEOPLE WILL BE ABLE TO RECLAIM THEIR HOMES AND LAND.
THEY'LL BE ABLE TO LIVE PEACEFULLY, WITHOUT HIS OPPRESSIVE REGIME.
BUT FOR NOW, WE HIDE HERE. AND CARRY OUT SABOTAGE MISSIONS.
YOU'RE REBELS. FIGHTING AGAINST A CORRUPT SYSTEM.
I CAN APPRECIATE THAT.
CORT...MIGHT I HAVE A WORD WITH YOU?
OF COURSE, MEYRICK.
YOU FOUND MORE OF THEM? AND BROUGHT THEM *HERE?*
SIR, PLEASE UNDERSTAND...
WAIT-- **MORE** OF US? WHAT DOES THAT MEAN? ARE THERE OTHERS?

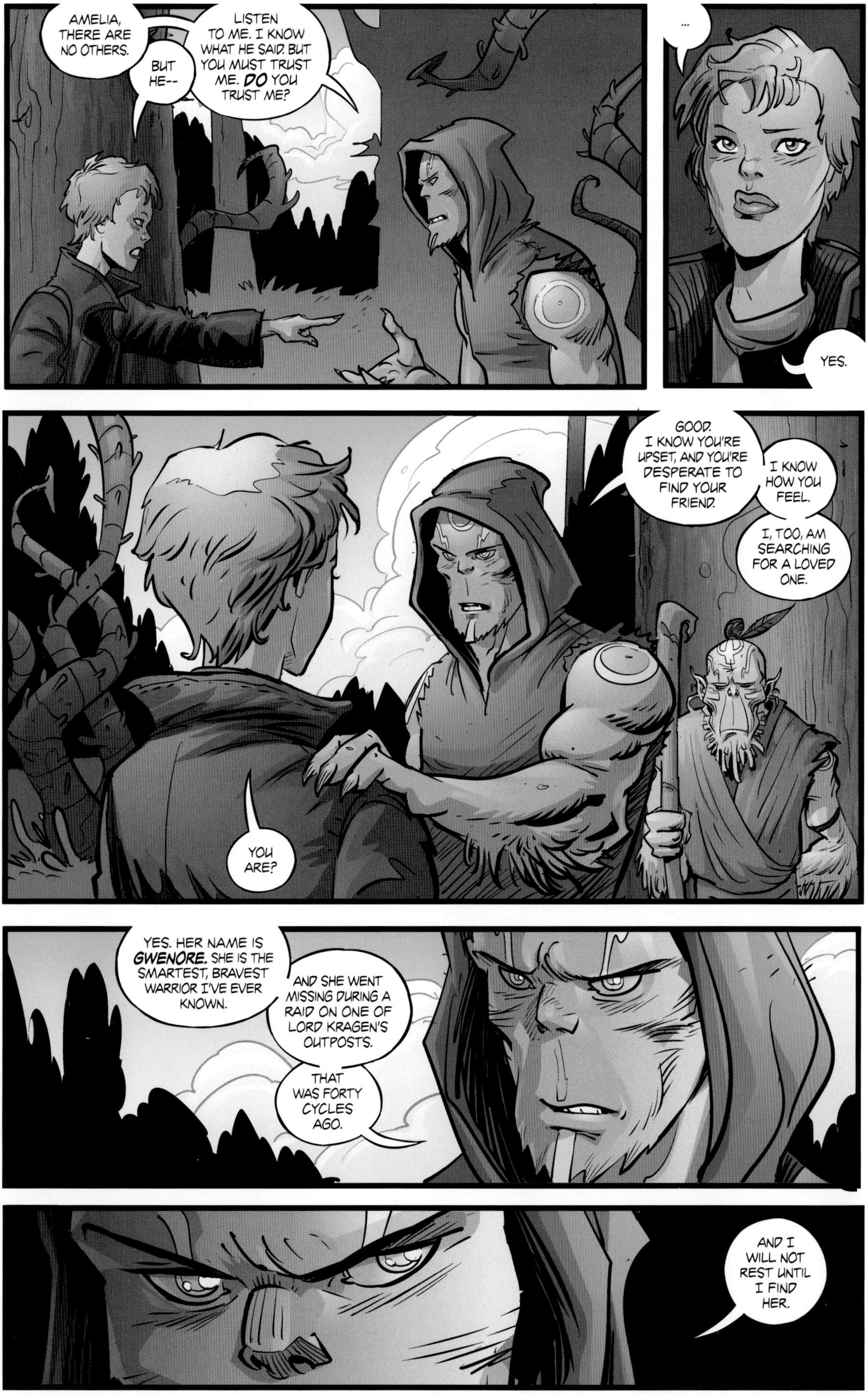
AMELIA, THERE ARE NO OTHERS.
BUT HE--
LISTEN TO ME. I KNOW WHAT HE SAID. BUT YOU MUST TRUST ME. DO YOU TRUST ME?
...
YES.
GOOD. I KNOW YOU'RE UPSET, AND YOU'RE DESPERATE TO FIND YOUR FRIEND.
I KNOW HOW YOU FEEL.
I, TOO, AM SEARCHING FOR A LOVED ONE.
YOU ARE?
YES. HER NAME IS GWENORE. SHE IS THE SMARTEST, BRAVEST WARRIOR I'VE EVER KNOWN.
AND SHE WENT MISSING DURING A RAID ON ONE OF LORD KRAGEN'S OUTPOSTS.
THAT WAS FORTY CYCLES AGO.
AND I WILL NOT REST UNTIL I FIND HER.

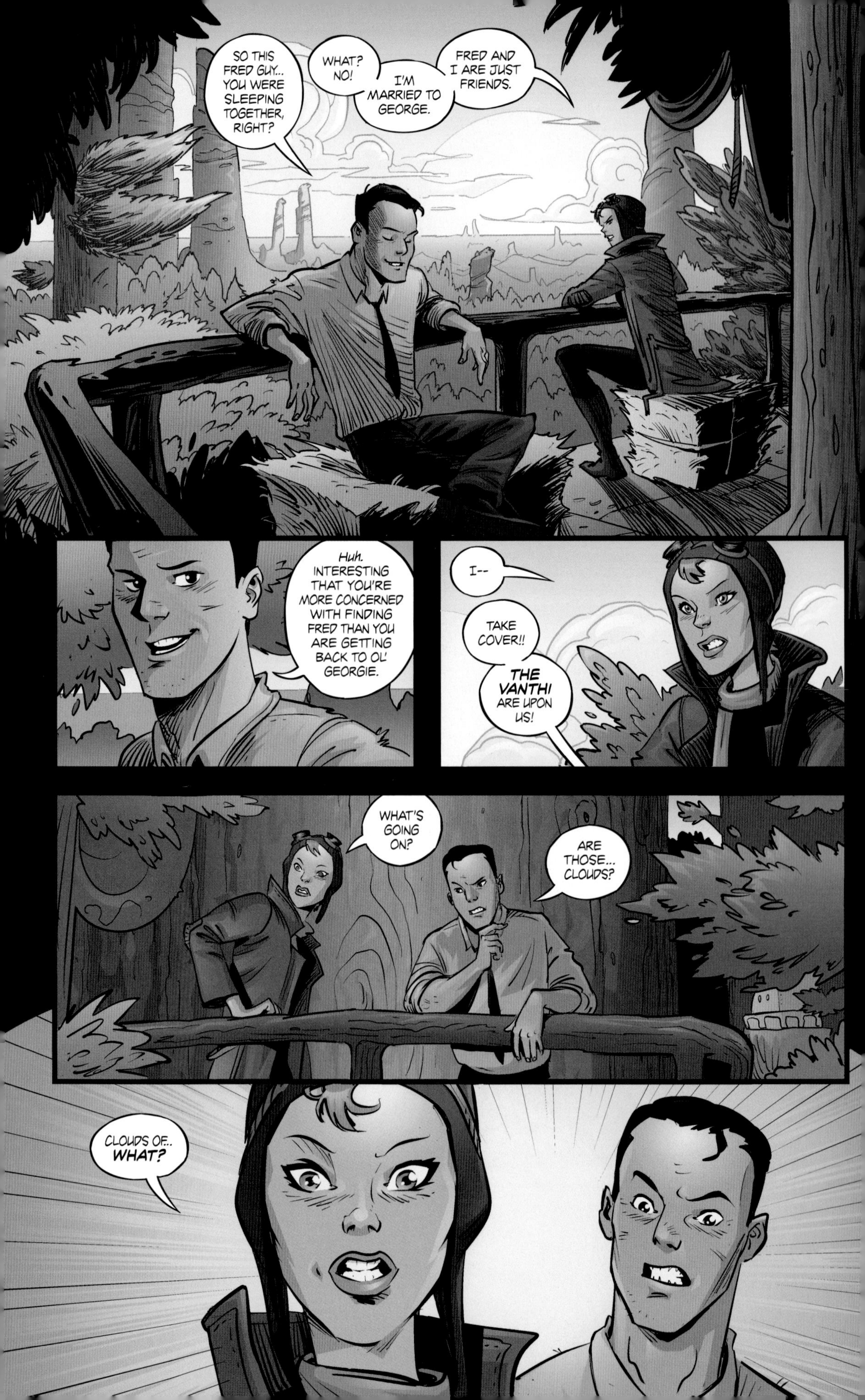
SO THIS FRED GUY... YOU WERE SLEEPING TOGETHER, RIGHT?
WHAT? NO!
I'M MARRIED TO GEORGE.
FRED AND I ARE JUST FRIENDS.
Huh. INTERESTING THAT YOU'RE MORE CONCERNED WITH FINDING FRED THAN YOU ARE GETTING BACK TO OL' GEORGIE.
I--
TAKE COVER!!
THE VANTHI ARE UPON US!
WHAT'S GOING ON?
ARE THOSE... CLOUDS?
CLOUDS OF.. WHAT?

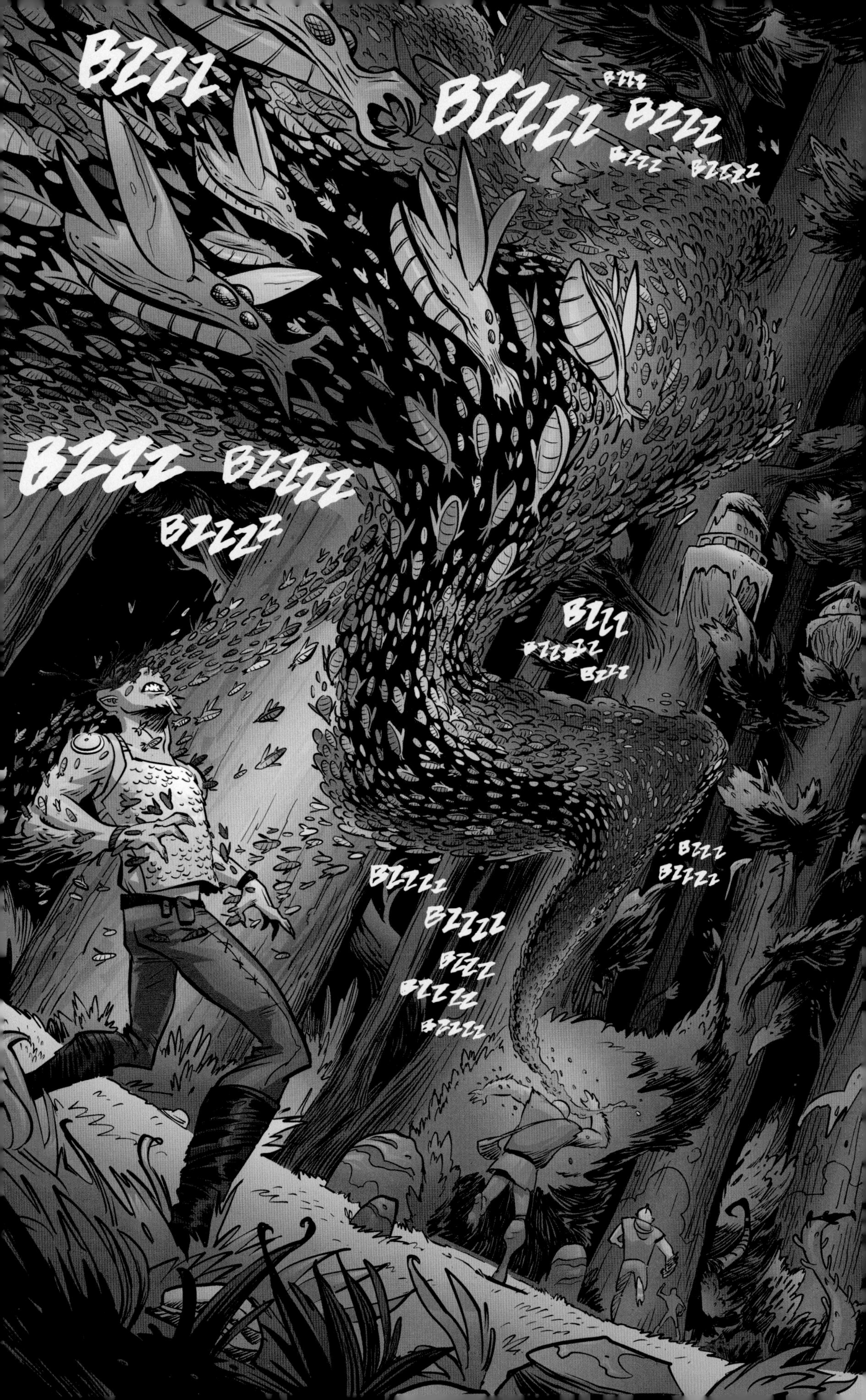
BZZZ
BZZZZ
BZZZ
BZZZ
BZZZ
BZZZZ
BZZZ
BZZZZZ
BZZZZ
BZZZ
BZZZZ
BZZZ
BZZZ
BZZZZ
BZZZZ
BZZZZ
BZZZ
BZZZZ
BZZZZ

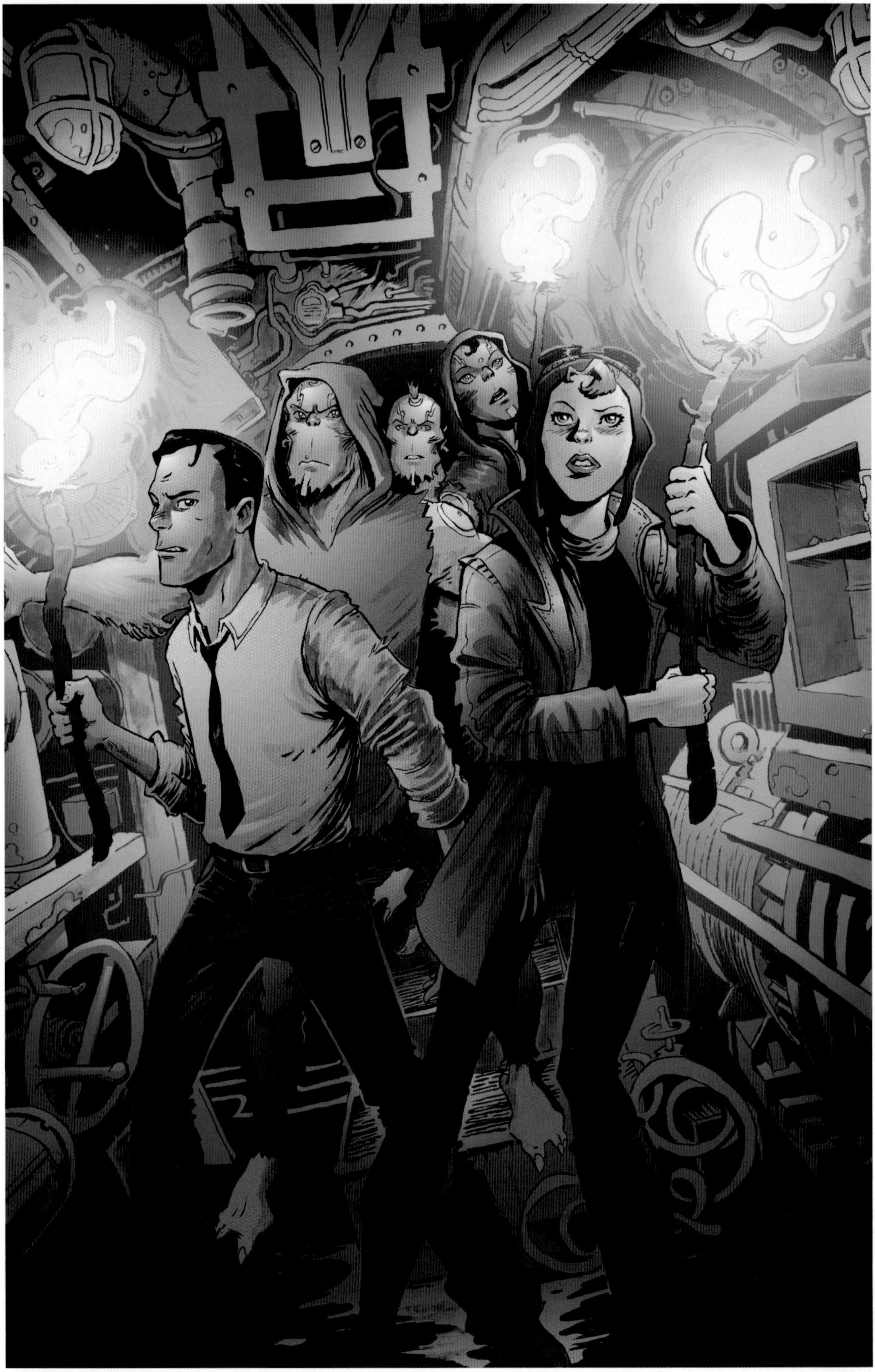

CHAPTER 3

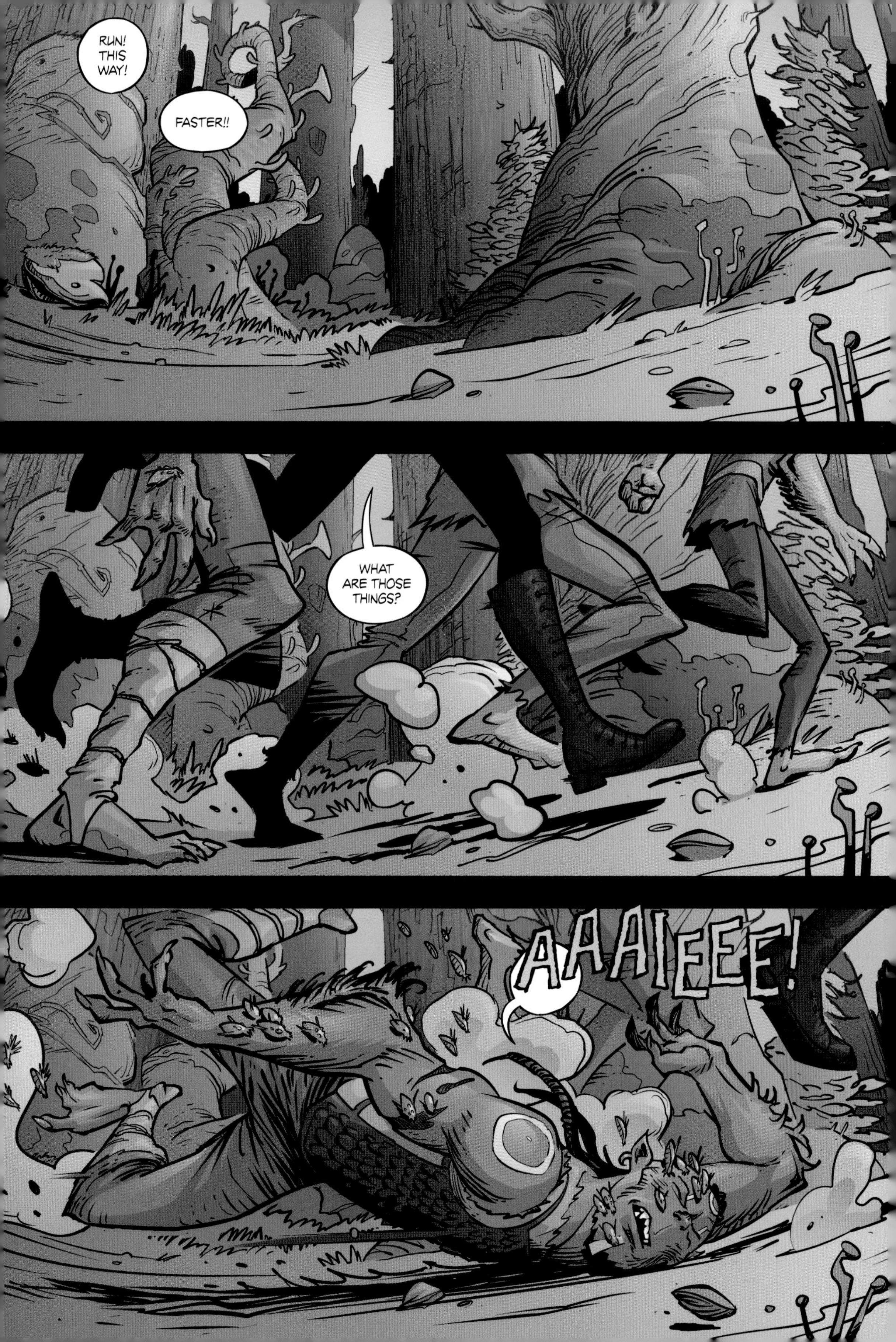
RUN! THIS WAY!
FASTER!!
WHAT ARE THOSE THINGS?
AAAIEEE!

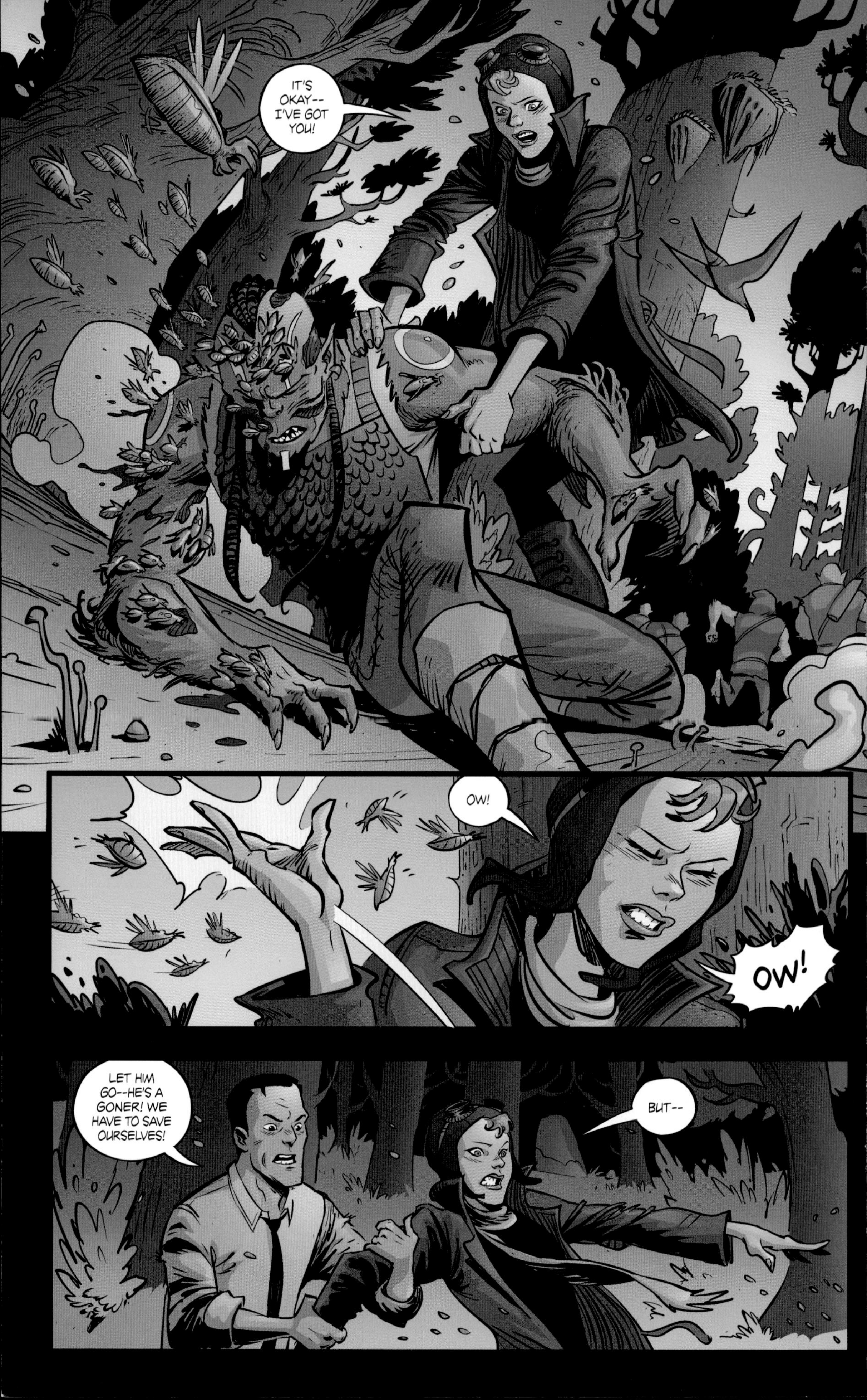
IT'S OKAY-- I'VE GOT YOU!
OW!
OW!
LET HIM GO--HE'S A GONER! WE HAVE TO SAVE OURSELVES!
BUT--

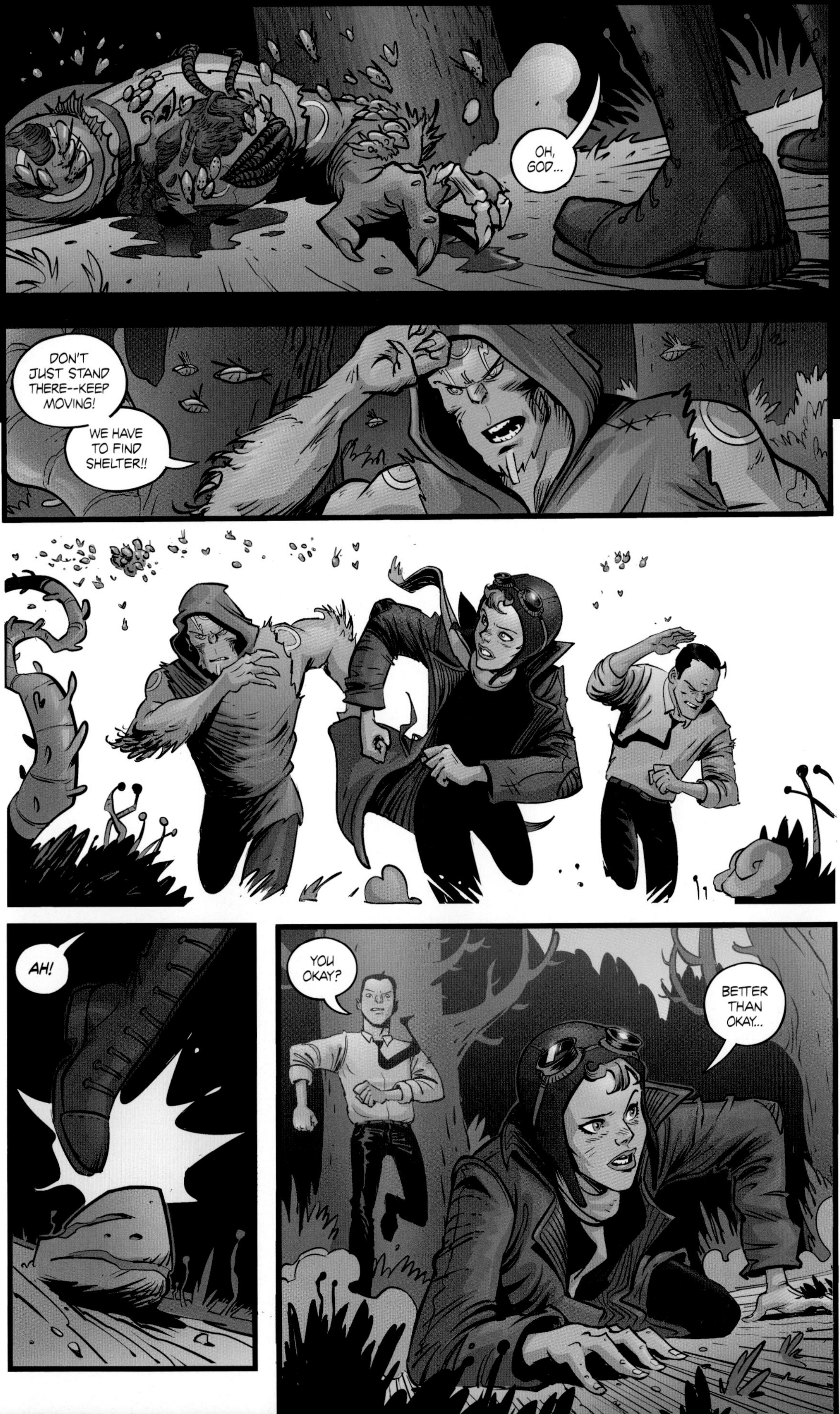
OH, GOD...
DON'T JUST STAND THERE--KEEP MOVING!
WE HAVE TO FIND SHELTER!!
AH!
YOU OKAY?
BETTER THAN OKAY...

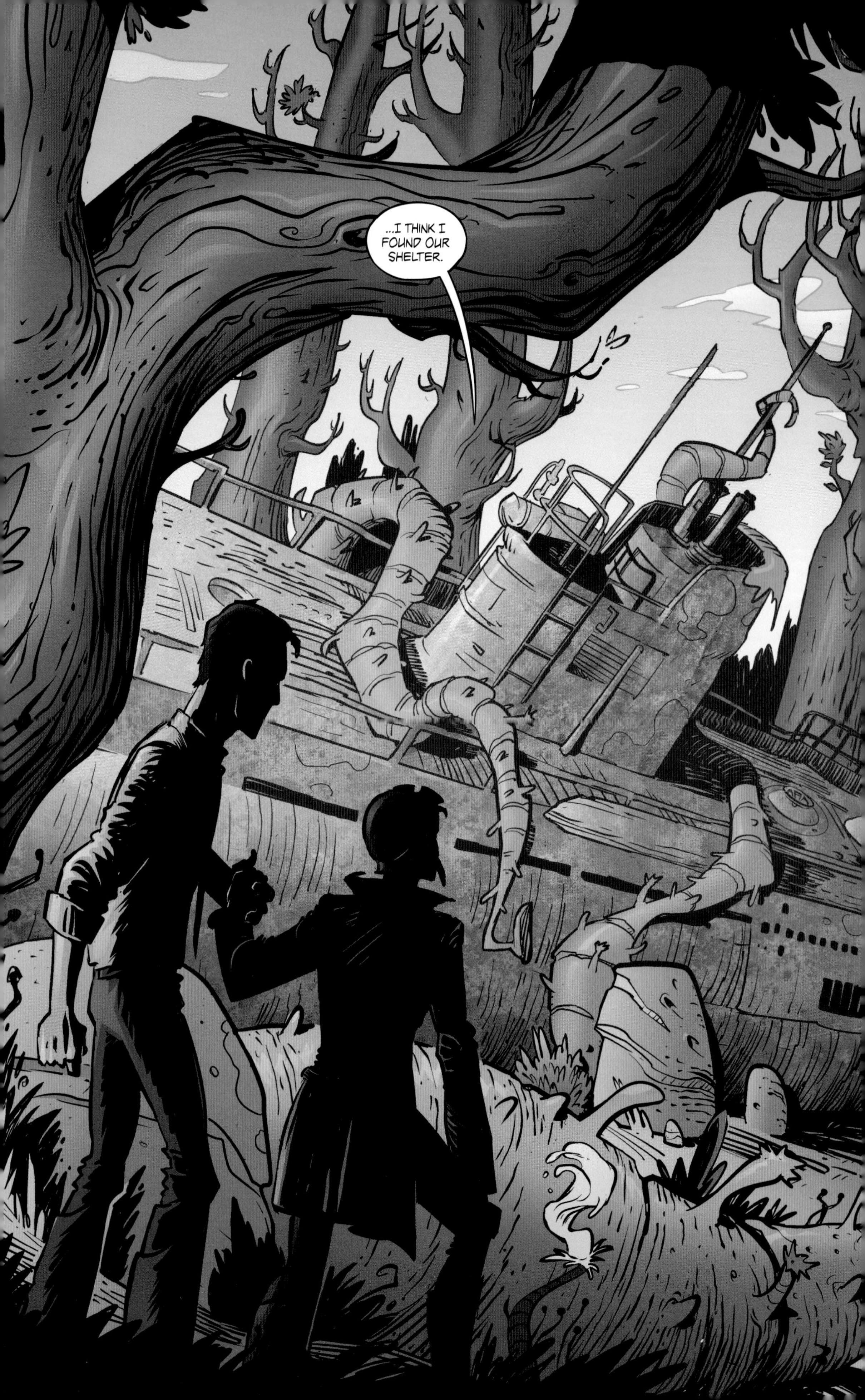
...I THINK I FOUND OUR SHELTER.

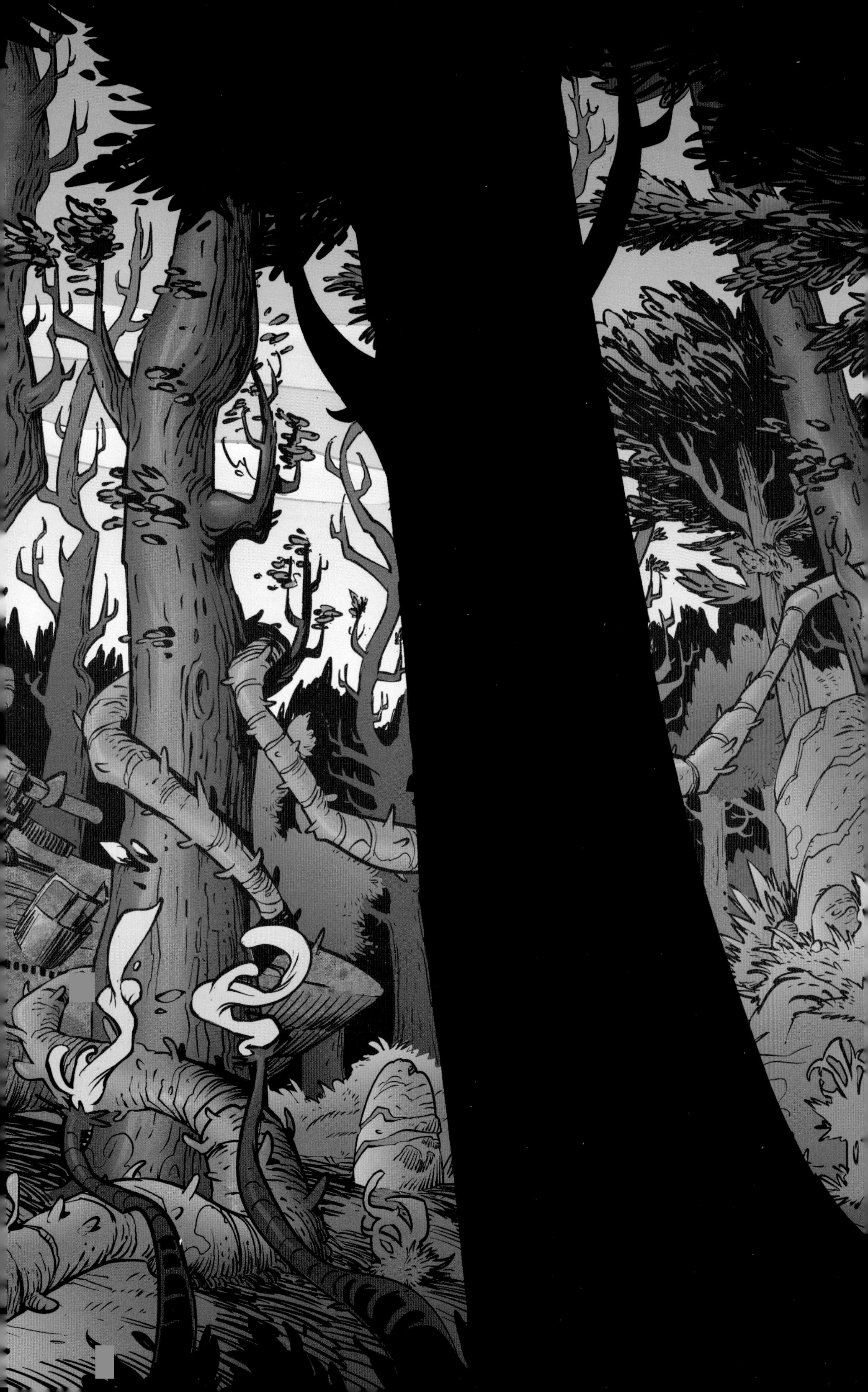

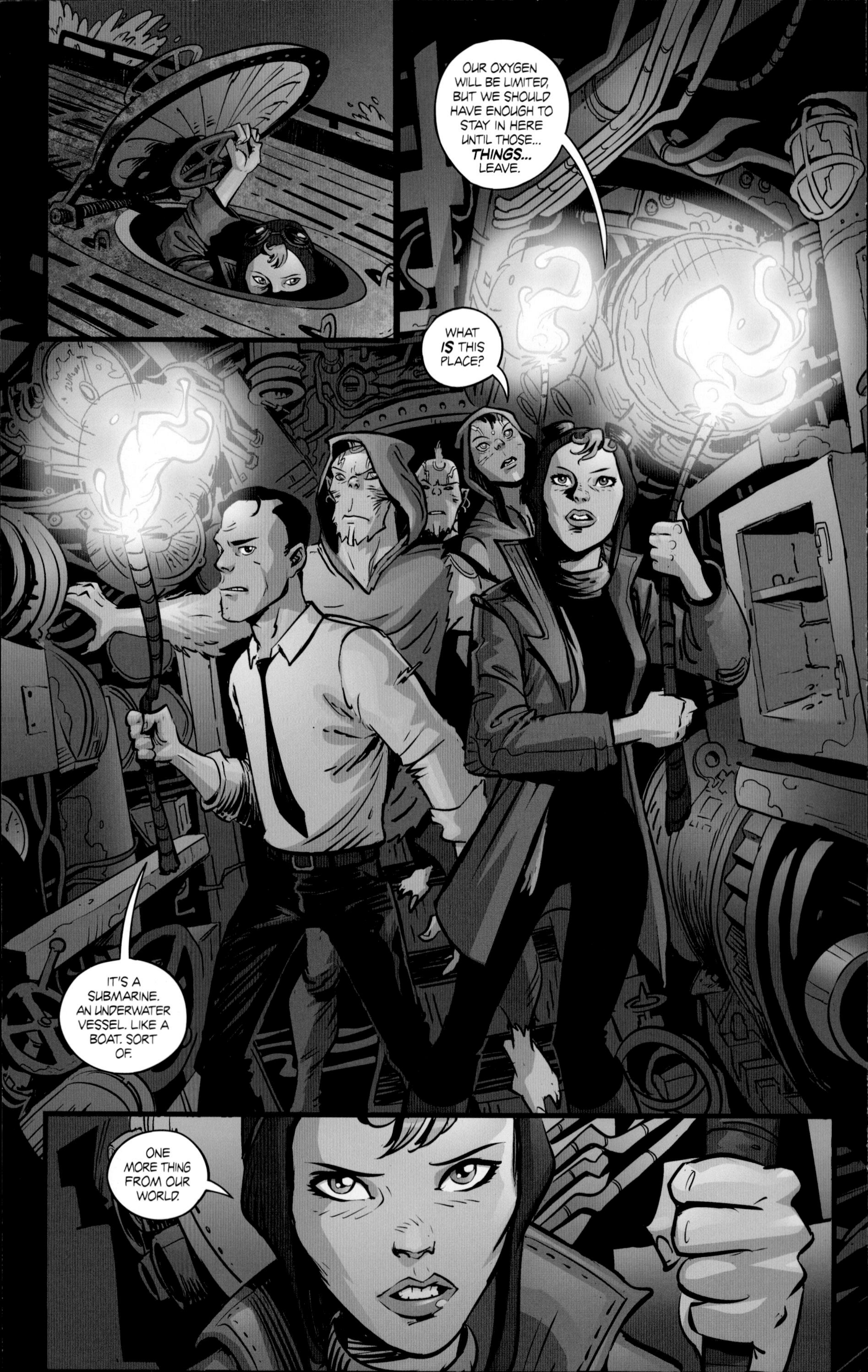
OUR OXYGEN WILL BE LIMITED, BUT WE SHOULD HAVE ENOUGH TO STAY IN HERE UNTIL THOSE... **THINGS...** LEAVE.
WHAT **IS** THIS PLACE?
IT'S A SUBMARINE. AN UNDERWATER VESSEL. LIKE A BOAT. SORT OF.
ONE MORE THING FROM OUR WORLD.

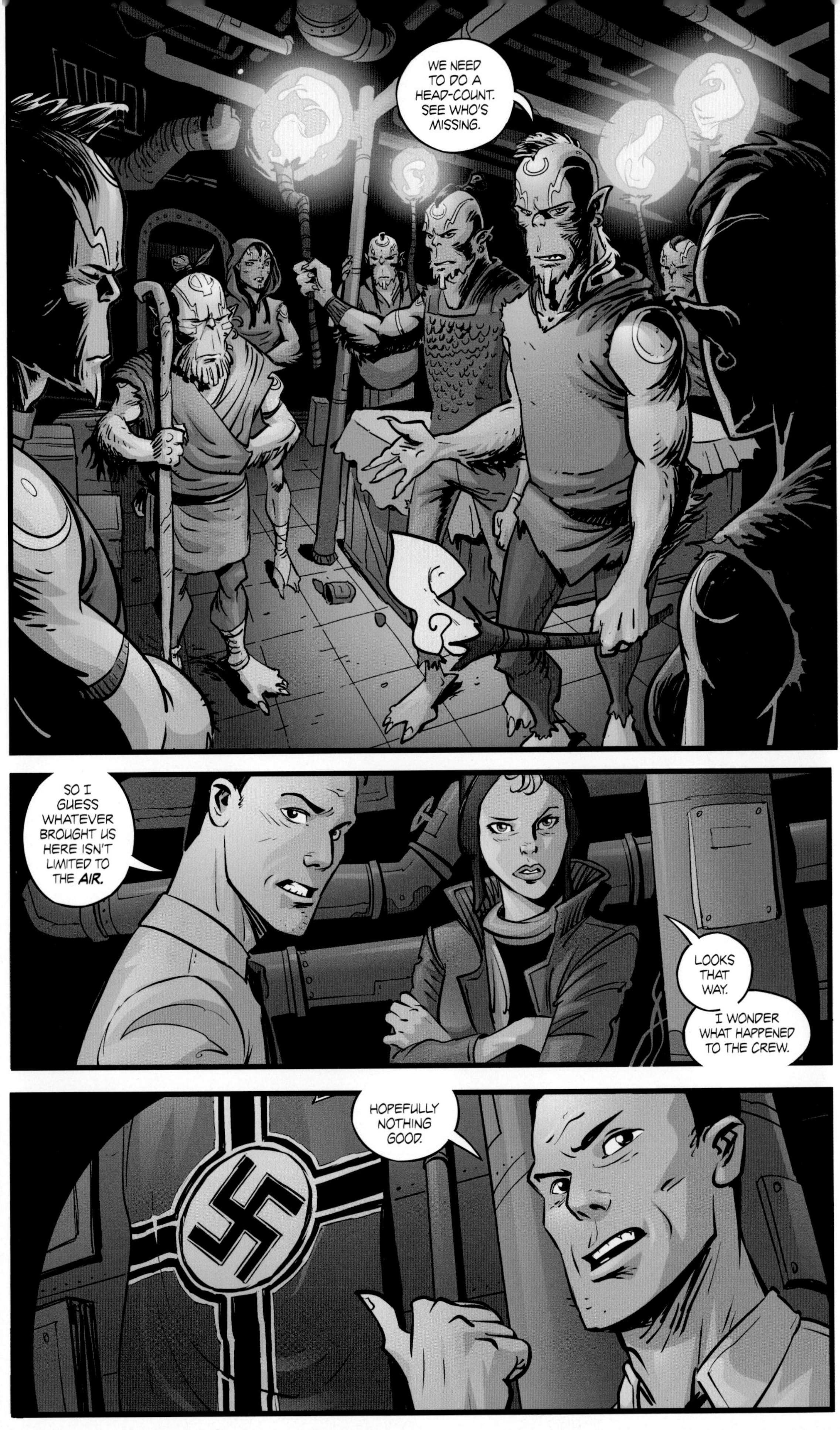
WE NEED TO DO A HEAD-COUNT. SEE WHO'S MISSING.
SO I GUESS WHATEVER BROUGHT US HERE ISN'T LIMITED TO THE *AIR.*
LOOKS THAT WAY.
I WONDER WHAT HAPPENED TO THE CREW.
HOPEFULLY NOTHING GOOD.

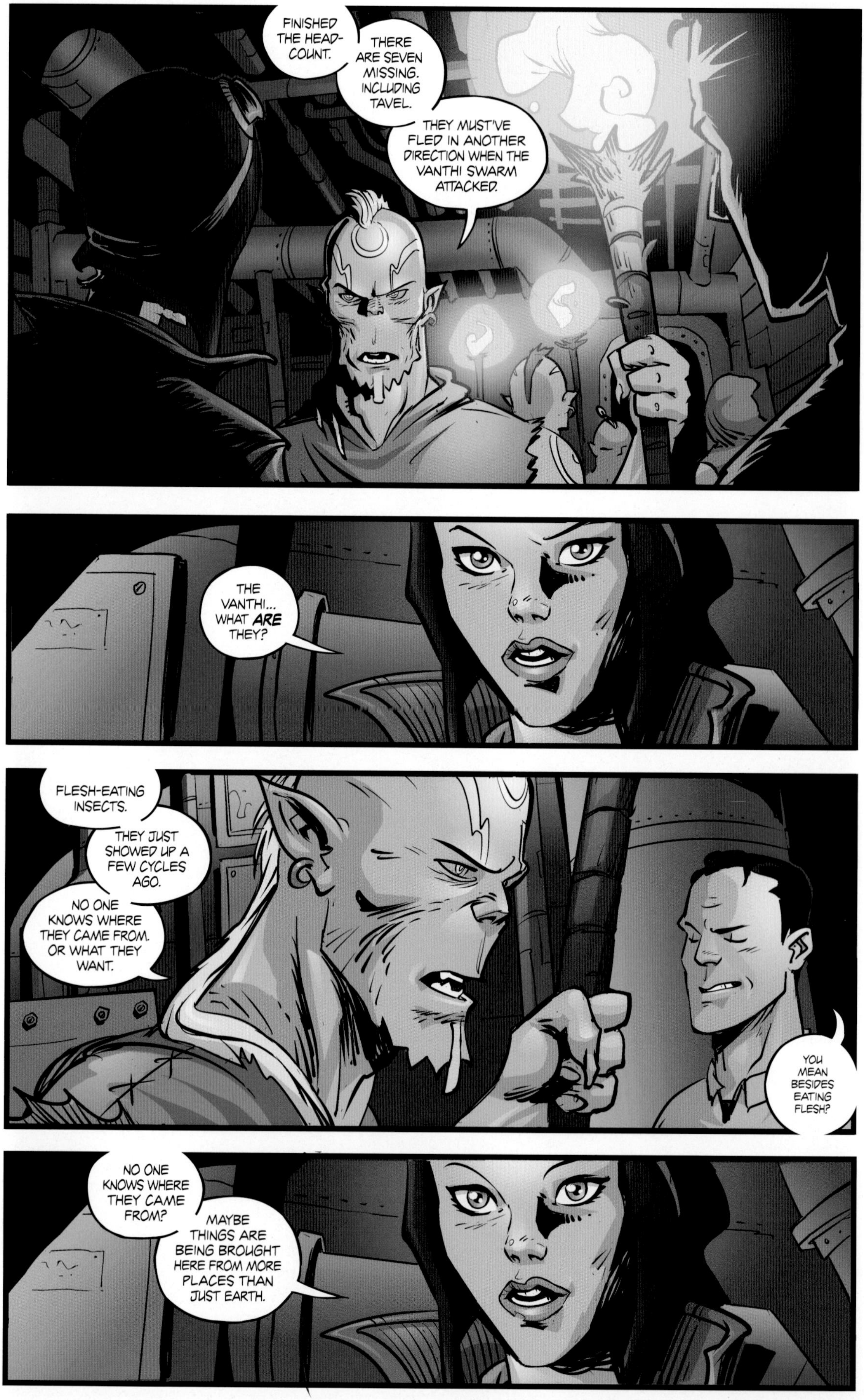
FINISHED THE HEAD-COUNT.
THERE ARE SEVEN MISSING. INCLUDING TAVEL.
THEY MUST'VE FLED IN ANOTHER DIRECTION WHEN THE VANTHI SWARM ATTACKED.
THE VANTHI... WHAT **ARE** THEY?
FLESH-EATING INSECTS.
THEY JUST SHOWED UP A FEW CYCLES AGO.
NO ONE KNOWS WHERE THEY CAME FROM. OR WHAT THEY WANT.
YOU MEAN BESIDES EATING FLESH?
NO ONE KNOWS WHERE THEY CAME FROM?
MAYBE THINGS ARE BEING BROUGHT HERE FROM MORE PLACES THAN JUST EARTH.

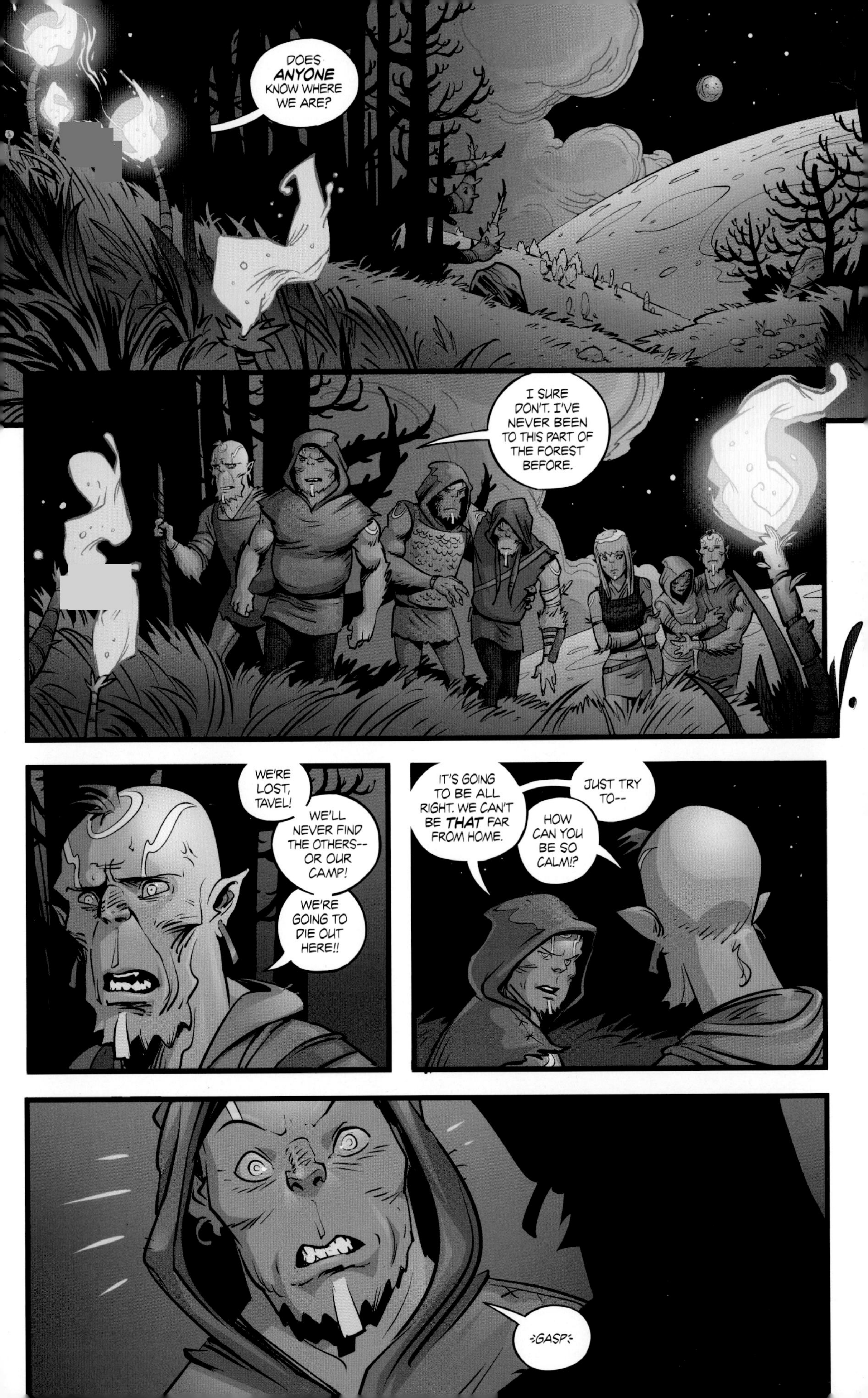
DOES ANYONE KNOW WHERE WE ARE?
I SURE DON'T. I'VE NEVER BEEN TO THIS PART OF THE FOREST BEFORE.
WE'RE LOST, TAVEL!
WE'LL NEVER FIND THE OTHERS-- OR OUR CAMP!
WE'RE GOING TO DIE OUT HERE!!
IT'S GOING TO BE ALL RIGHT. WE CAN'T BE THAT FAR FROM HOME.
JUST TRY TO--
HOW CAN YOU BE SO CALM!?
GASP

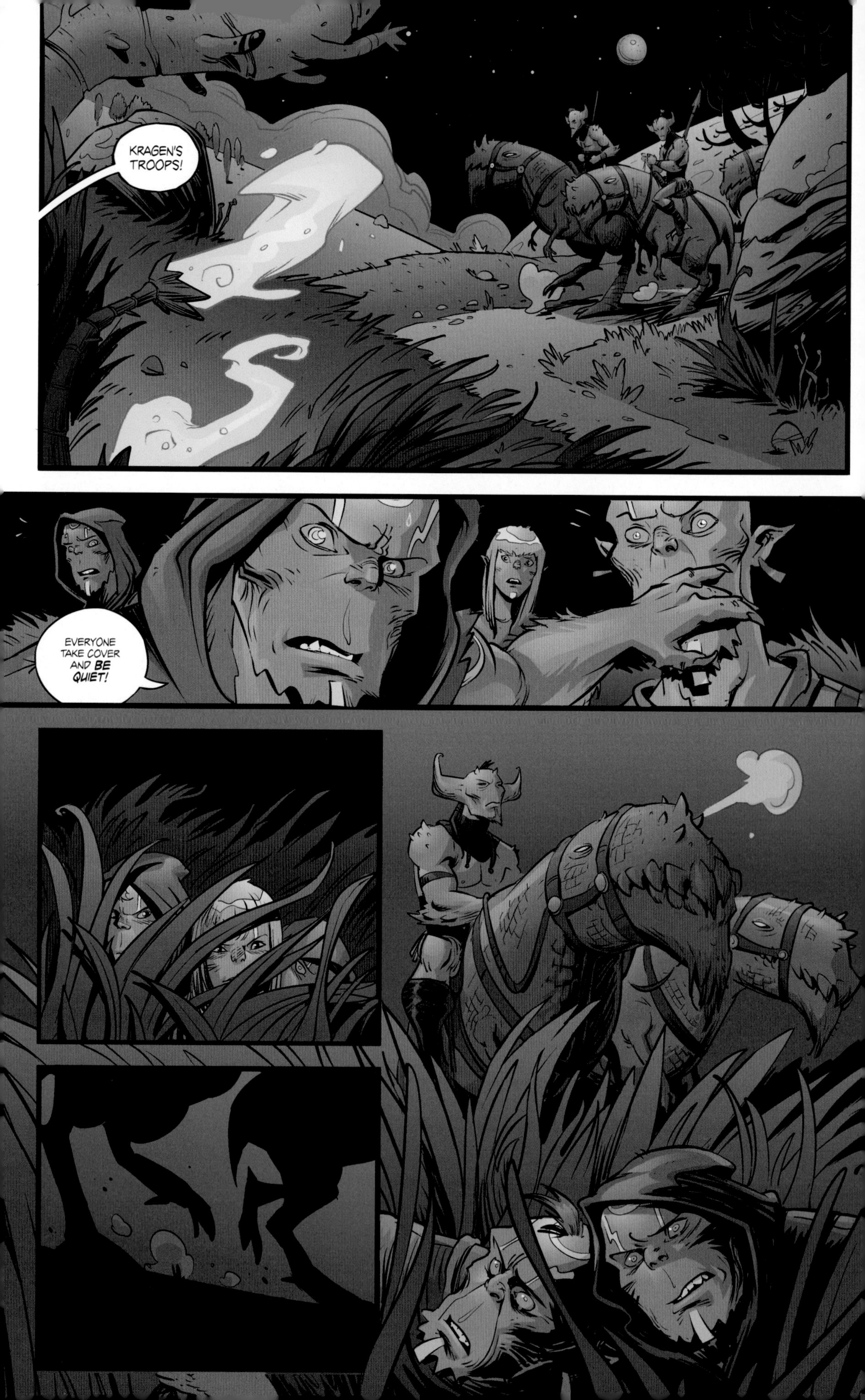
KRAGEN'S TROOPS!
EVERYONE TAKE COVER AND **BE QUIET!**

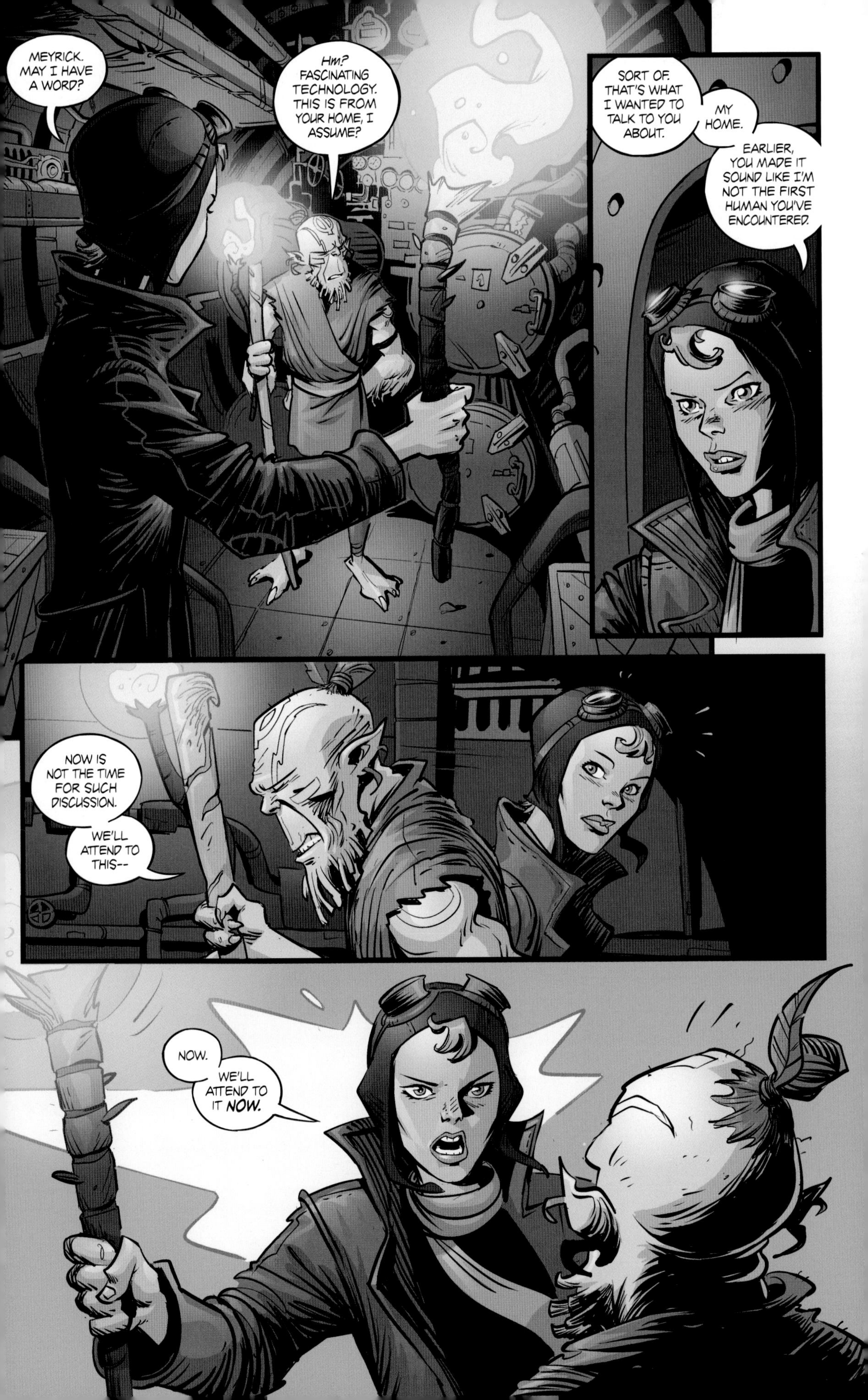
MEYRICK. MAY I HAVE A WORD?
Hm? FASCINATING TECHNOLOGY. THIS IS FROM YOUR HOME, I ASSUME?
SORT OF. THAT'S WHAT I WANTED TO TALK TO YOU ABOUT.
MY HOME.
EARLIER, YOU MADE IT SOUND LIKE I'M NOT THE FIRST HUMAN YOU'VE ENCOUNTERED.
NOW IS NOT THE TIME FOR SUCH DISCUSSION.
WE'LL ATTEND TO THIS--
NOW.
WE'LL ATTEND TO IT NOW.

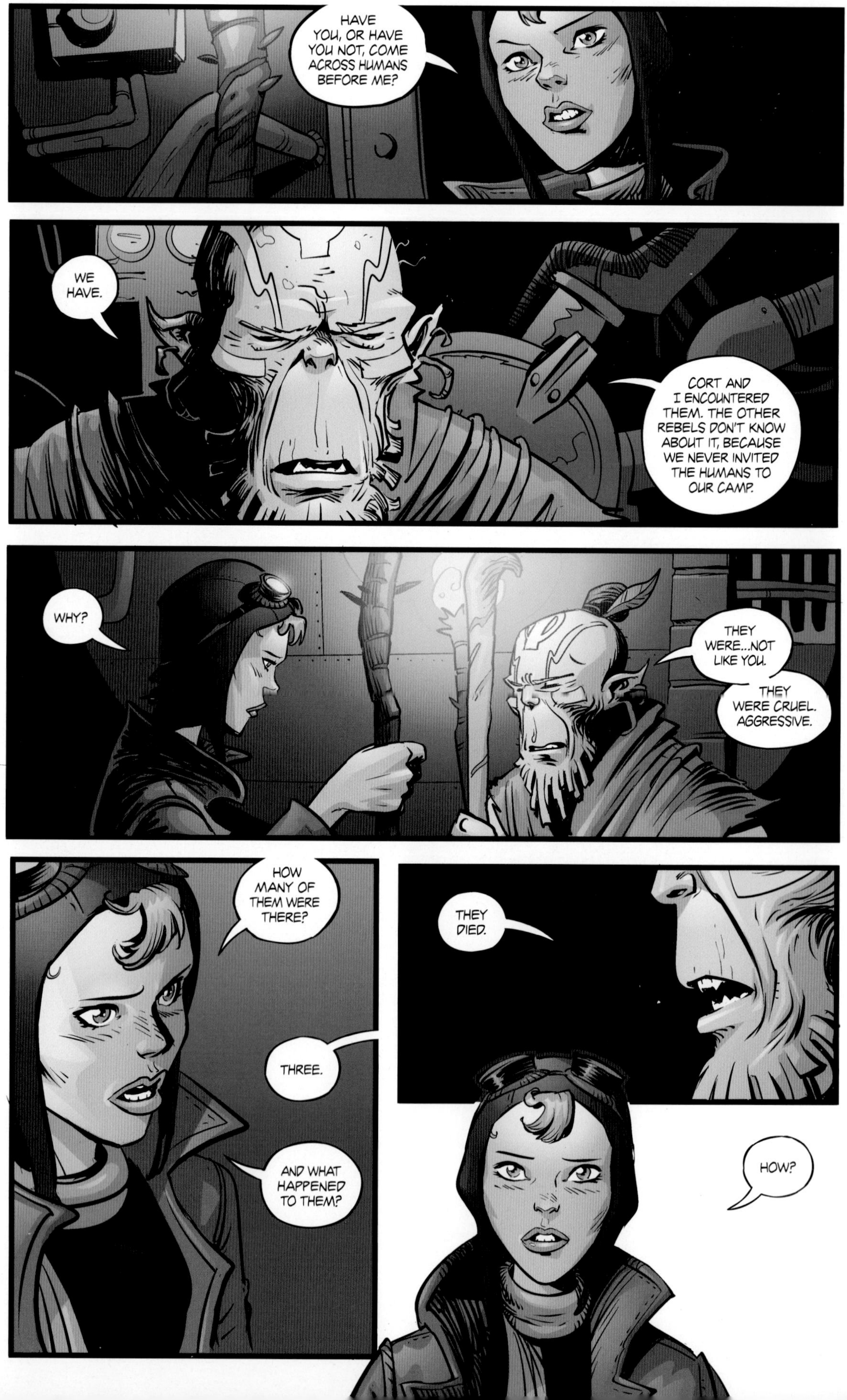
HAVE YOU, OR HAVE YOU NOT, COME ACROSS HUMANS BEFORE ME?
WE HAVE.
CORT AND I ENCOUNTERED THEM. THE OTHER REBELS DON'T KNOW ABOUT IT, BECAUSE WE NEVER INVITED THE HUMANS TO OUR CAMP.
WHY?
THEY WERE...NOT LIKE YOU.
THEY WERE CRUEL. AGGRESSIVE.
HOW MANY OF THEM WERE THERE?
THREE.
AND WHAT HAPPENED TO THEM?
THEY DIED.
HOW?

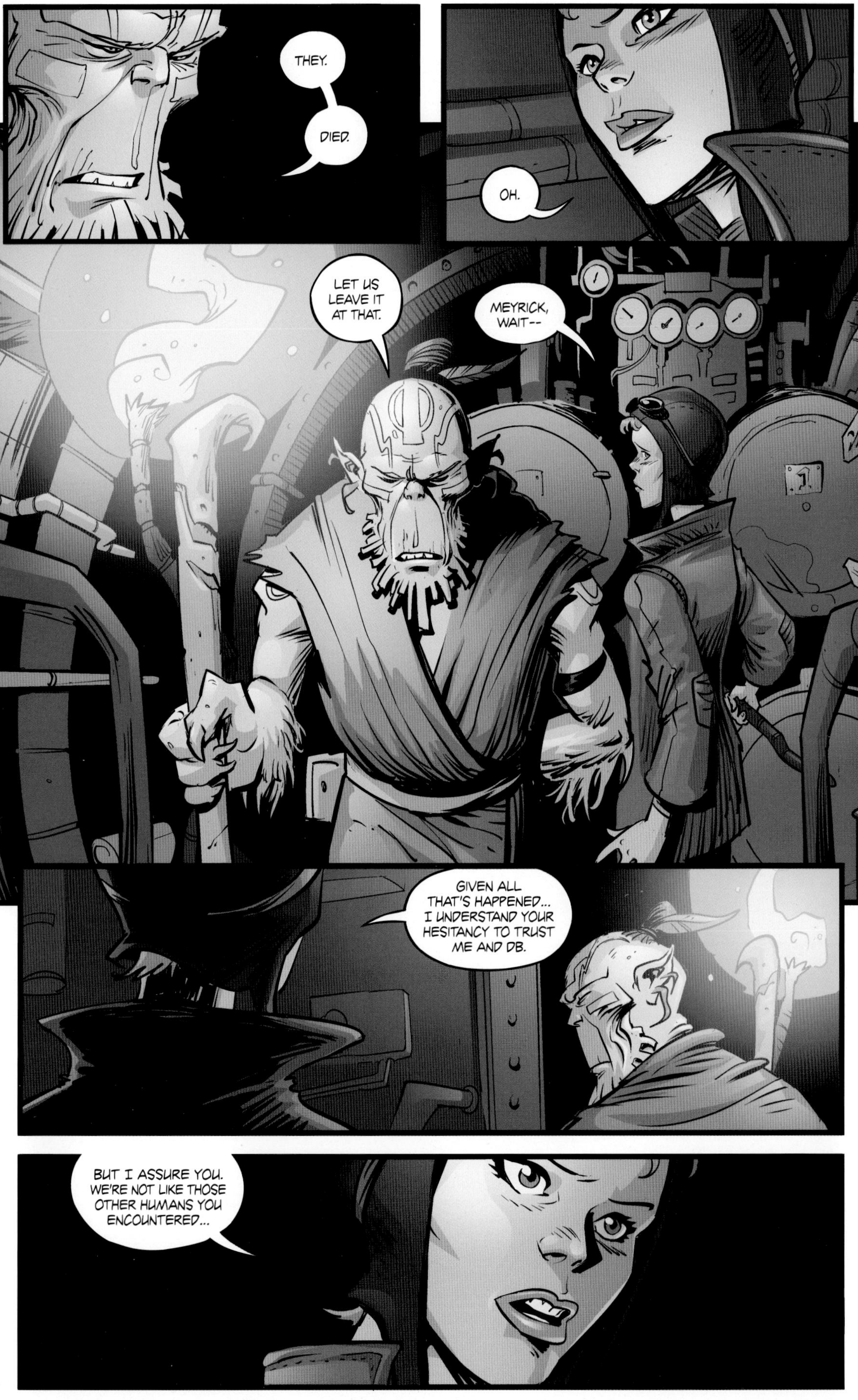
THEY.
DIED.
OH.
LET US LEAVE IT AT THAT.
MEYRICK, WAIT--
GIVEN ALL THAT'S HAPPENED... I UNDERSTAND YOUR HESITANCY TO TRUST ME AND DB.
BUT I ASSURE YOU. WE'RE NOT LIKE THOSE OTHER HUMANS YOU ENCOUNTERED...

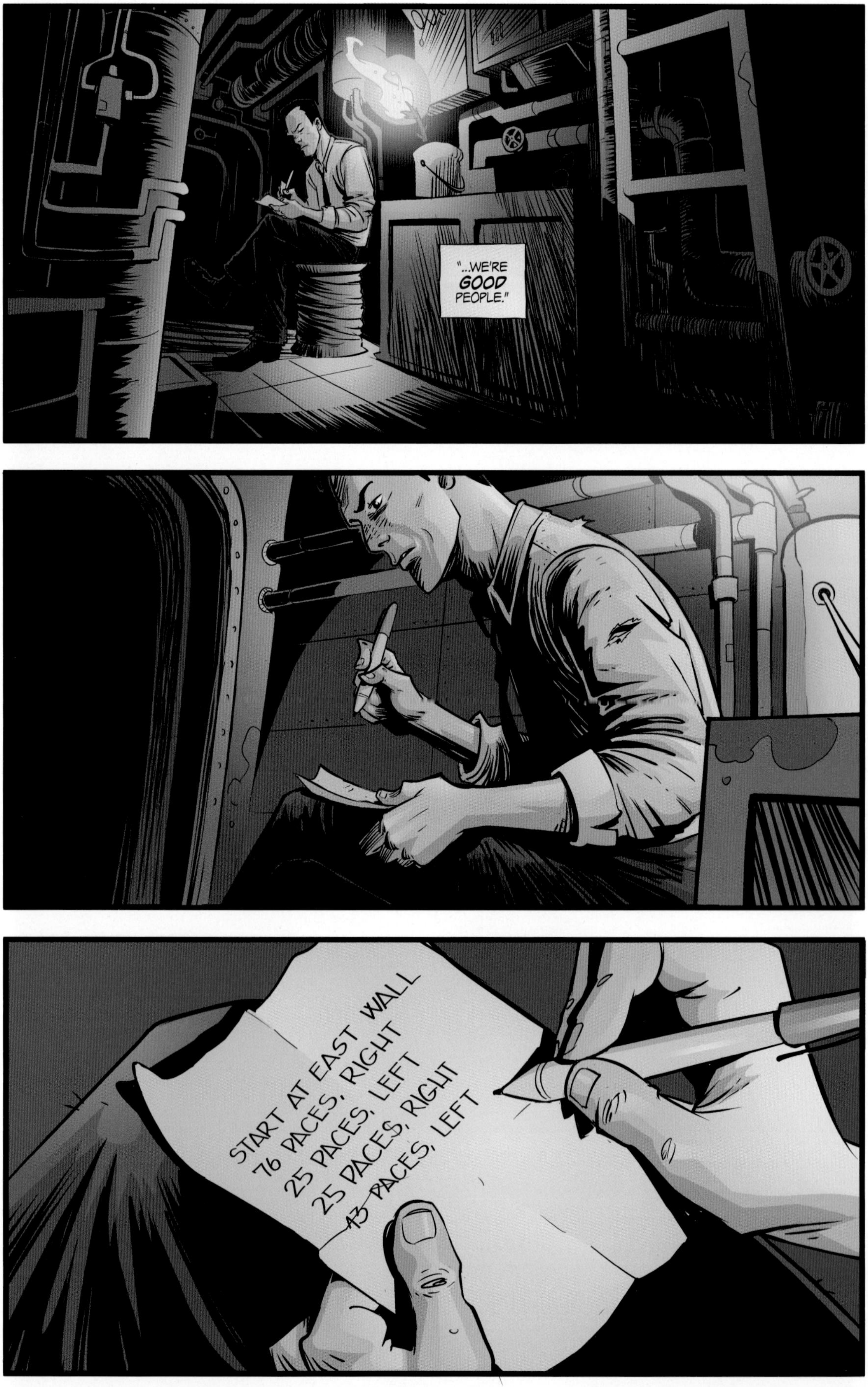
"...WE'RE GOOD PEOPLE."
START AT EAST WALL
76 PACES, RIGHT
25 PACES, LEFT
25 PACES, RIGHT
43 PACES, LEFT

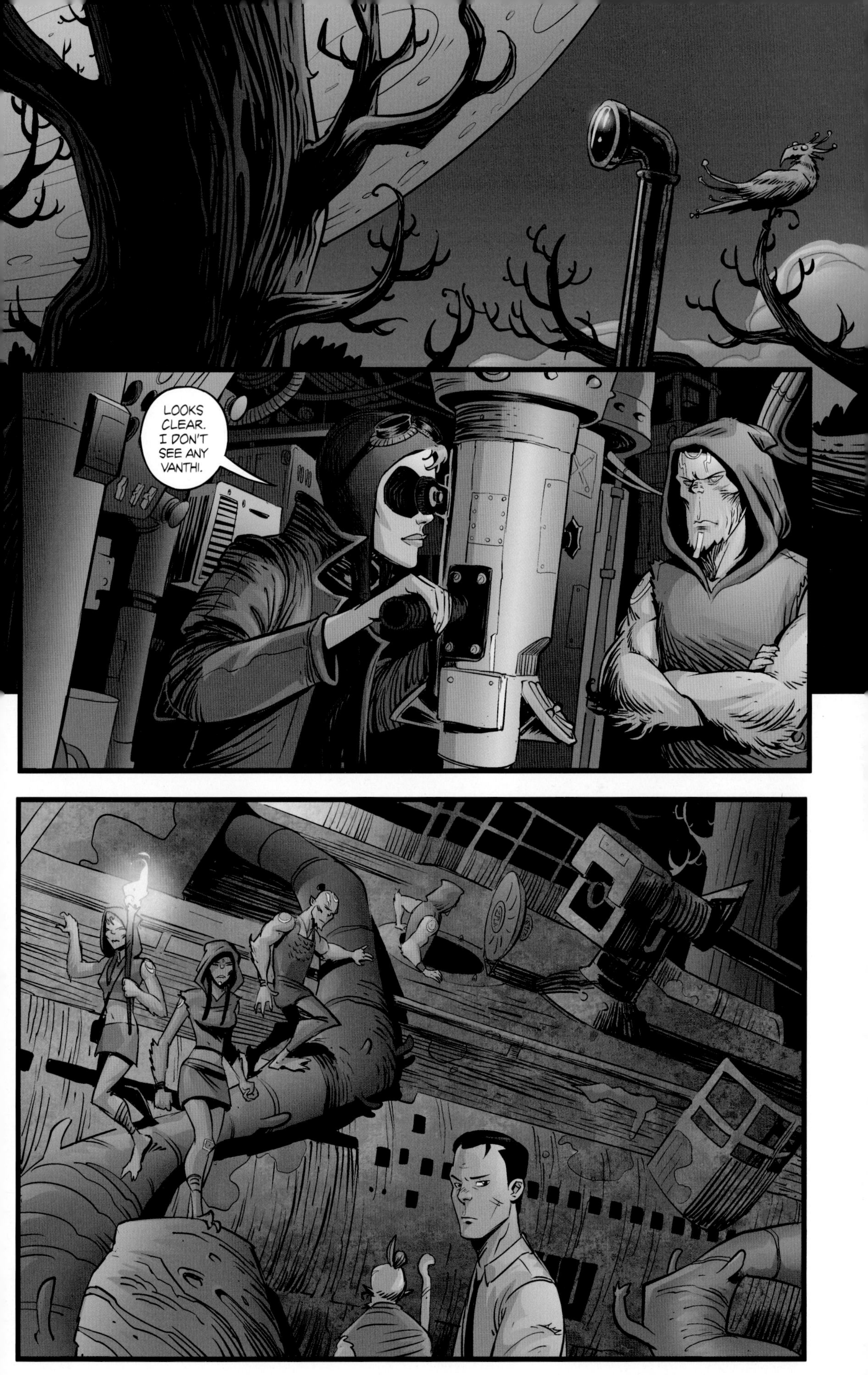
LOOKS CLEAR. I DON'T SEE ANY VANTHI.

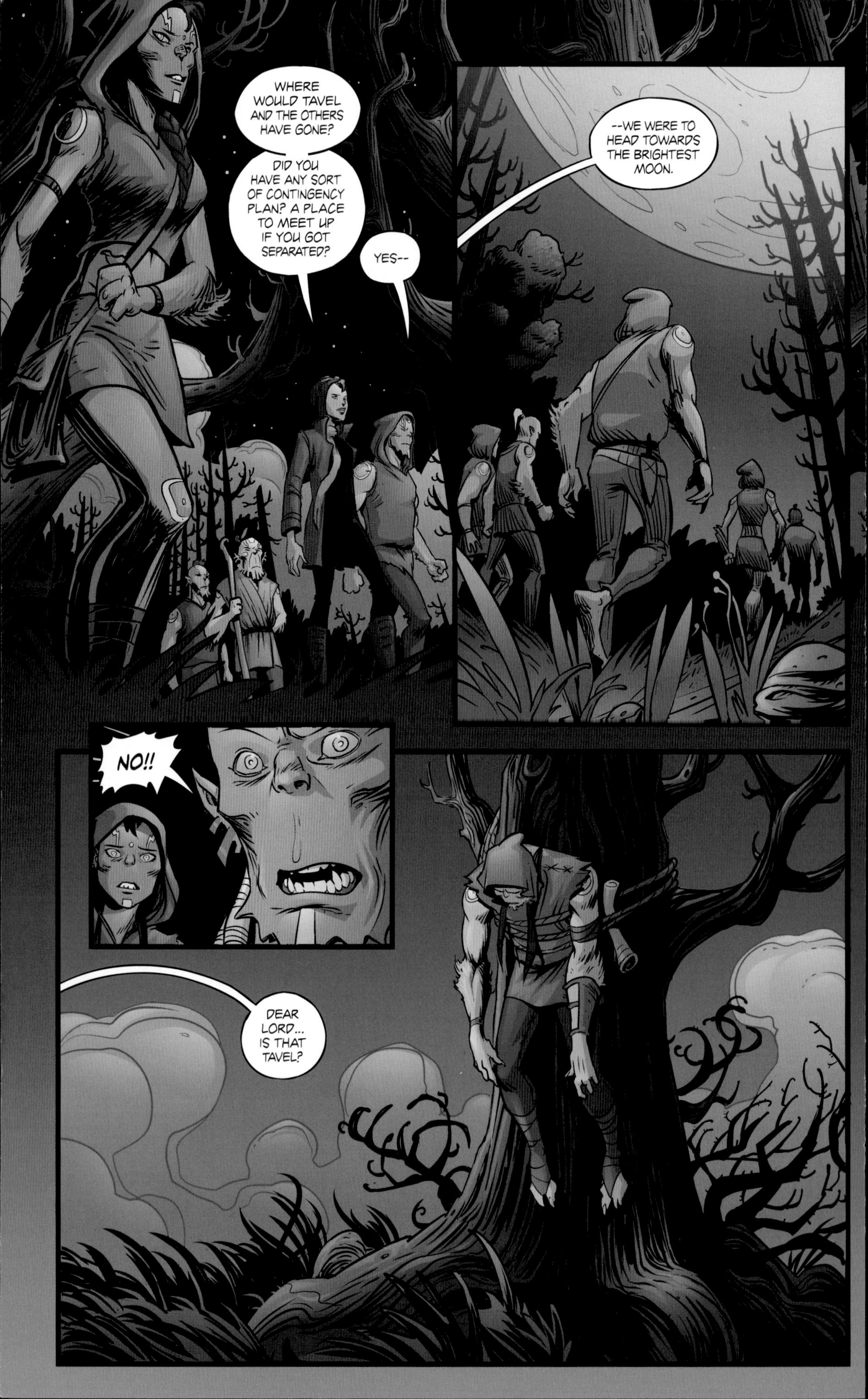
WHERE WOULD TAVEL AND THE OTHERS HAVE GONE?
DID YOU HAVE ANY SORT OF CONTINGENCY PLAN? A PLACE TO MEET UP IF YOU GOT SEPARATED?
YES--
--WE WERE TO HEAD TOWARDS THE BRIGHTEST MOON.
NO!!
DEAR LORD... IS THAT TAVEL?

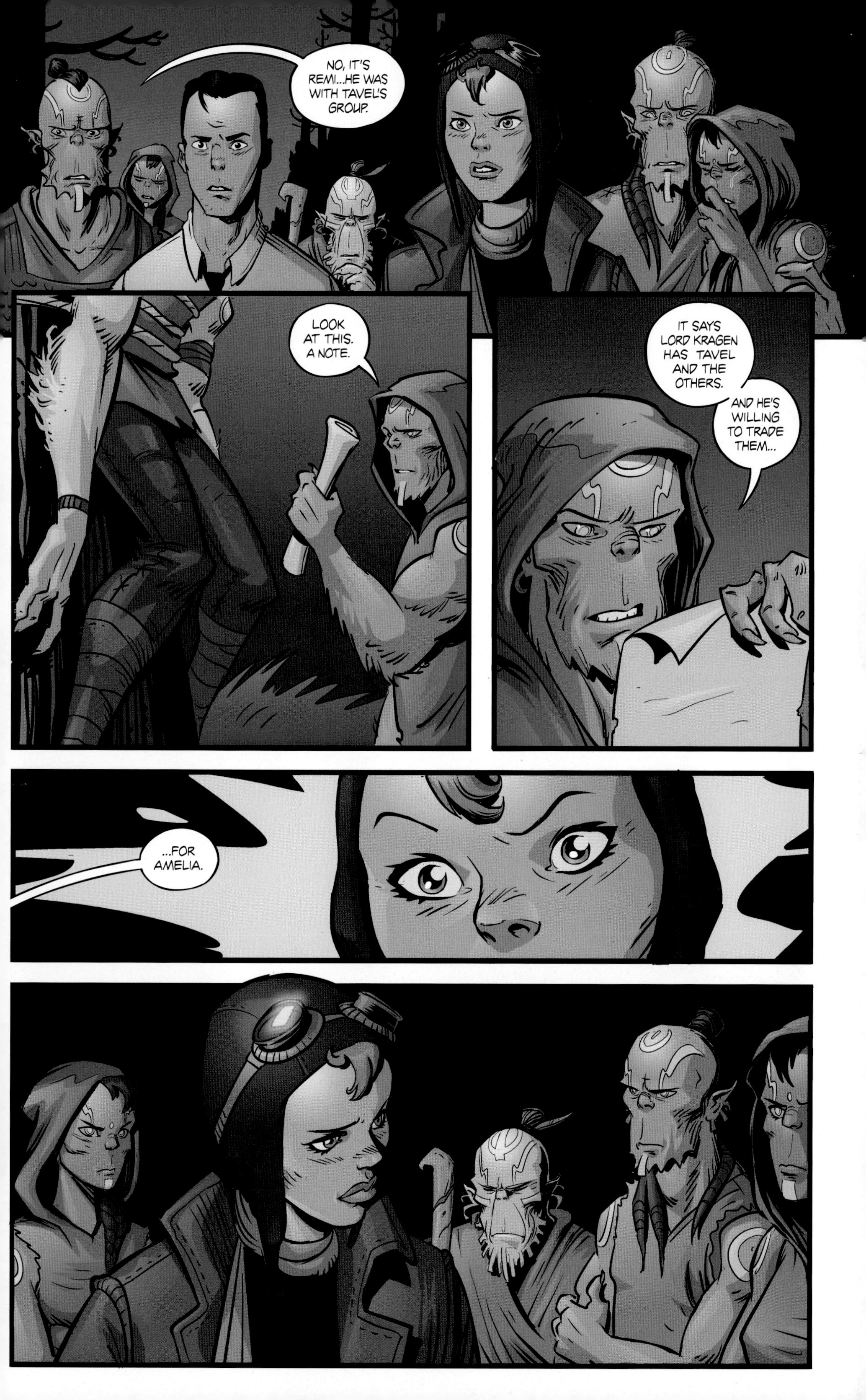
NO, IT'S REMI...HE WAS WITH TAVEL'S GROUP.
LOOK AT THIS. A NOTE.
IT SAYS LORD KRAGEN HAS TAVEL AND THE OTHERS.
AND HE'S WILLING TO TRADE THEM...
...FOR AMELIA.

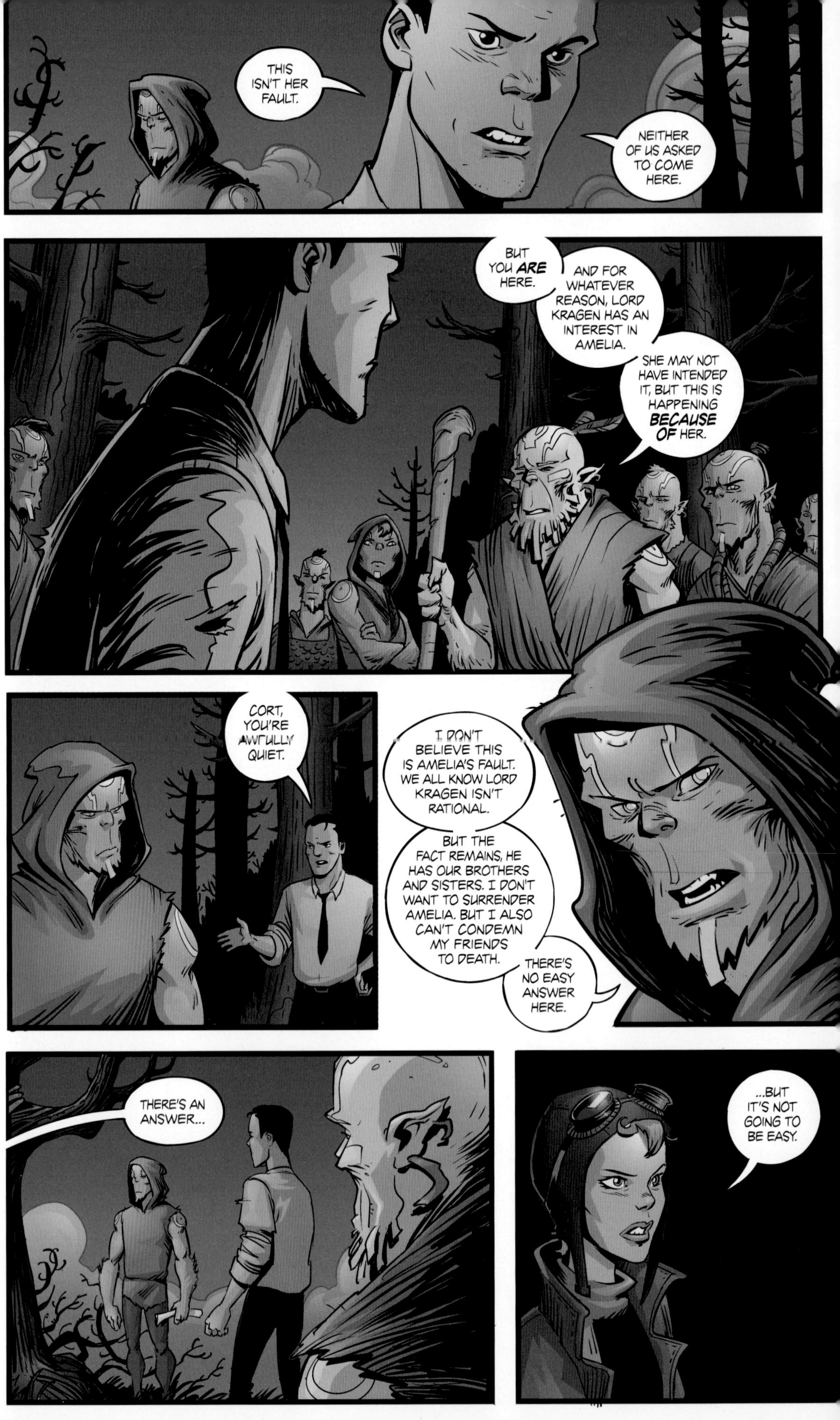
THIS ISN'T HER FAULT.
NEITHER OF US ASKED TO COME HERE.
BUT YOU **ARE** HERE.
AND FOR WHATEVER REASON, LORD KRAGEN HAS AN INTEREST IN AMELIA.
SHE MAY NOT HAVE INTENDED IT, BUT THIS IS HAPPENING **BECAUSE OF** HER.
CORT, YOU'RE AWFULLY QUIET.
I DON'T BELIEVE THIS IS AMELIA'S FAULT. WE ALL KNOW LORD KRAGEN ISN'T RATIONAL.
BUT THE FACT REMAINS, HE HAS OUR BROTHERS AND SISTERS. I DON'T WANT TO SURRENDER AMELIA. BUT I ALSO CAN'T CONDEMN MY FRIENDS TO DEATH.
THERE'S NO EASY ANSWER HERE.
THERE'S AN ANSWER...
...BUT IT'S NOT GOING TO BE EASY.

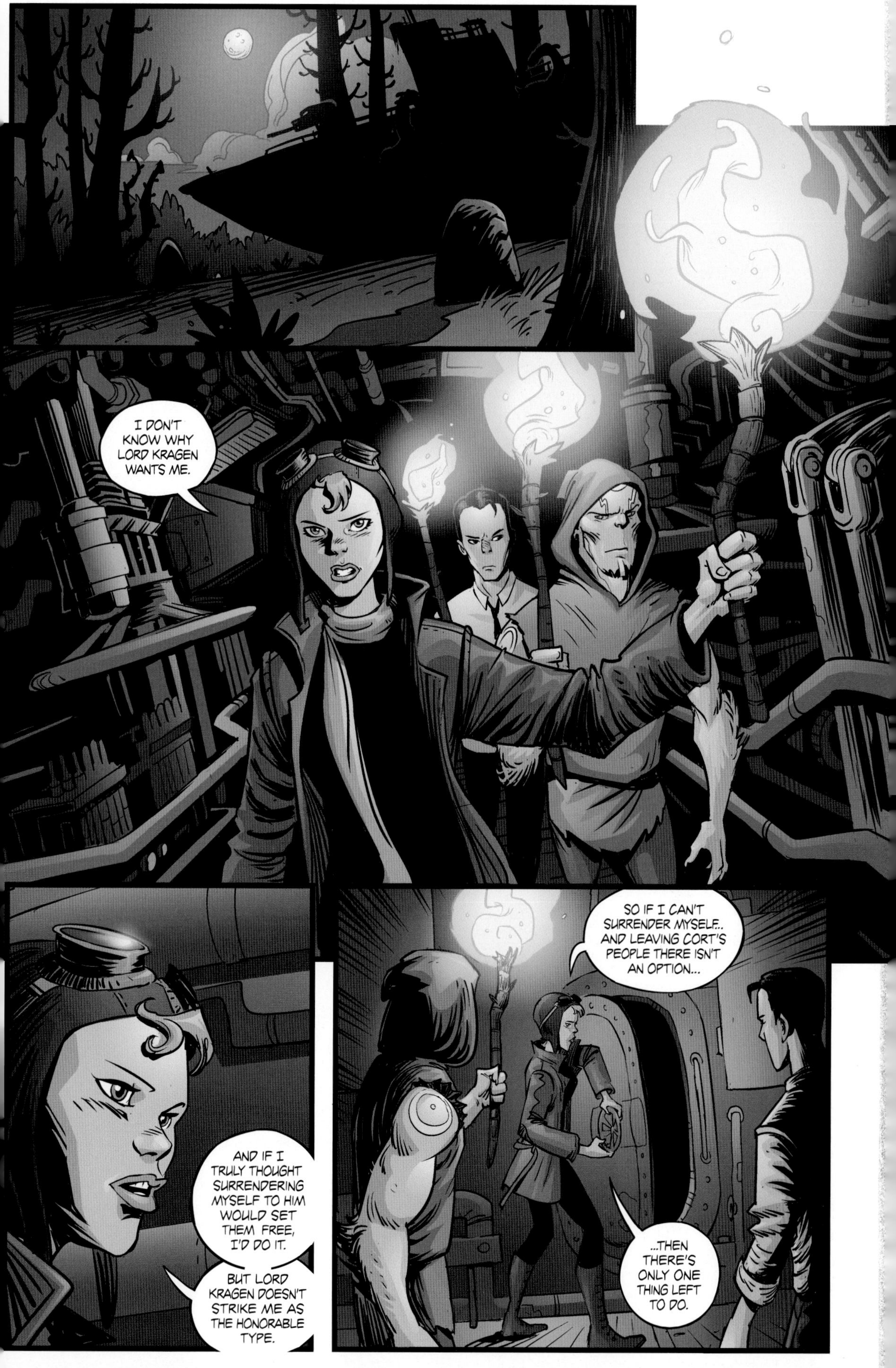
I DON'T KNOW WHY LORD KRAGEN WANTS ME.
AND IF I TRULY THOUGHT SURRENDERING MYSELF TO HIM WOULD SET THEM FREE, I'D DO IT.
BUT LORD KRAGEN DOESN'T STRIKE ME AS THE HONORABLE TYPE.
SO IF I CAN'T SURRENDER MYSELF.. AND LEAVING CORT'S PEOPLE THERE ISN'T AN OPTION...
...THEN THERE'S ONLY ONE THING LEFT TO DO.

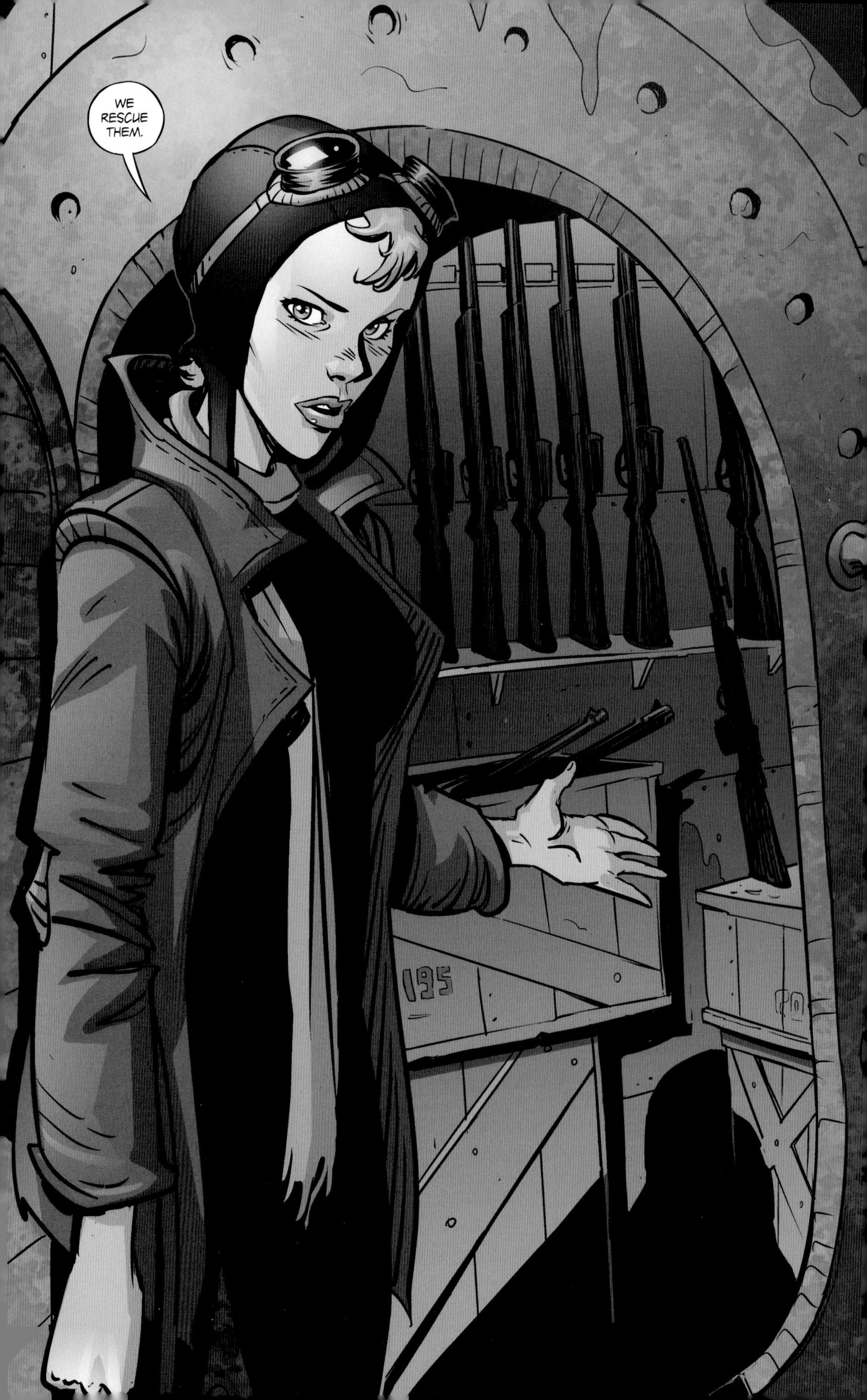
WE RESCUE THEM.

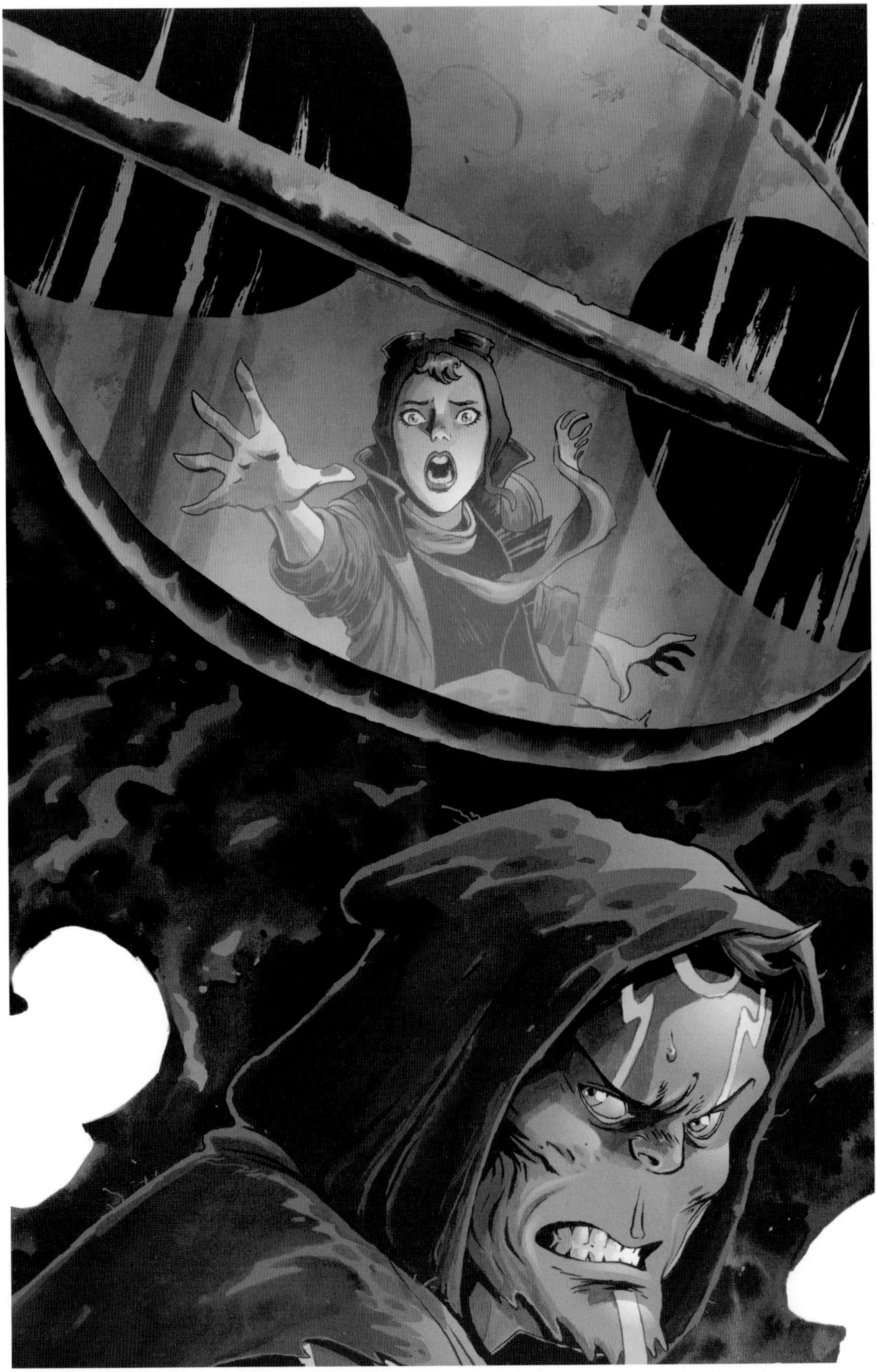

CHAPTER 4

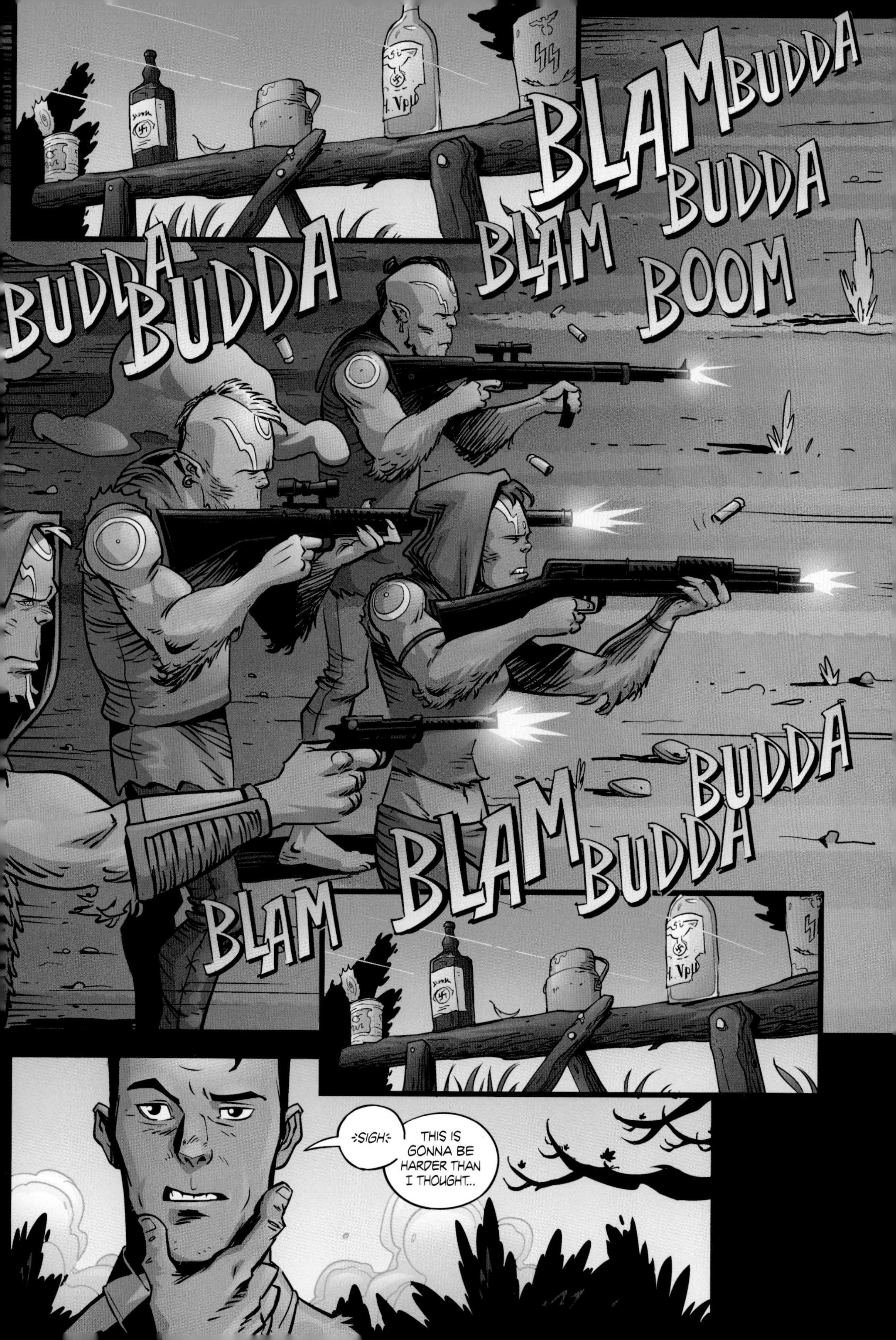
BLAM BUDDA
BLAM BUDDA
BUDDA BUDDA BUDDA
BOOM
BLAM BLAM BUDDA BUDDA
-SIGH-
THIS IS GONNA BE HARDER THAN I THOUGHT...

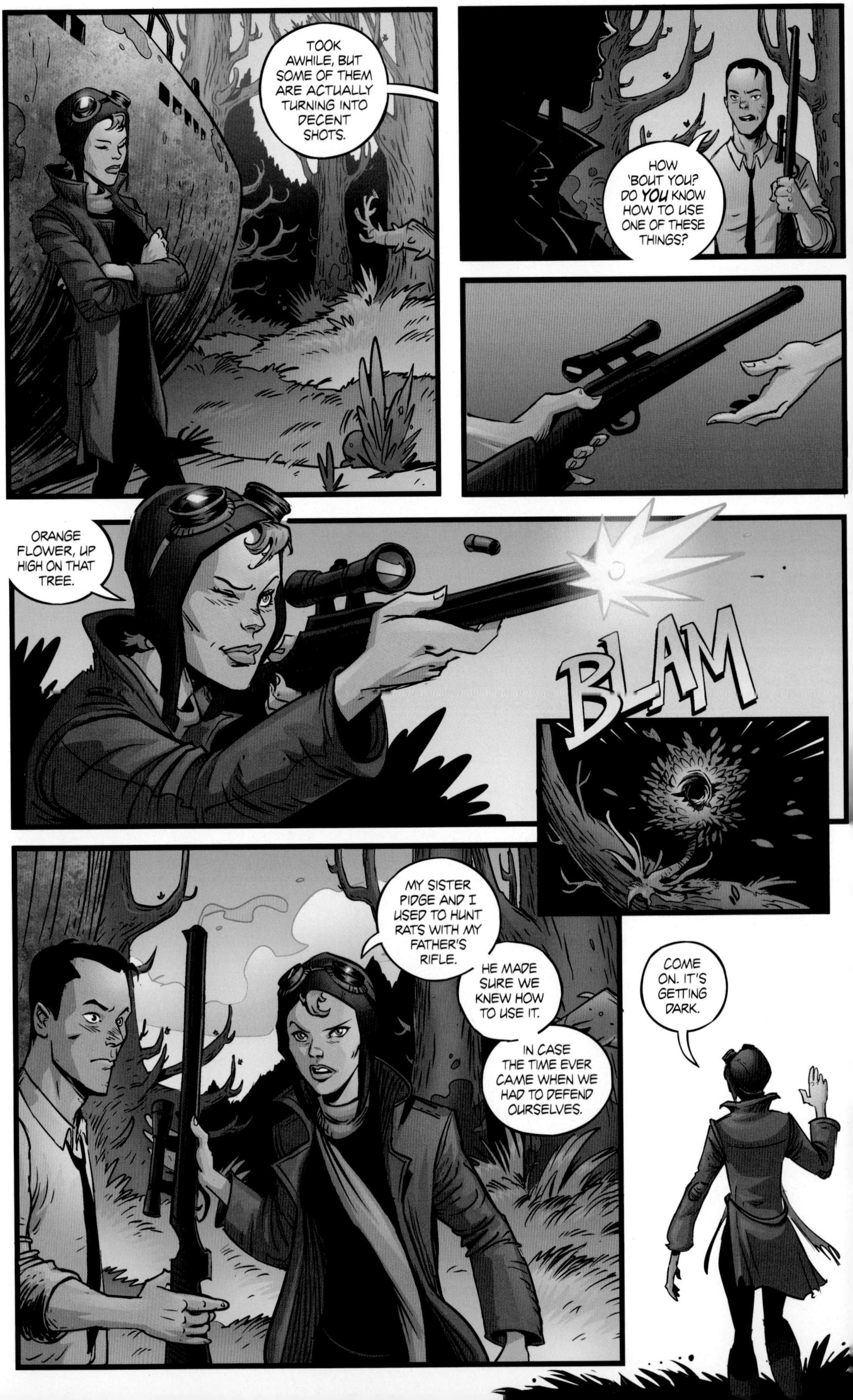
TOOK AWHILE, BUT SOME OF THEM ARE ACTUALLY TURNING INTO DECENT SHOTS.
HOW 'BOUT YOU? DO **YOU** KNOW HOW TO USE ONE OF THESE THINGS?
ORANGE FLOWER, UP HIGH ON THAT TREE.
BLAM
MY SISTER PIDGE AND I USED TO HUNT RATS WITH MY FATHER'S RIFLE.
HE MADE SURE WE KNEW HOW TO USE IT.
IN CASE THE TIME EVER CAME WHEN WE HAD TO DEFEND OURSELVES.
COME ON. IT'S GETTING DARK.

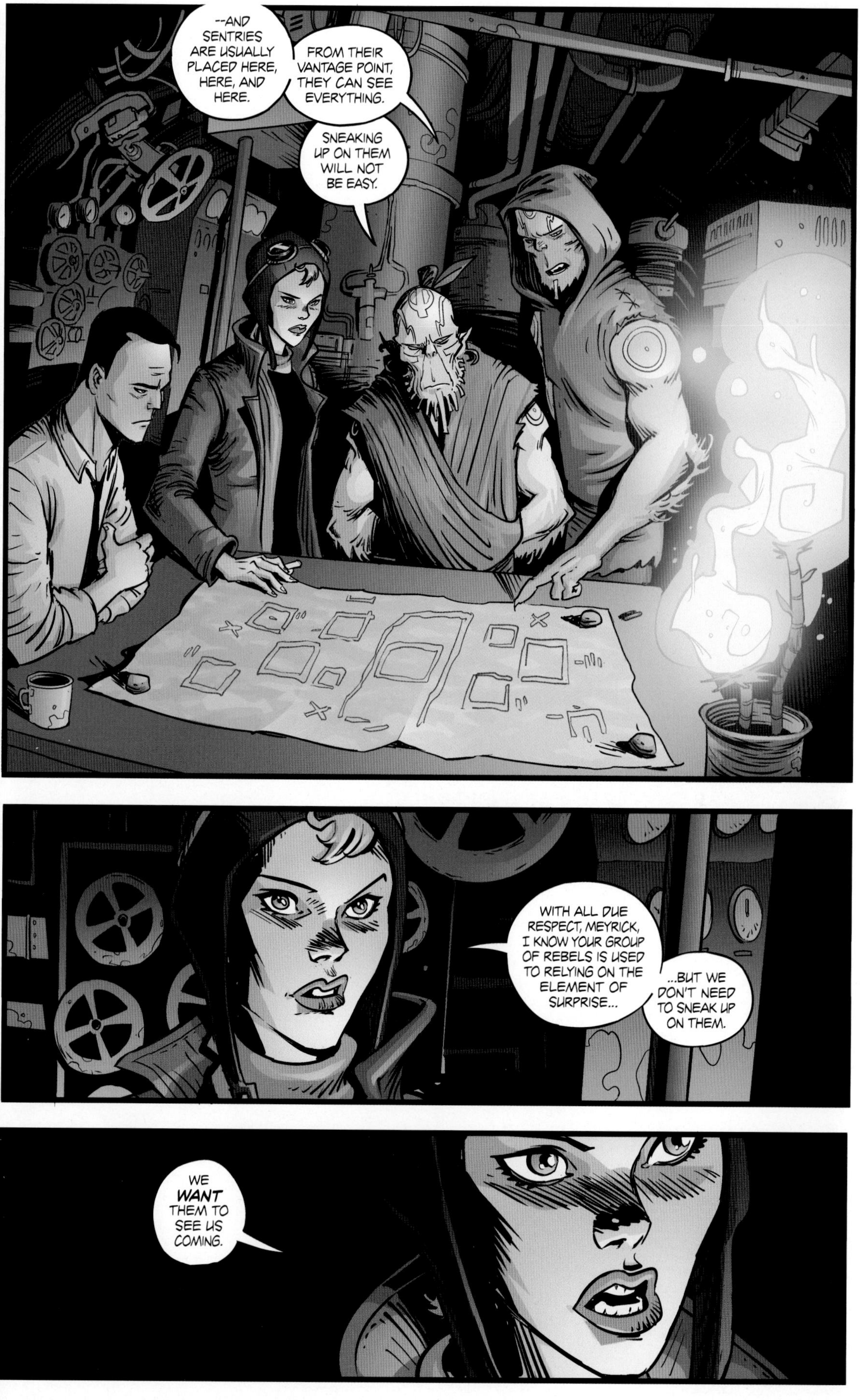
--AND SENTRIES ARE USUALLY PLACED HERE, HERE, AND HERE.
FROM THEIR VANTAGE POINT, THEY CAN SEE EVERYTHING.
SNEAKING UP ON THEM WILL NOT BE EASY.
WITH ALL DUE RESPECT, MEYRICK, I KNOW YOUR GROUP OF REBELS IS USED TO RELYING ON THE ELEMENT OF SURPRISE...
...BUT WE DON'T NEED TO SNEAK UP ON THEM.
WE *WANT* THEM TO SEE US COMING.

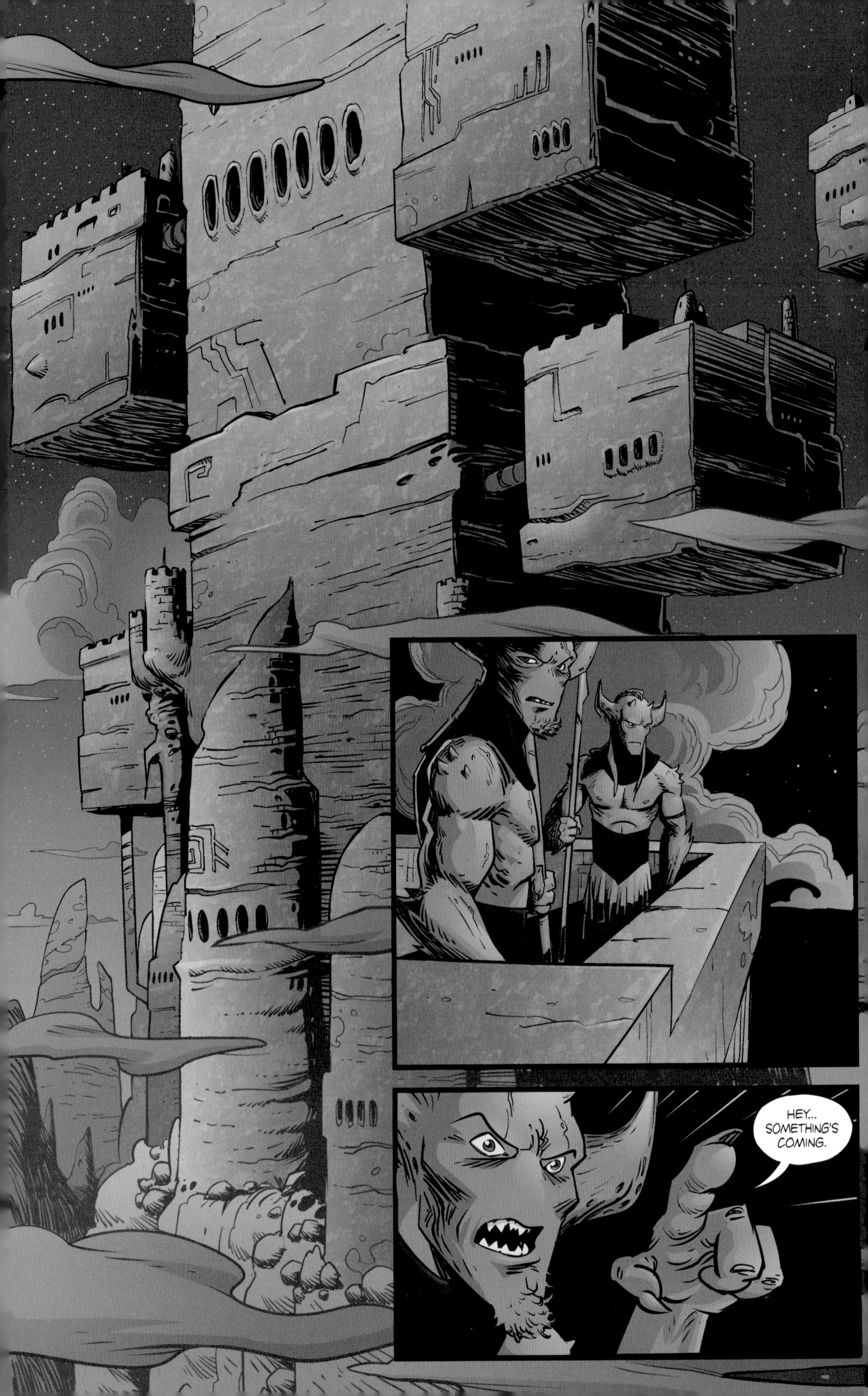
HEY... SOMETHING'S COMING.

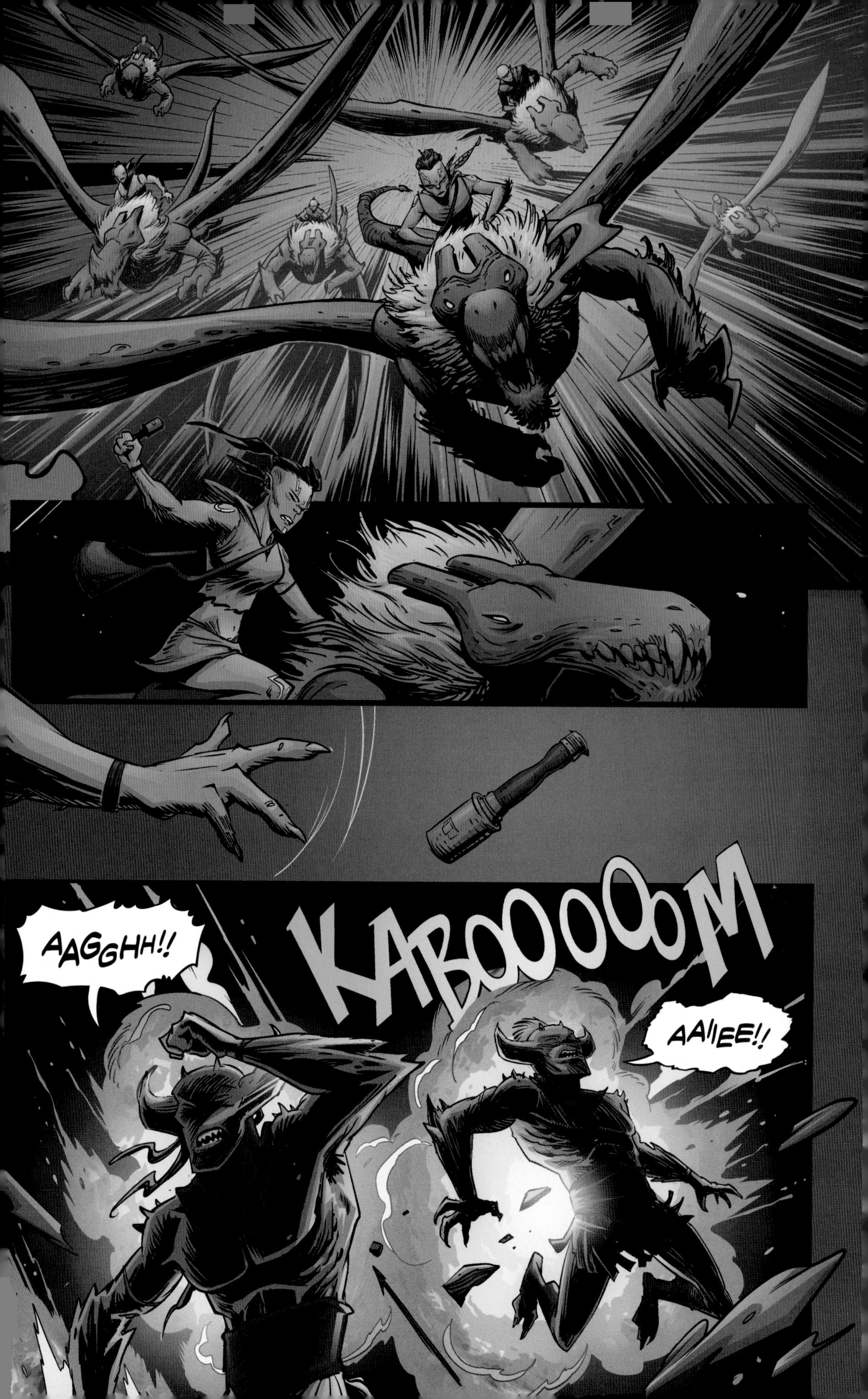
AAGGHH!!
KABOOOOOM
AAIIEE!!

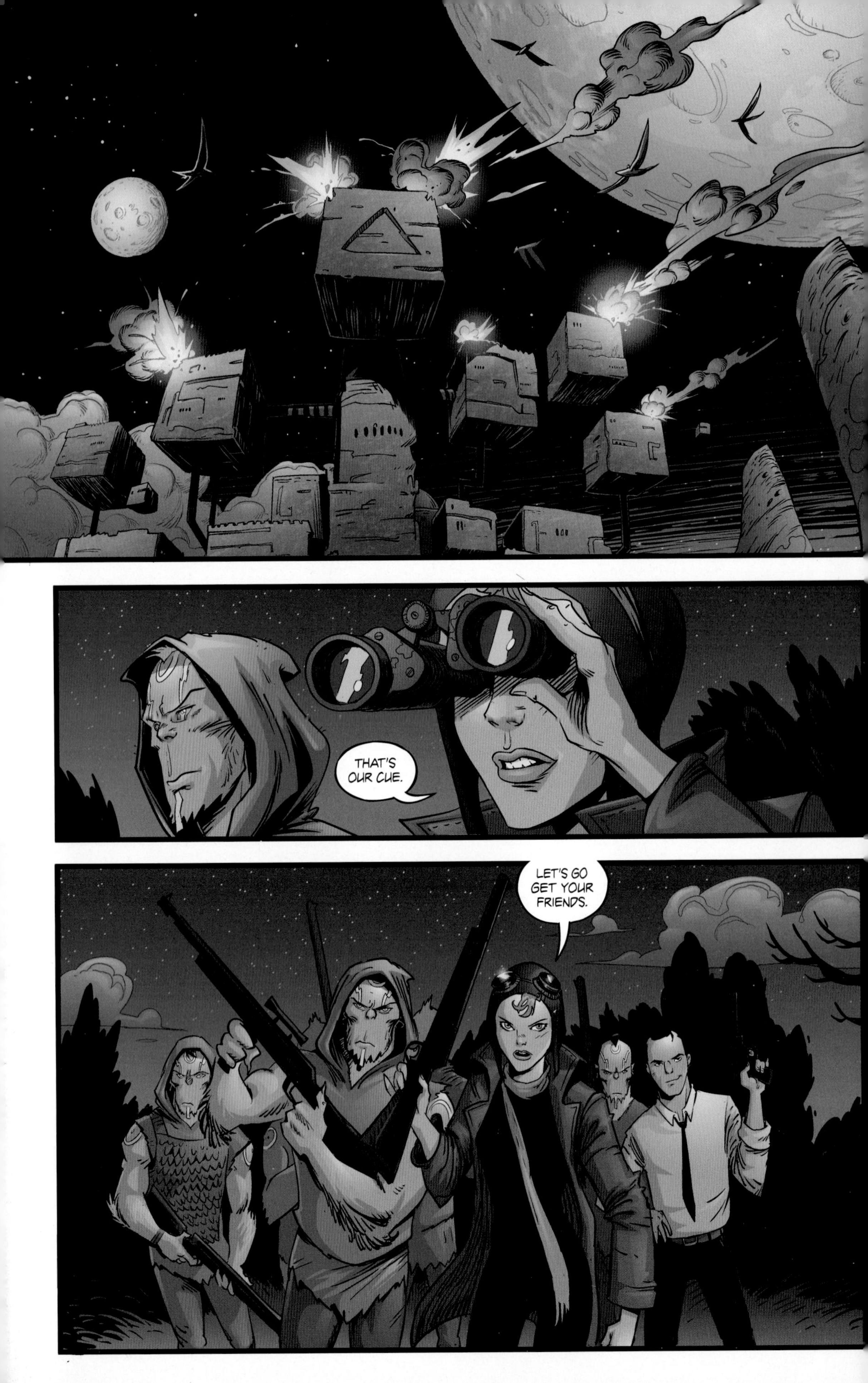
THAT'S OUR CUE.
LET'S GO GET YOUR FRIENDS.

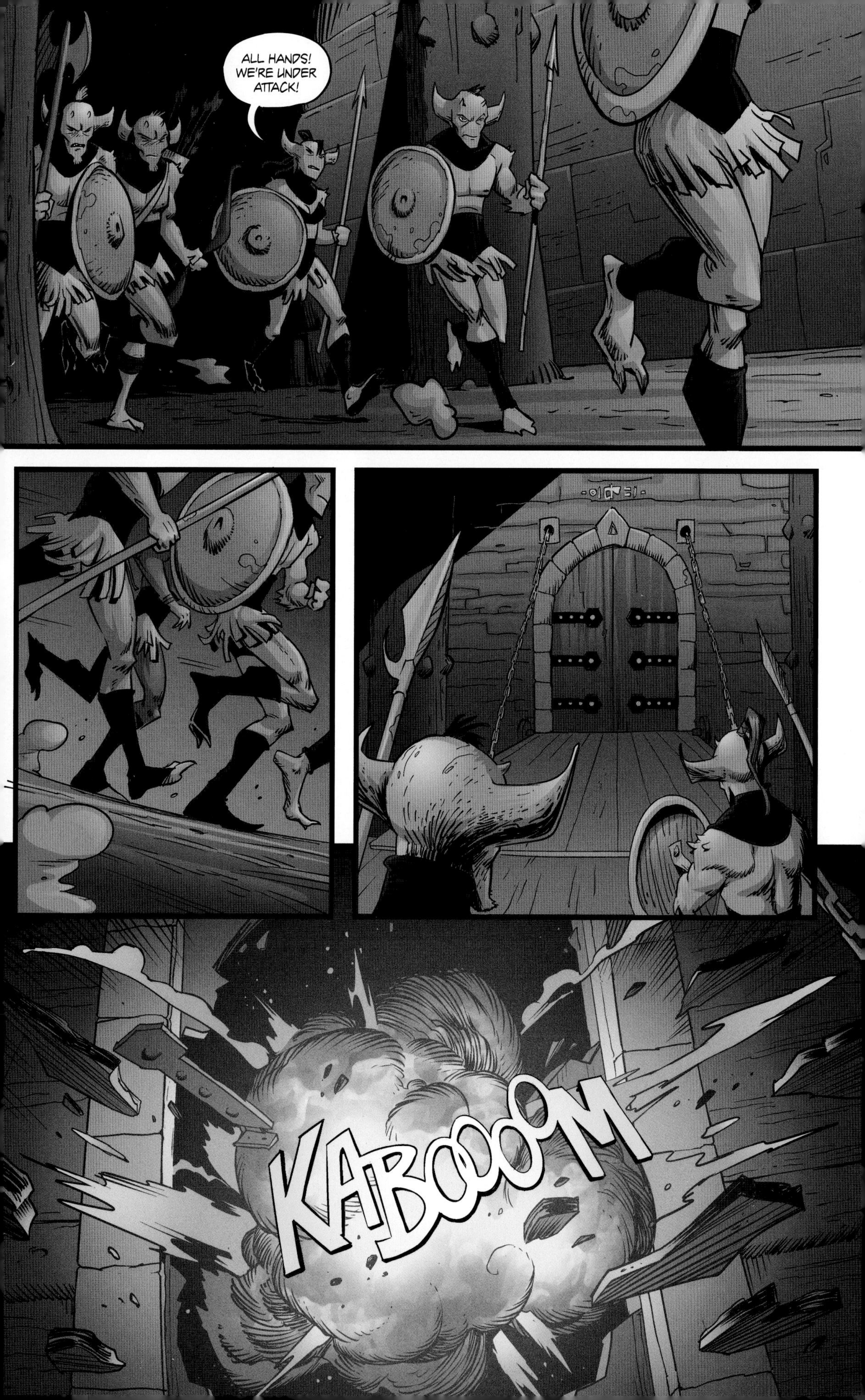
ALL HANDS! WE'RE UNDER ATTACK!
KABOOOM

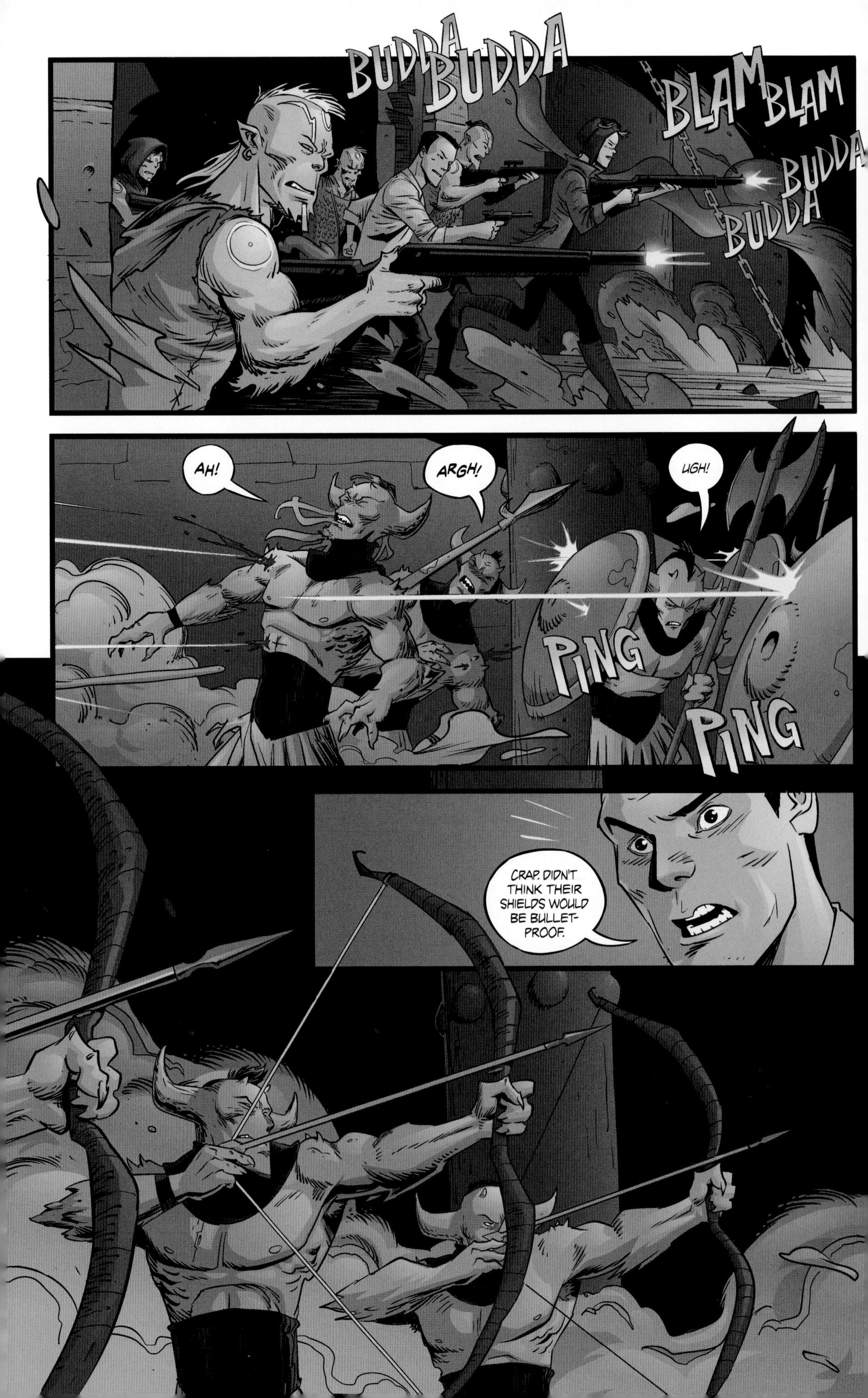

BUDDA BUDDA
BLAM BLAM
BUDDA BUDDA
AH!
ARGH!
UGH!
PING
PING
CRAP. DIDN'T THINK THEIR SHIELDS WOULD BE BULLET-PROOF.

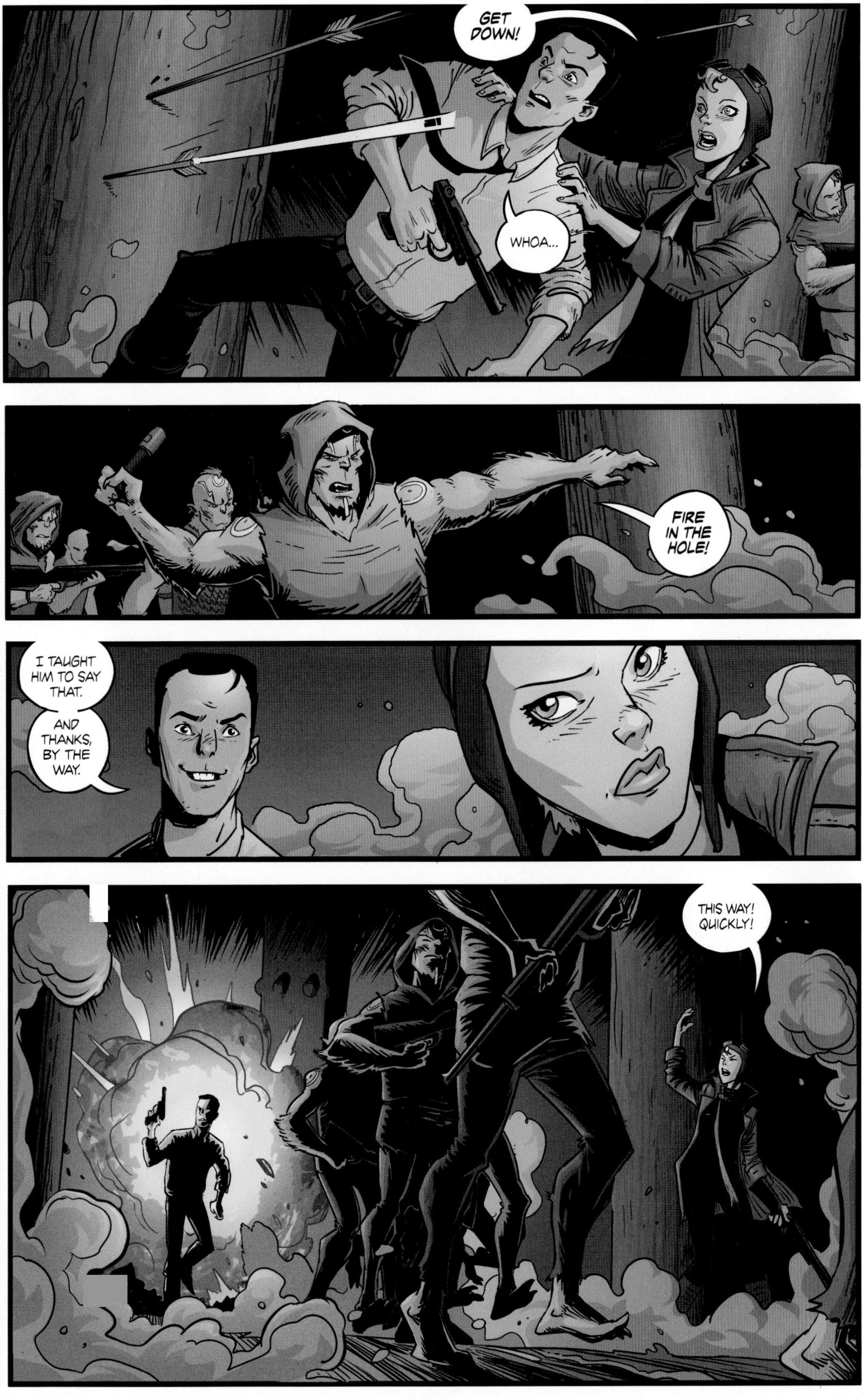
GET DOWN!
WHOA...
FIRE IN THE HOLE!
I TAUGHT HIM TO SAY THAT.
AND THANKS, BY THE WAY.
THIS WAY! QUICKLY!

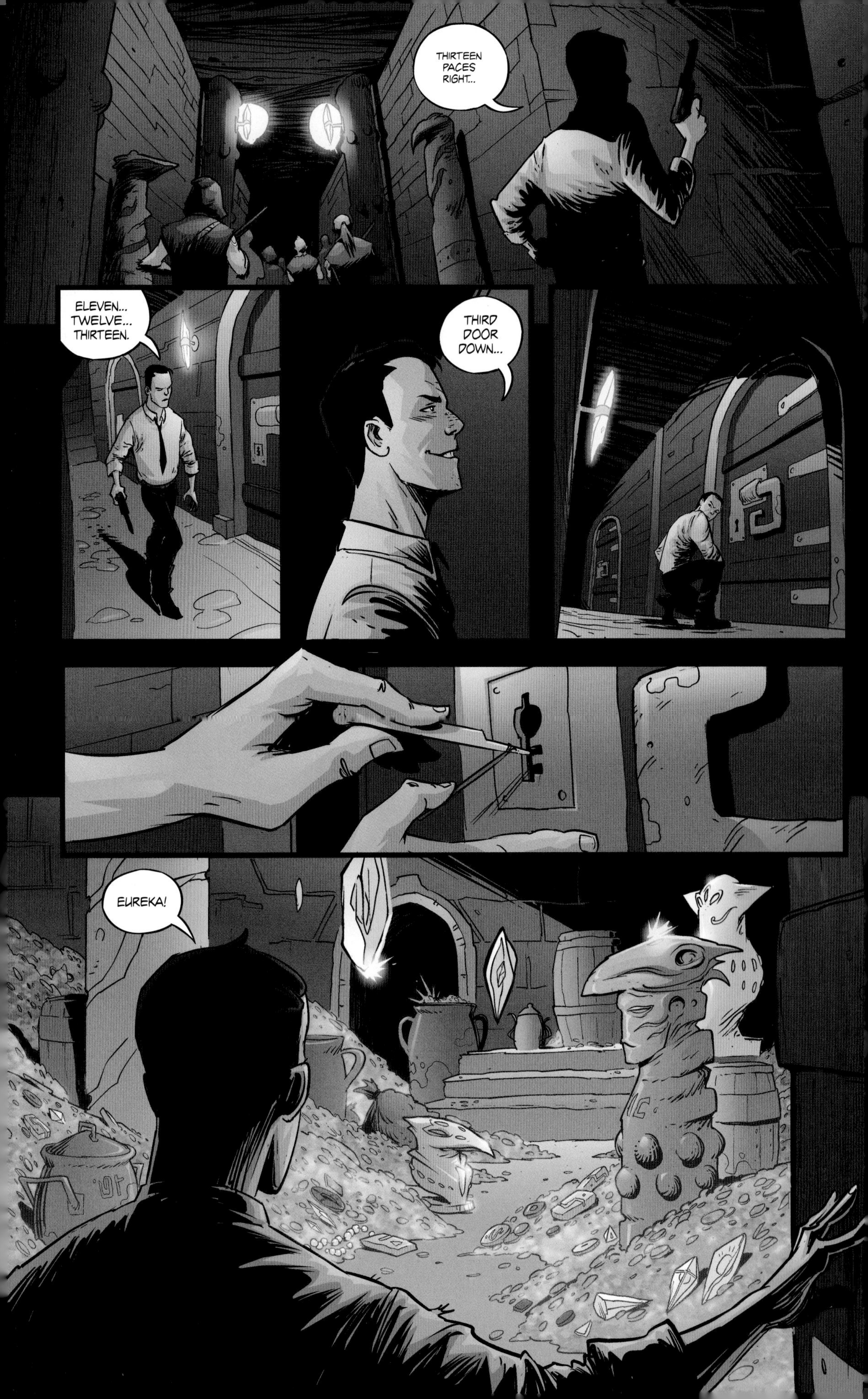
THIRTEEN PACES RIGHT...
ELEVEN... TWELVE... THIRTEEN.
THIRD DOOR DOWN...
EUREKA!

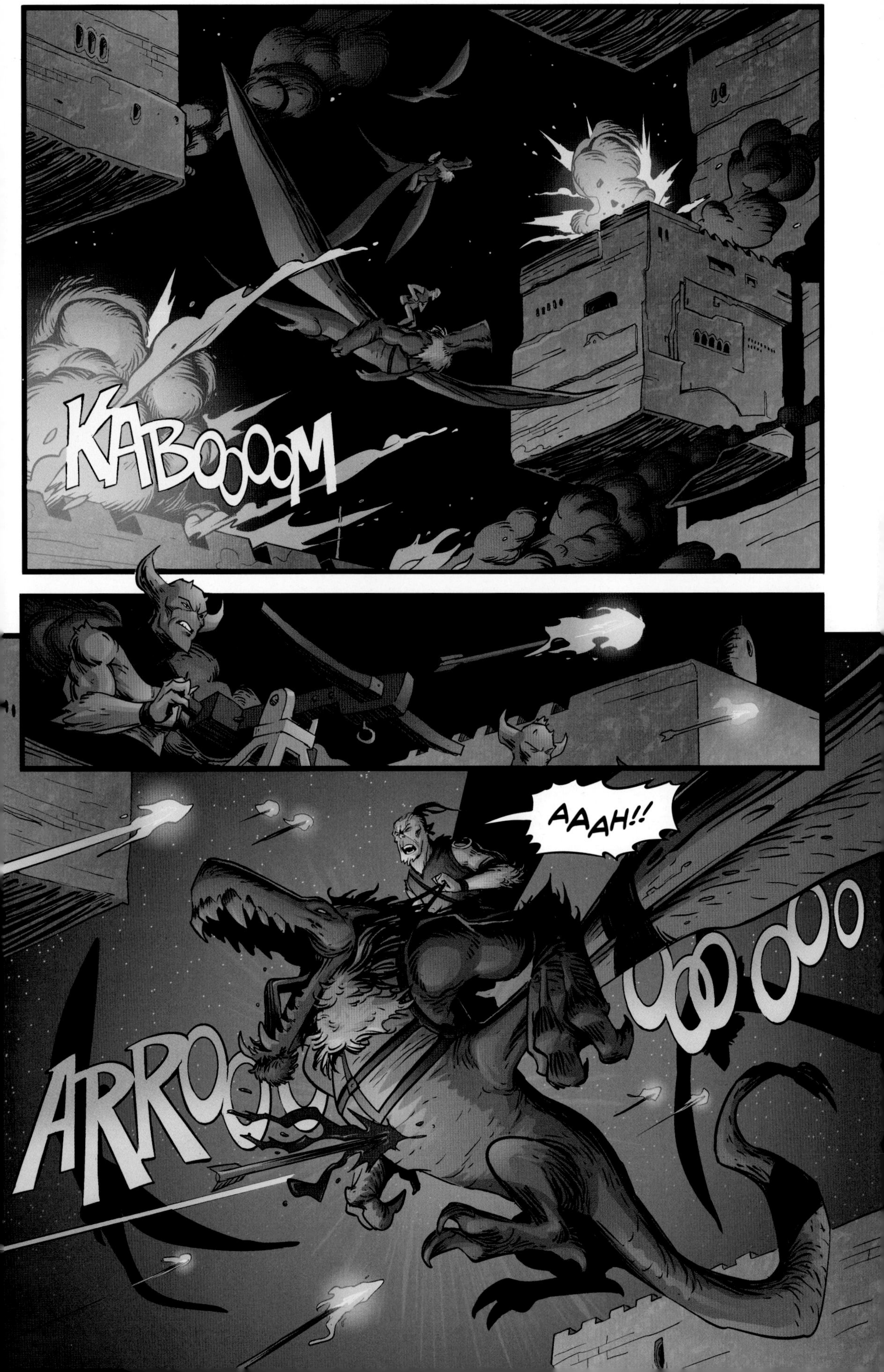
KABOOOOM
AAAH!!
ARROOO
OOO OOO

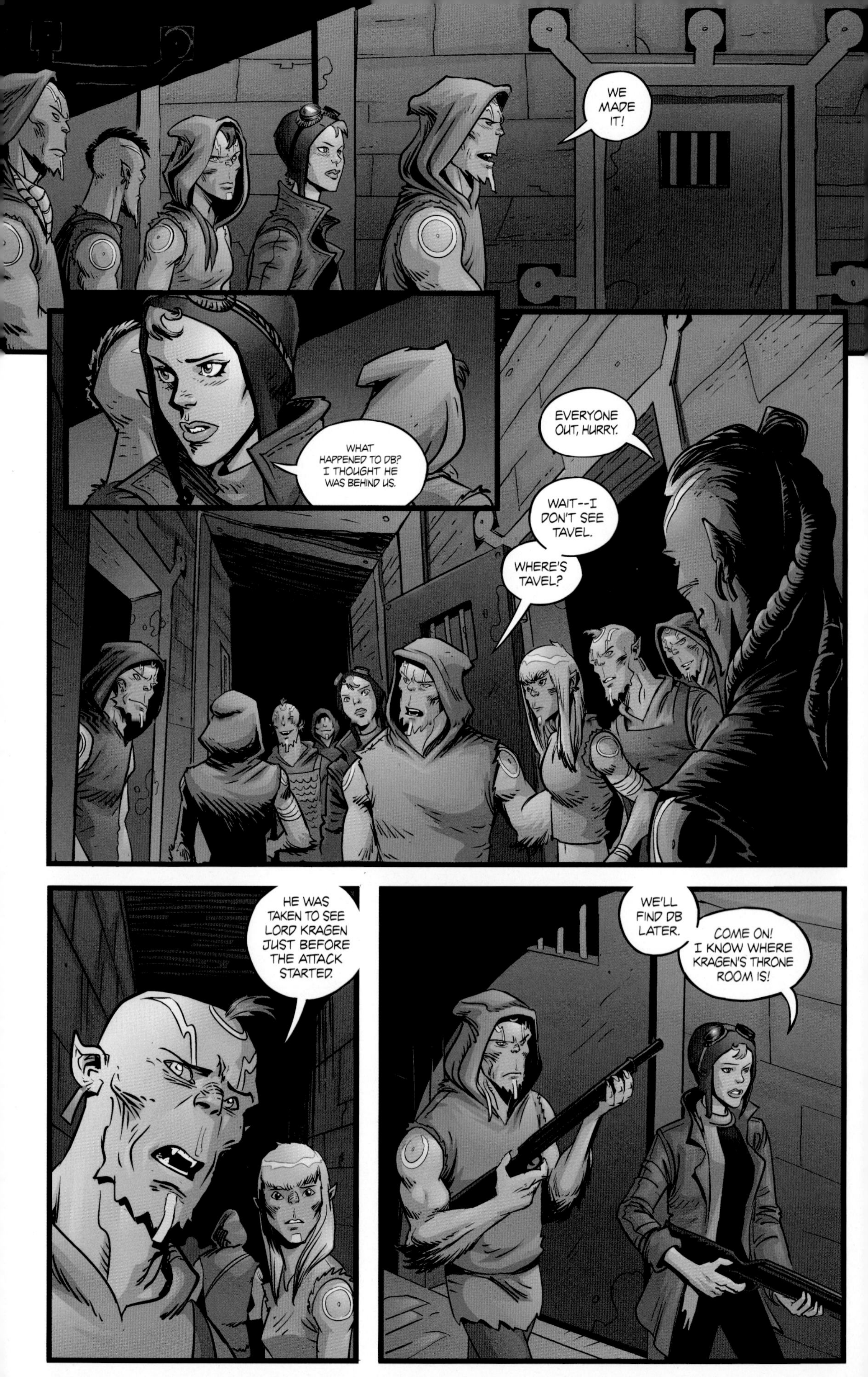
WE MADE IT!
WHAT HAPPENED TO DB? I THOUGHT HE WAS BEHIND US.
EVERYONE OUT, HURRY.
WAIT--I DON'T SEE TAVEL.
WHERE'S TAVEL?
HE WAS TAKEN TO SEE LORD KRAGEN JUST BEFORE THE ATTACK STARTED.
WE'LL FIND DB LATER.
COME ON! I KNOW WHERE KRAGEN'S THRONE ROOM IS!

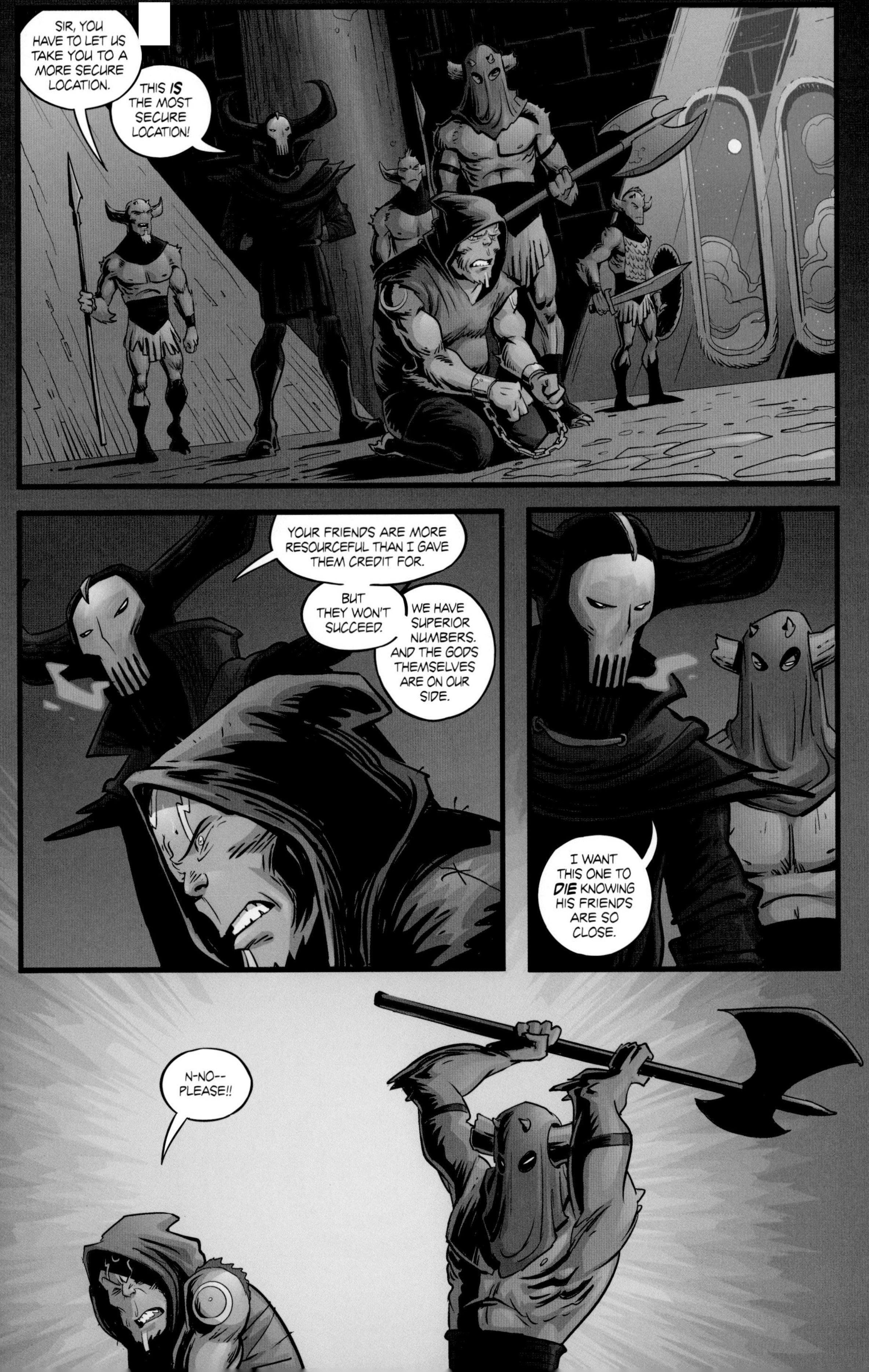
SIR, YOU HAVE TO LET US TAKE YOU TO A MORE SECURE LOCATION.
THIS IS THE MOST SECURE LOCATION!
YOUR FRIENDS ARE MORE RESOURCEFUL THAN I GAVE THEM CREDIT FOR.
BUT THEY WON'T SUCCEED.
WE HAVE SUPERIOR NUMBERS. AND THE GODS THEMSELVES ARE ON OUR SIDE.
I WANT THIS ONE TO DIE KNOWING HIS FRIENDS ARE SO CLOSE.
N-NO-- PLEASE!!

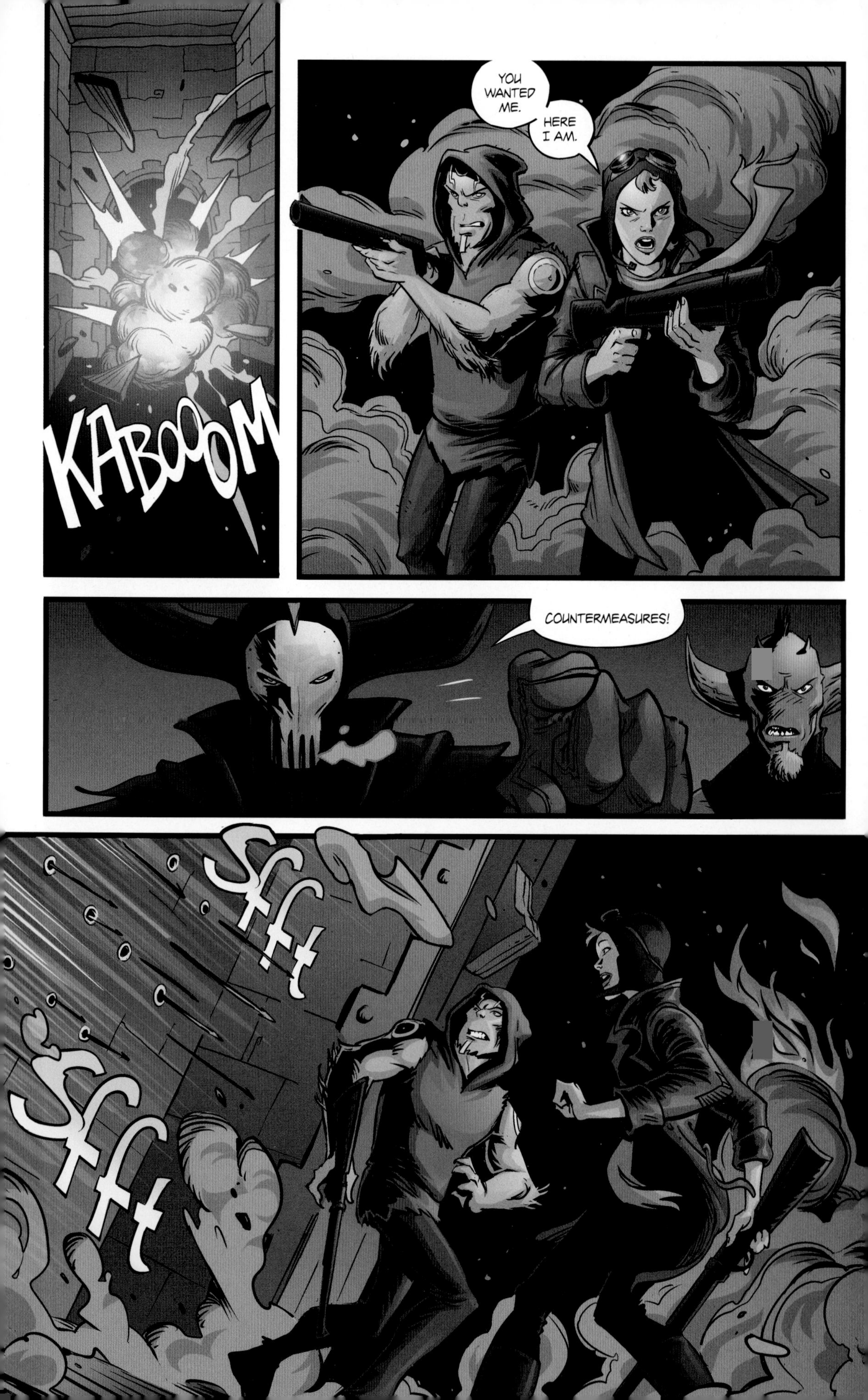
KABOOOM
YOU WANTED ME.
HERE I AM.
COUNTERMEASURES!
SFFT
SFFT

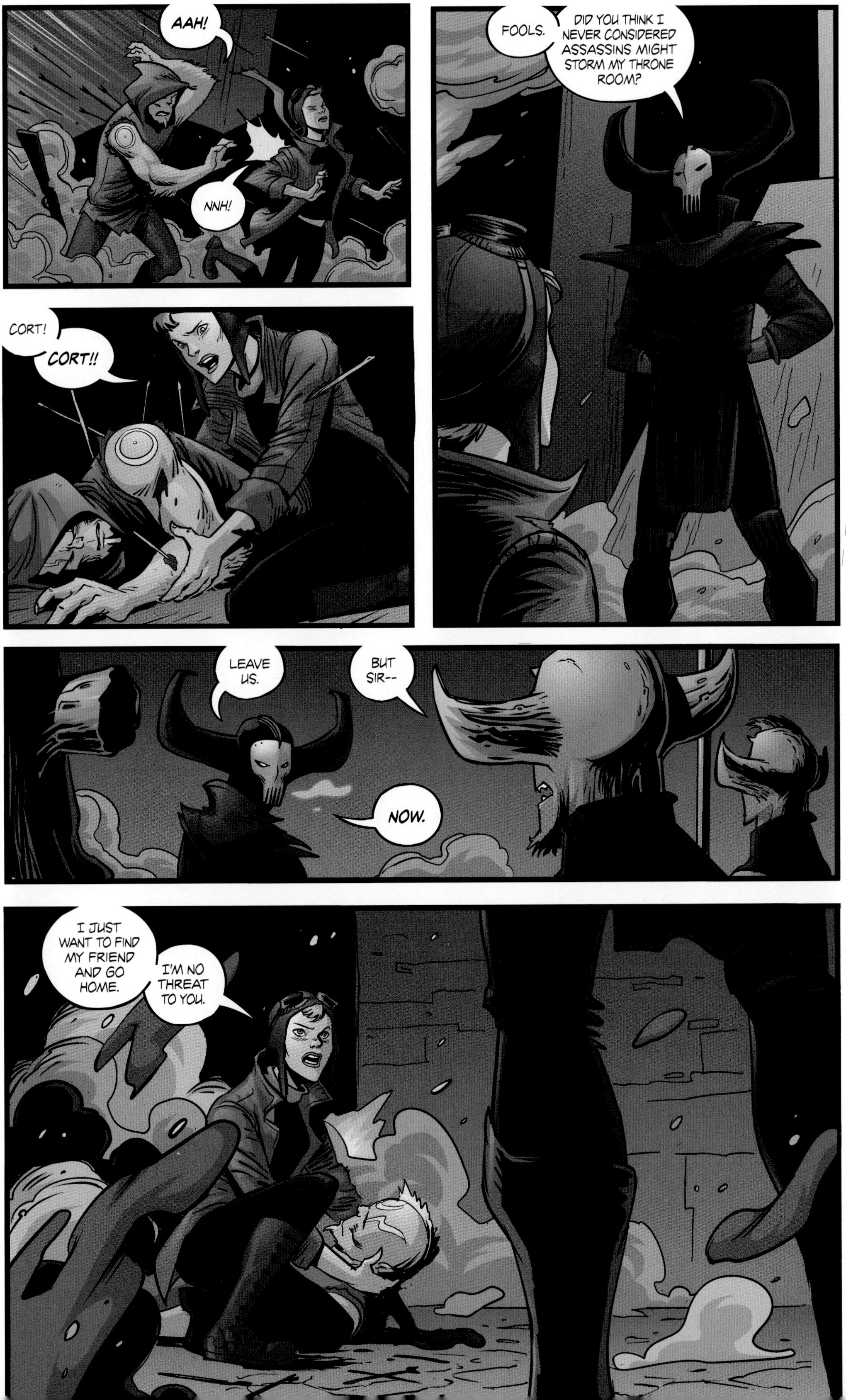
AAH!
NNH!
FOOLS.
DID YOU THINK I NEVER CONSIDERED ASSASSINS MIGHT STORM MY THRONE ROOM?
CORT!
CORT!!
LEAVE US.
BUT SIR--
NOW.
I JUST WANT TO FIND MY FRIEND AND GO HOME.
I'M NO THREAT TO YOU.

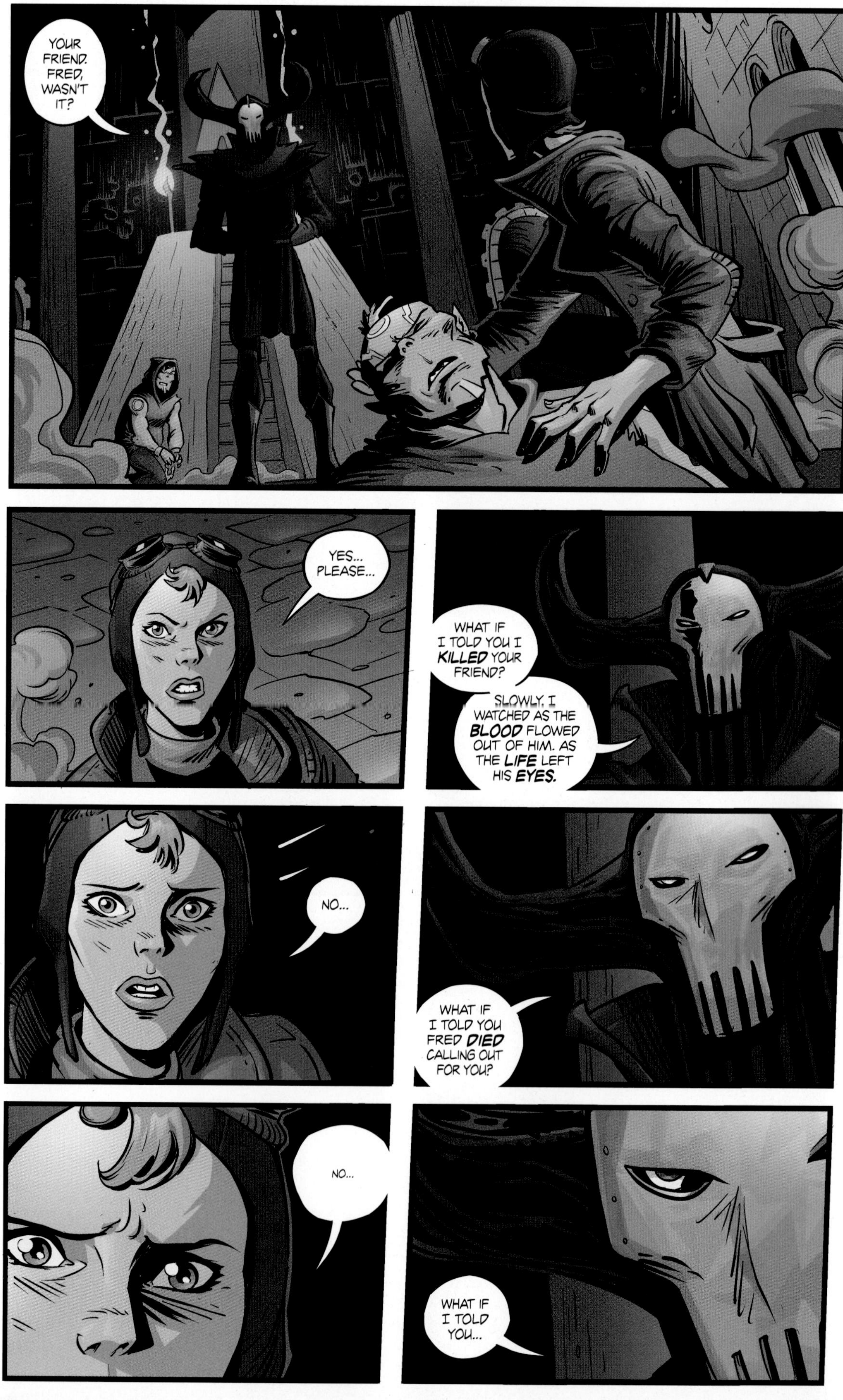

YOUR FRIEND. FRED, WASN'T IT?
YES... PLEASE...
WHAT IF I TOLD YOU I KILLED YOUR FRIEND?
SLOWLY. I WATCHED AS THE BLOOD FLOWED OUT OF HIM. AS THE LIFE LEFT HIS EYES.
NO...
WHAT IF I TOLD YOU FRED DIED CALLING OUT FOR YOU?
NO...
WHAT IF I TOLD YOU...

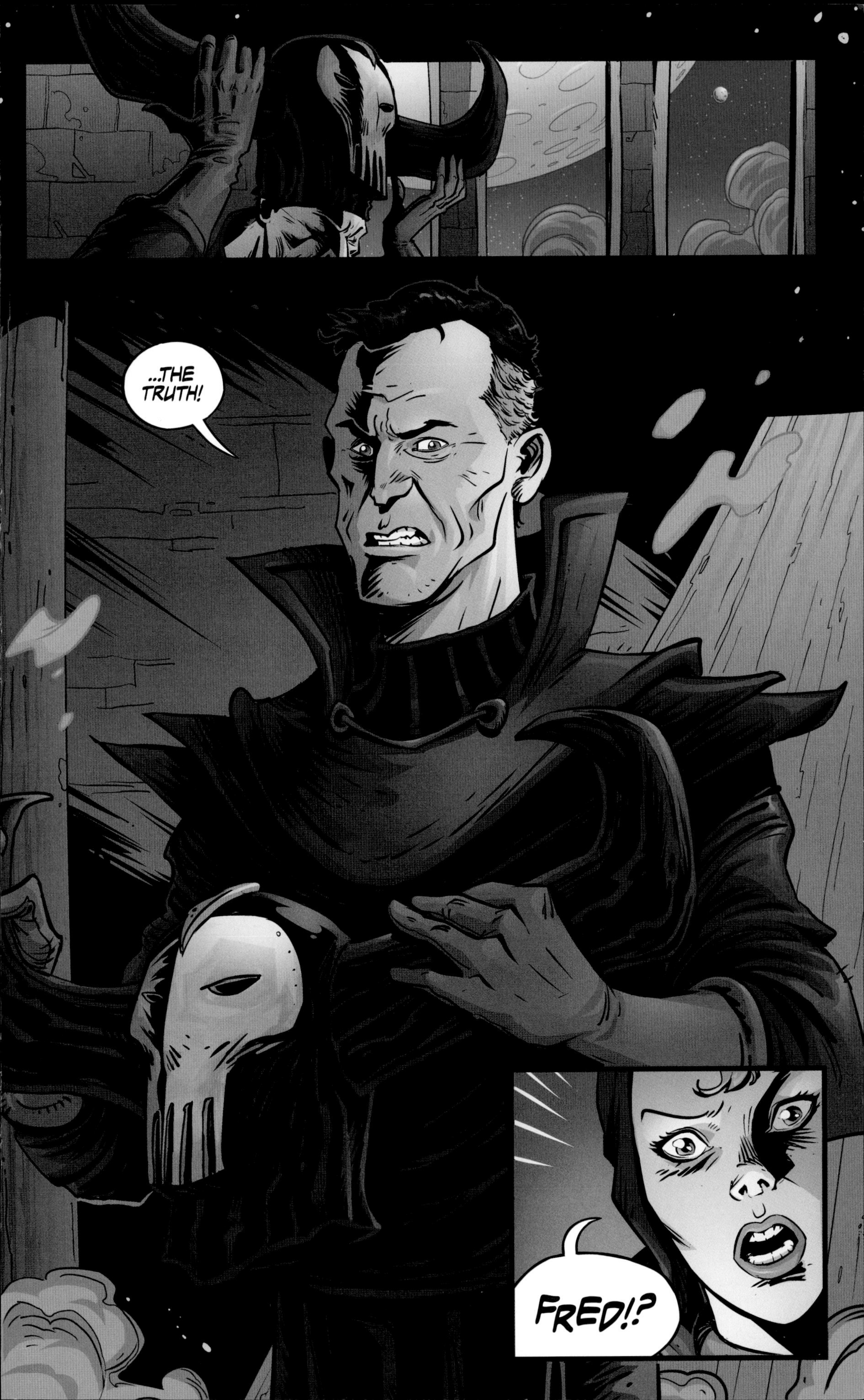
...THE TRUTH!
FRED!?

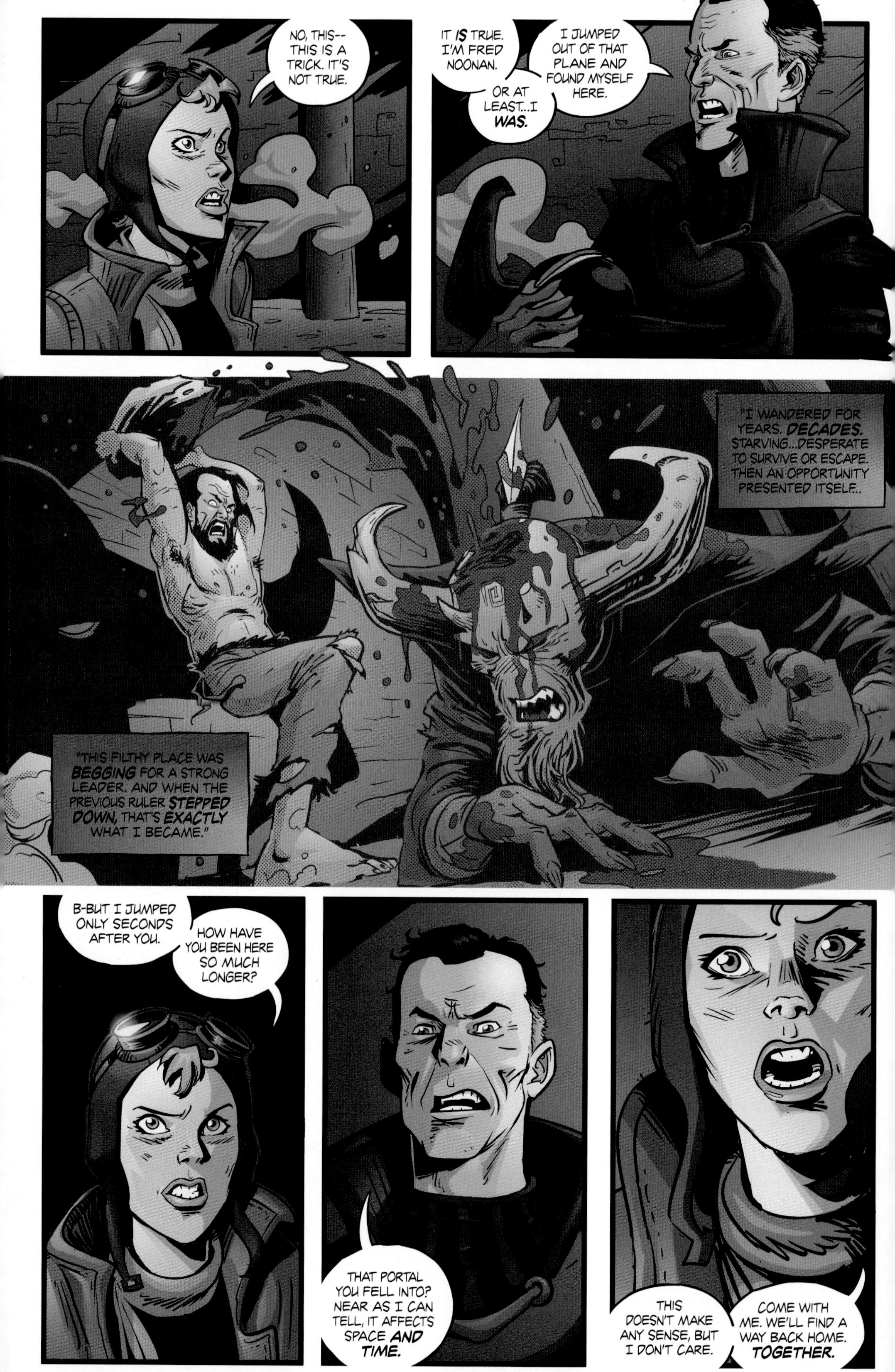
NO, THIS--
THIS IS A TRICK. IT'S NOT TRUE.
IT *IS* TRUE. I'M FRED NOONAN.
OR AT LEAST...I **WAS.**
I JUMPED OUT OF THAT PLANE AND FOUND MYSELF HERE.
"I WANDERED FOR YEARS. ***DECADES.*** STARVING...DESPERATE TO SURVIVE OR ESCAPE. THEN AN OPPORTUNITY PRESENTED ITSELF...
"THIS FILTHY PLACE WAS ***BEGGING*** FOR A STRONG LEADER. AND WHEN THE PREVIOUS RULER ***STEPPED DOWN,*** THAT'S ***EXACTLY*** WHAT I BECAME."
B-BUT I JUMPED ONLY SECONDS AFTER YOU.
HOW HAVE YOU BEEN HERE SO MUCH LONGER?
THAT PORTAL YOU FELL INTO? NEAR AS I CAN TELL, IT AFFECTS SPACE ***AND TIME.***
THIS DOESN'T MAKE ANY SENSE, BUT I DON'T CARE.
COME WITH ME. WE'LL FIND A WAY BACK HOME. ***TOGETHER.***

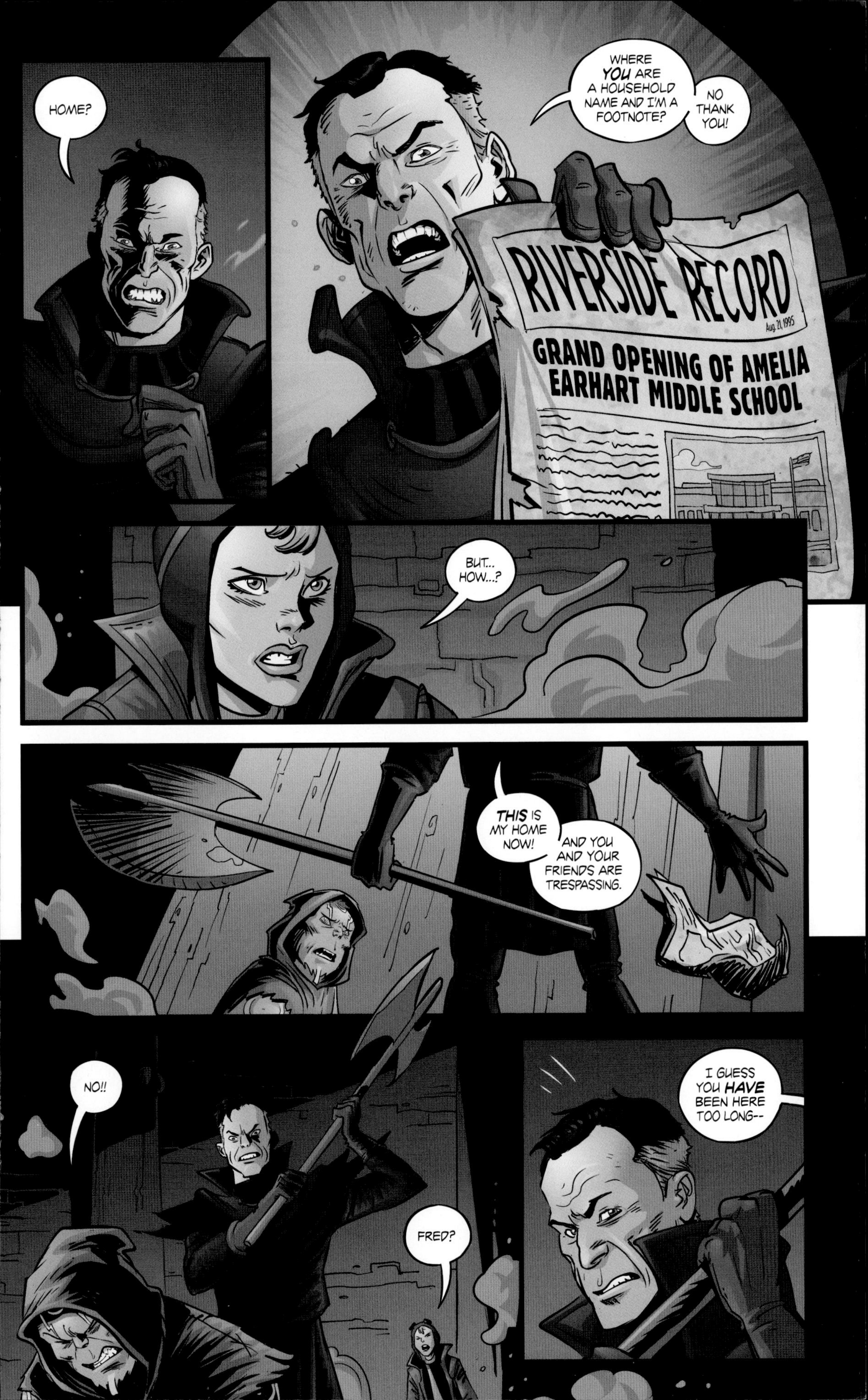
HOME?
WHERE YOU ARE A HOUSEHOLD NAME AND I'M A FOOTNOTE?
NO THANK YOU!
RIVERSIDE RECORD
Aug. 21, 1995
GRAND OPENING OF AMELIA EARHART MIDDLE SCHOOL
BUT... HOW...?
THIS IS MY HOME NOW!
AND YOU AND YOUR FRIENDS ARE TRESPASSING.
NO!!
FRED?
I GUESS YOU HAVE BEEN HERE TOO LONG--

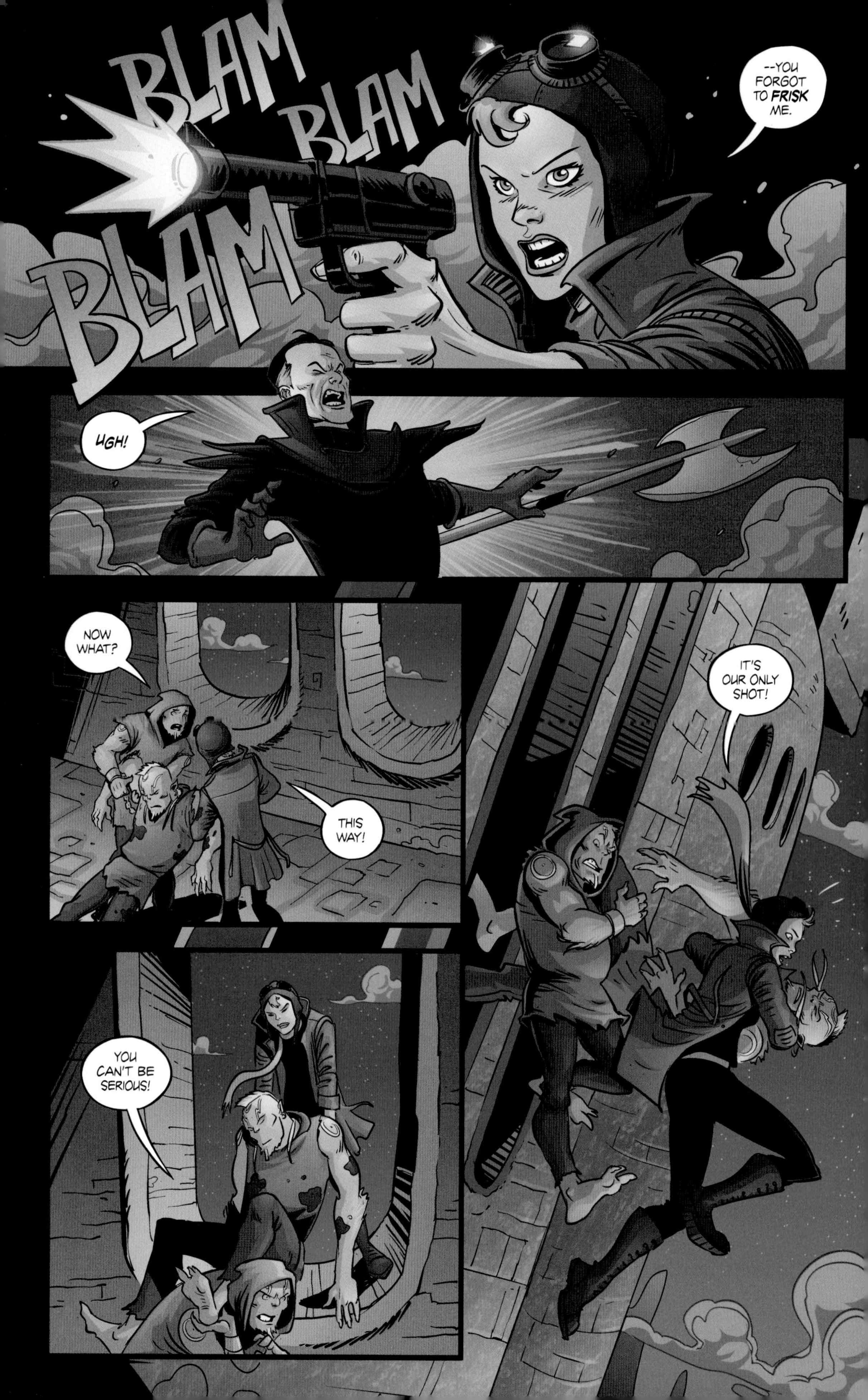
BLAM
BLAM
BLAM
--YOU FORGOT TO FRISK ME.
UGH!
NOW WHAT?
THIS WAY!
IT'S OUR ONLY SHOT!
YOU CAN'T BE SERIOUS!

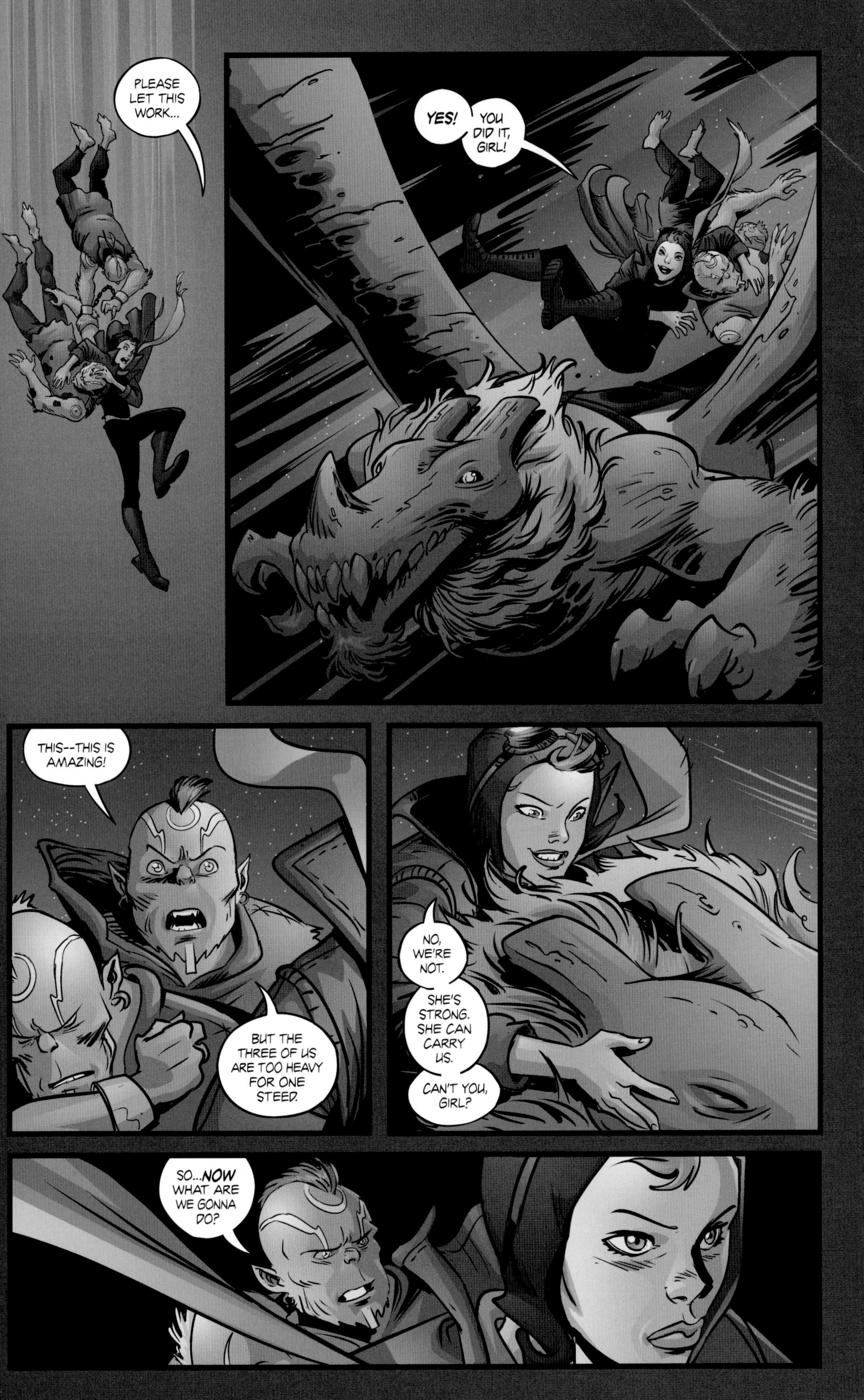
PLEASE LET THIS WORK...
YES!
YOU DID IT, GIRL!
THIS--THIS IS AMAZING!
BUT THE THREE OF US ARE TOO HEAVY FOR ONE STEED.
NO, WE'RE NOT.
SHE'S STRONG. SHE CAN CARRY US.
CAN'T YOU, GIRL?
SO...**NOW** WHAT ARE WE GONNA DO?

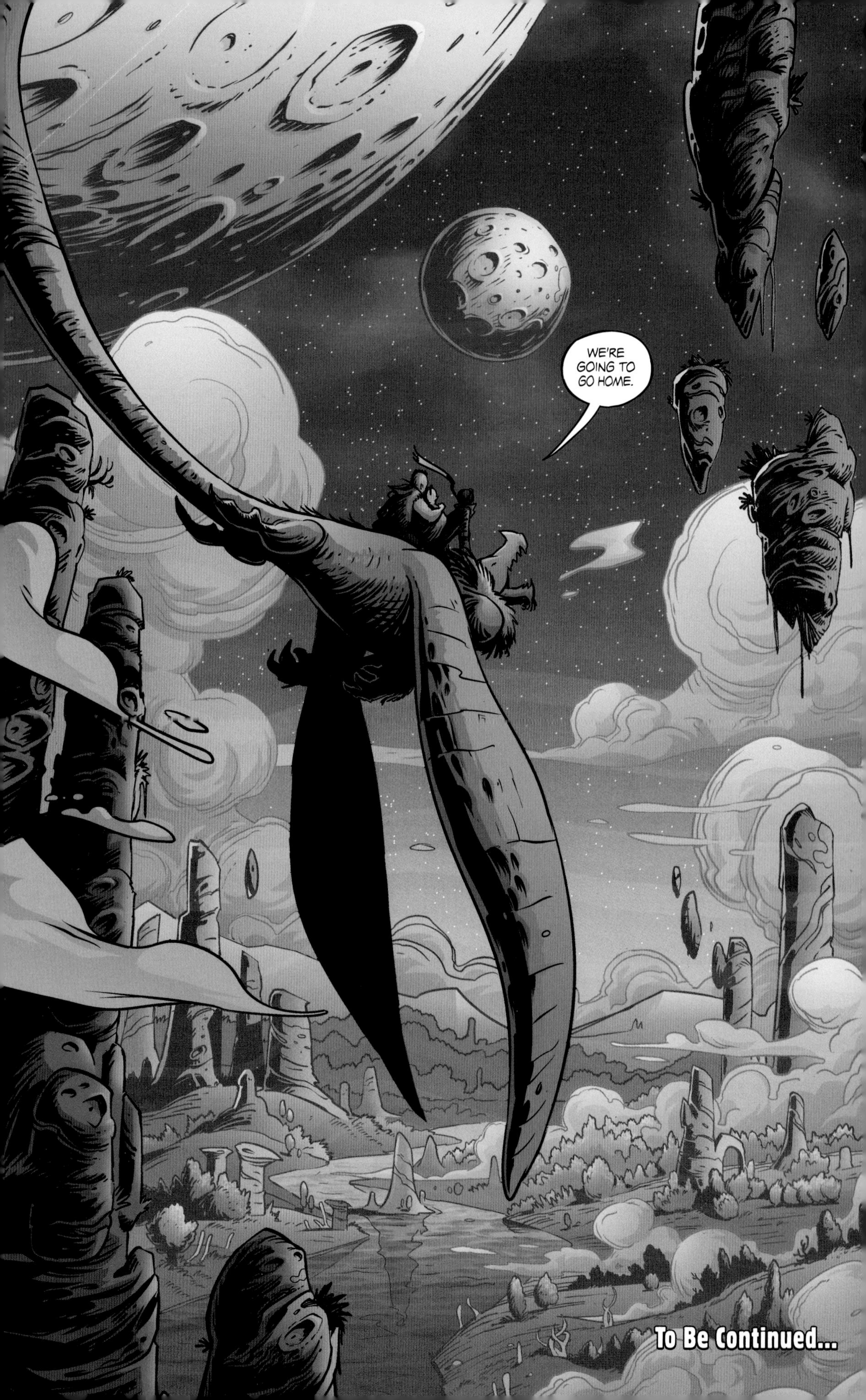
WE'RE GOING TO GO HOME.
To Be Continued...

BEHIND THE SCENES

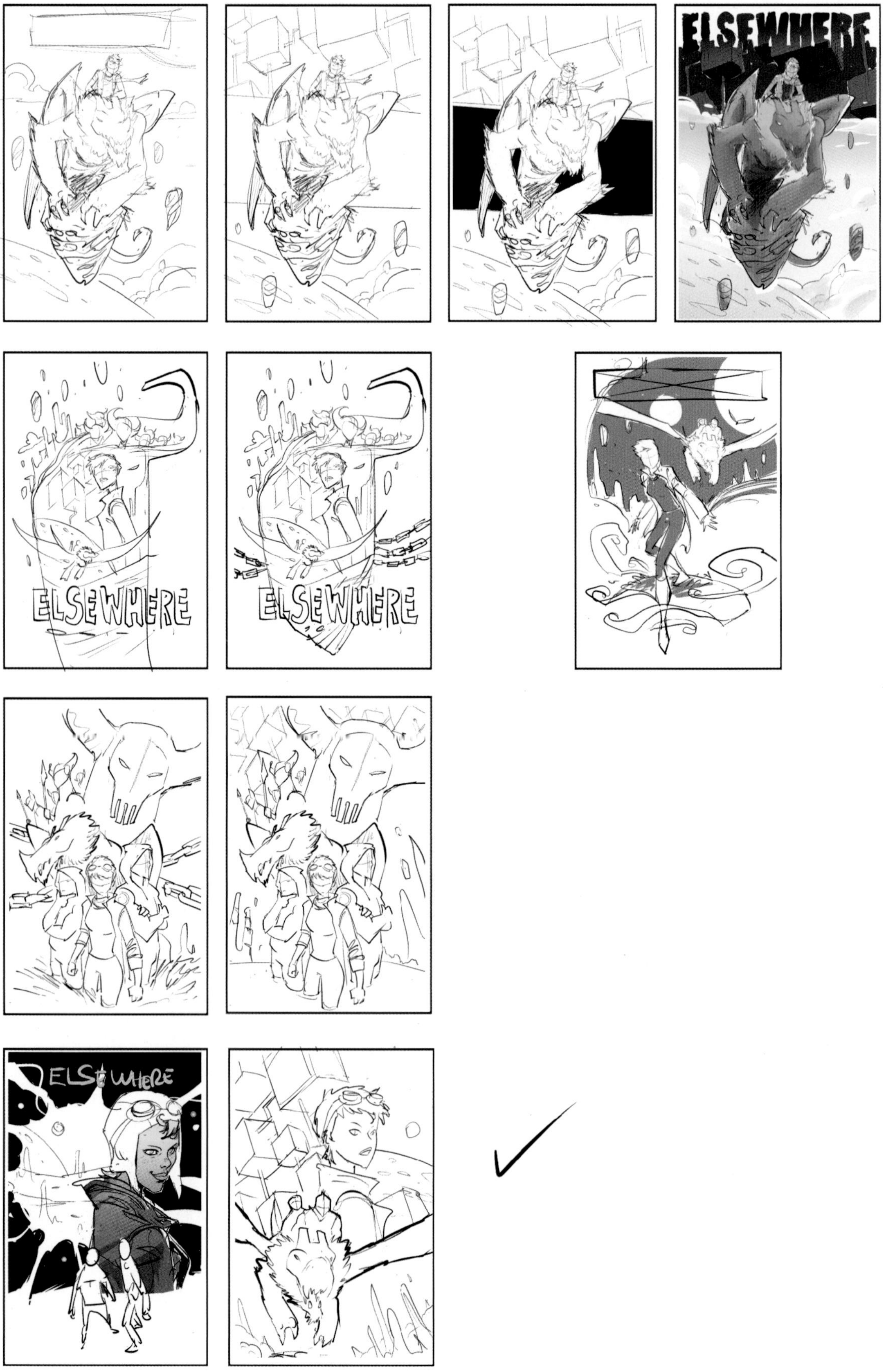
ELSEWHERE
ELSEWHERE
ELSEWHERE
ELSEWHERE

Cover Concepts for Issue 1 & Graytones of the Final Cover (opposite)

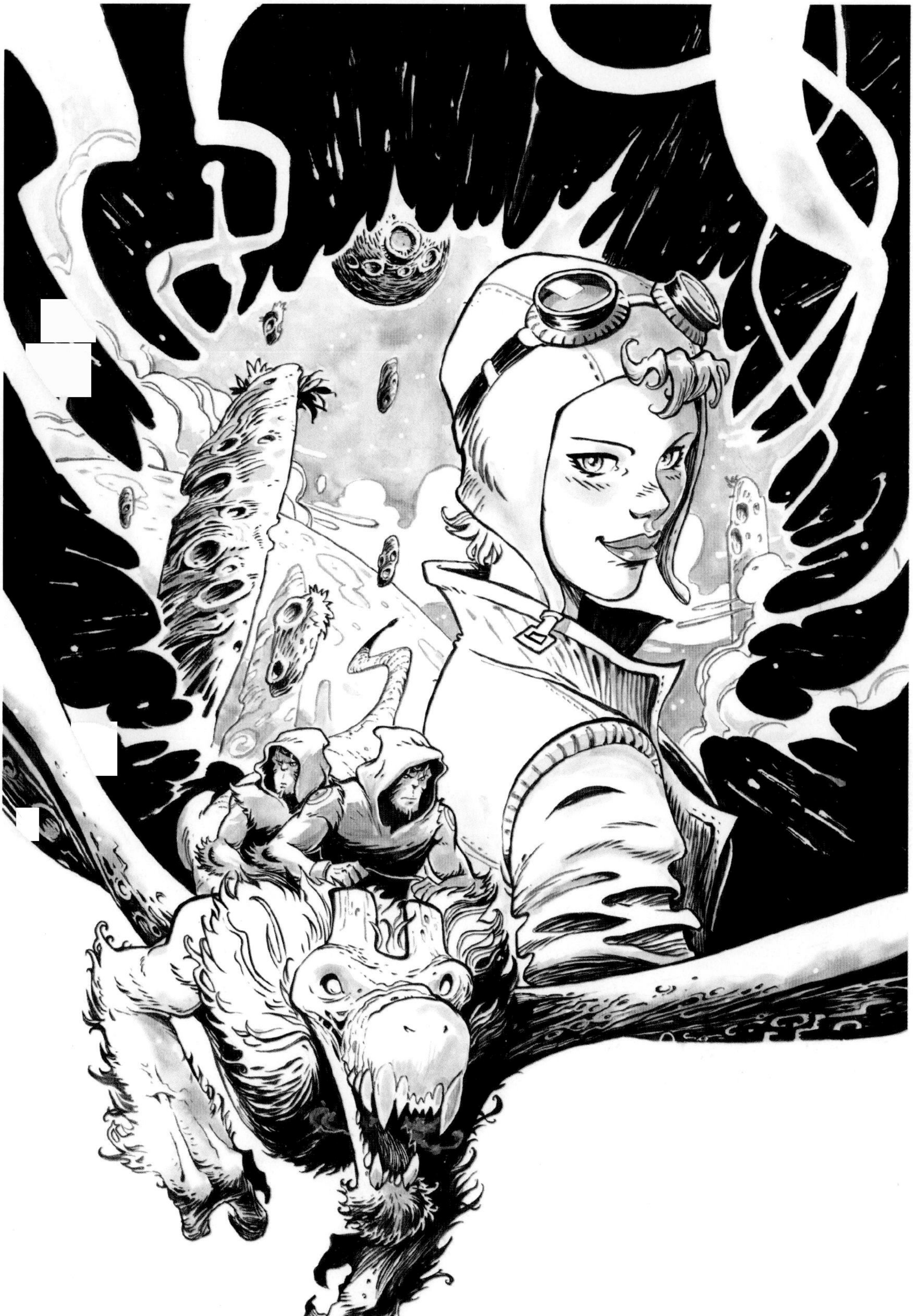

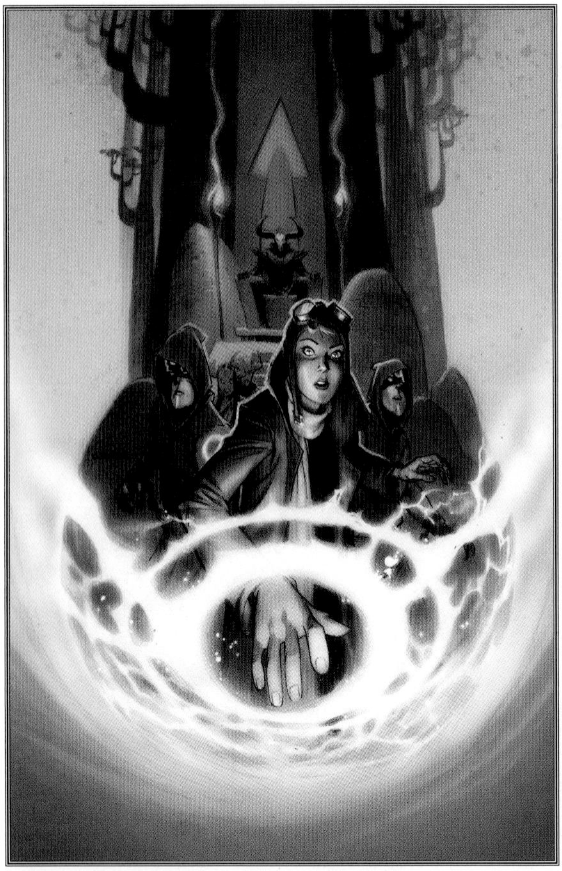

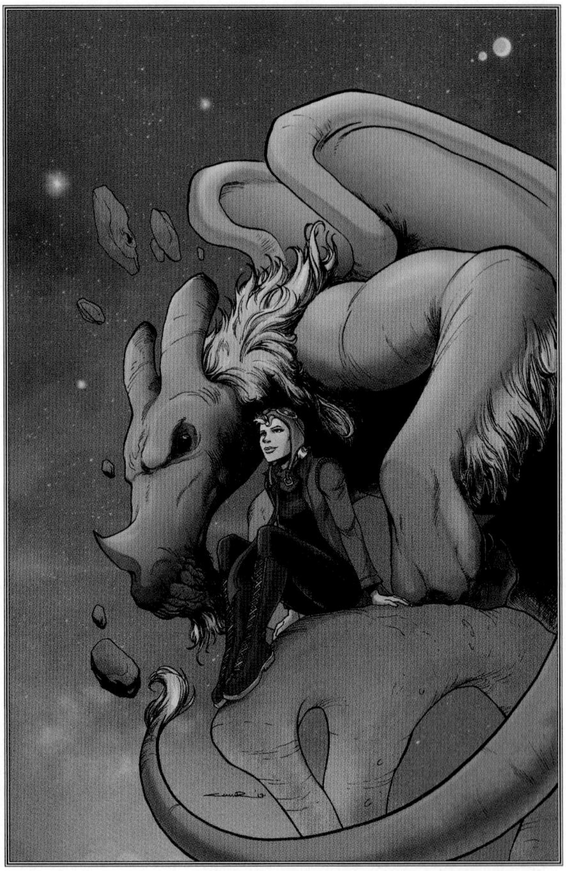

Issue 1 Variant Cover by Andrew Robinson

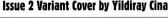

Issue 2 Variant Cover by Yildiray Cinar

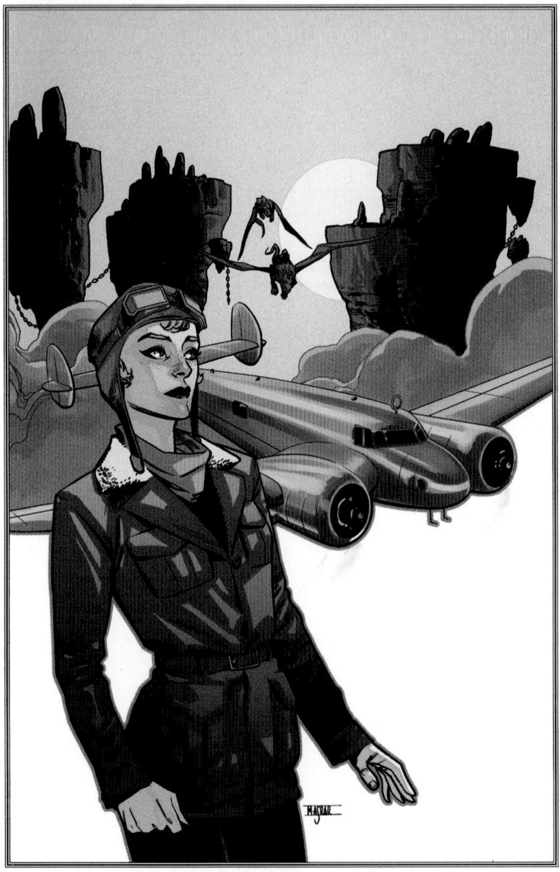

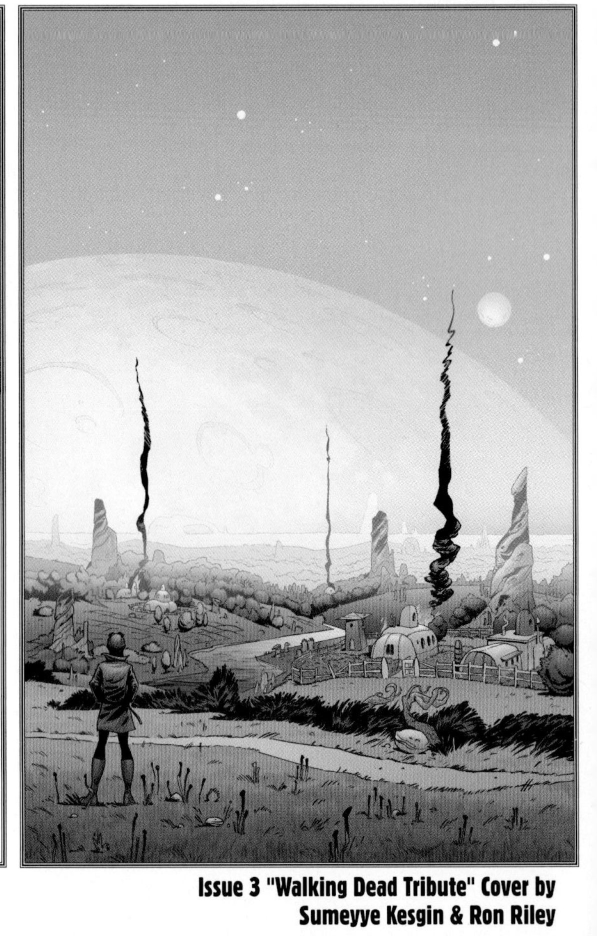

Issue 3 Variant Cover by Mahmud Asrar

Issue 3 "Walking Dead Tribute" Cover by
Sumeyye Kesgin & Ron Riley

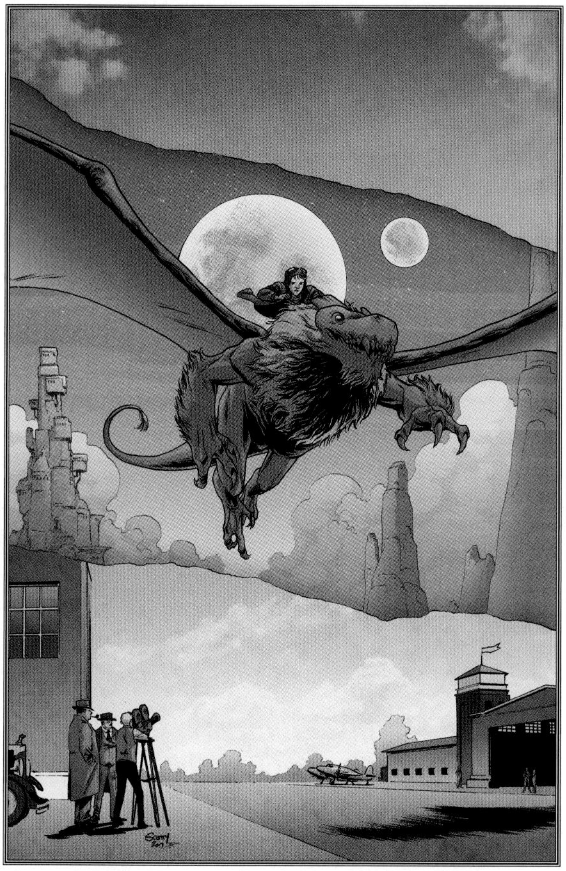

Issue 4 Variant Cover by Scott Godlewski & Ron Riley

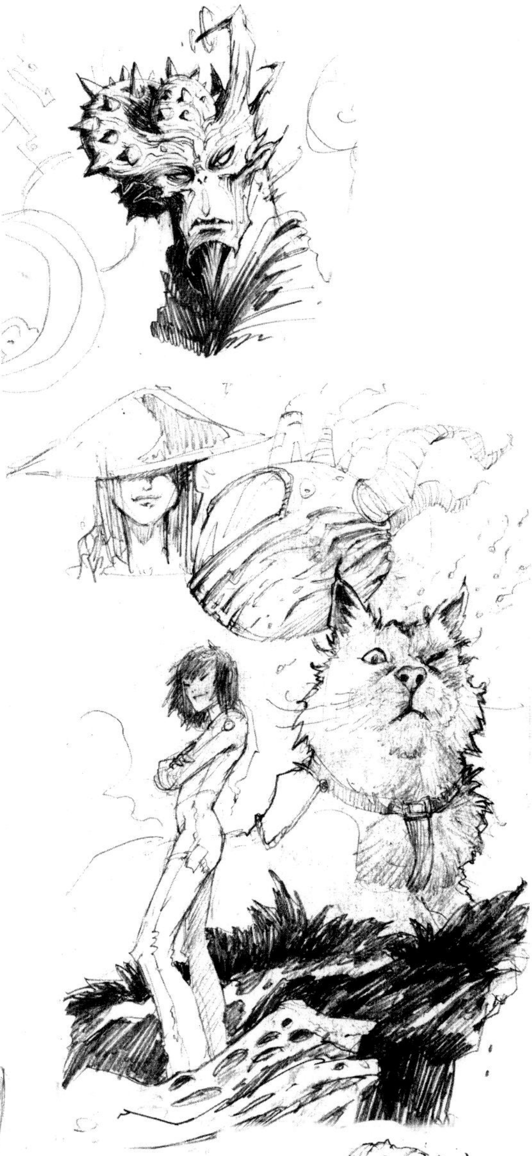

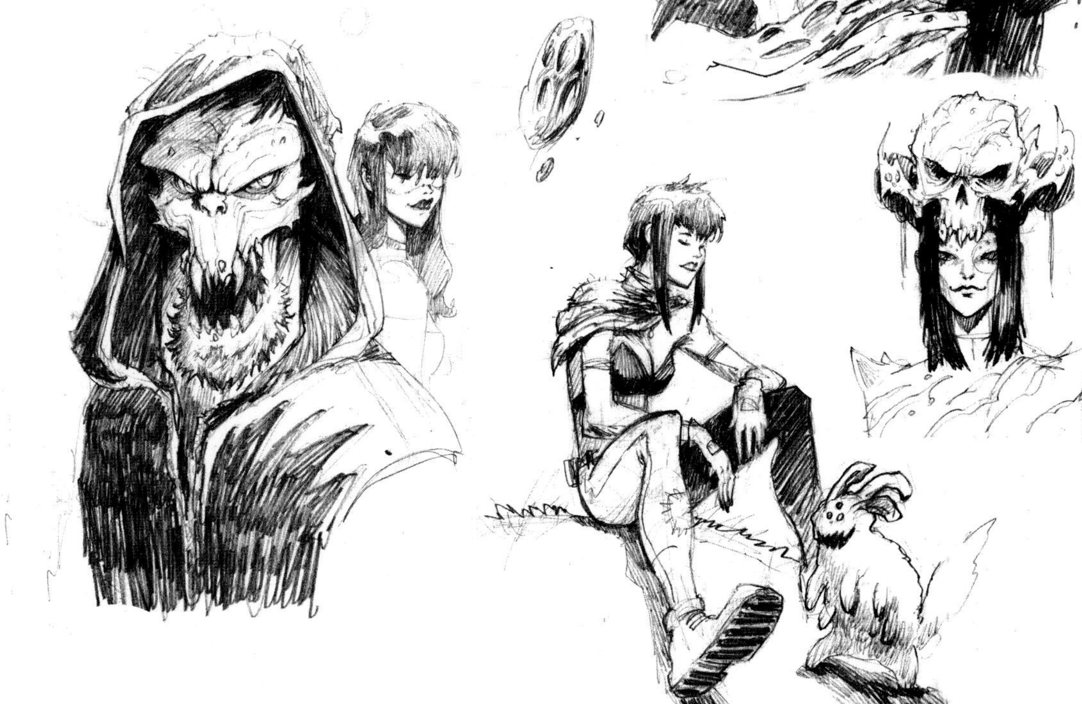

Early concept art by Sumeyye Kesgin

From script to final colors:
Issue 1 page 6

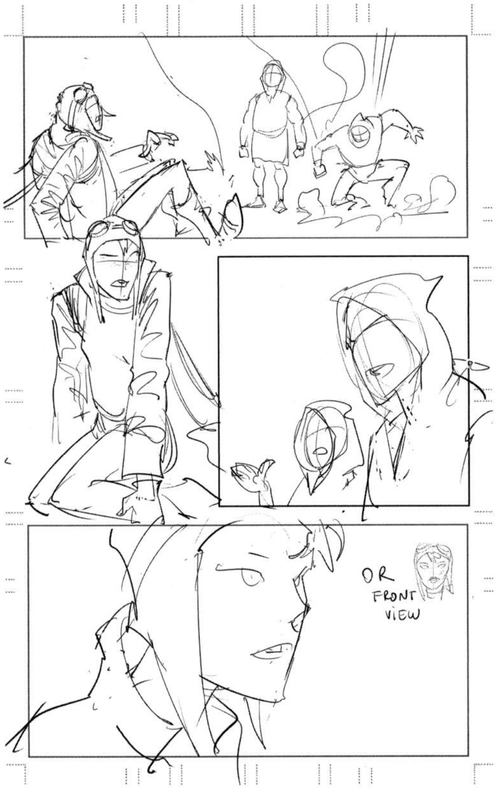
OR
FRONT
VIEW

PAGE 6, Panel One
Cort jumps down next to Tavel, as Amelia scrambles away from them.

AMELIA: Stay back, you... you....

TAVEL: Heroes?

CORT: Really? Plural?

PAGE 6, Panel Two
On Amelia, terrified.

AMELIA: Who-- WHAT are you?
Where AM I?

PAGE 6, Panel Three
On Cort and Tavel.

CORT: I am CORT and
this is TAVEL.

TAVEL: And you're in KORVATH.

CORT: Who are YOU?

PAGE 6, Panel Four
Big panel on Amelia, for this moment when we hear her name for the first time.

AMELIA: I'm Amelia.
AMELIA: AMELIA EARHART.

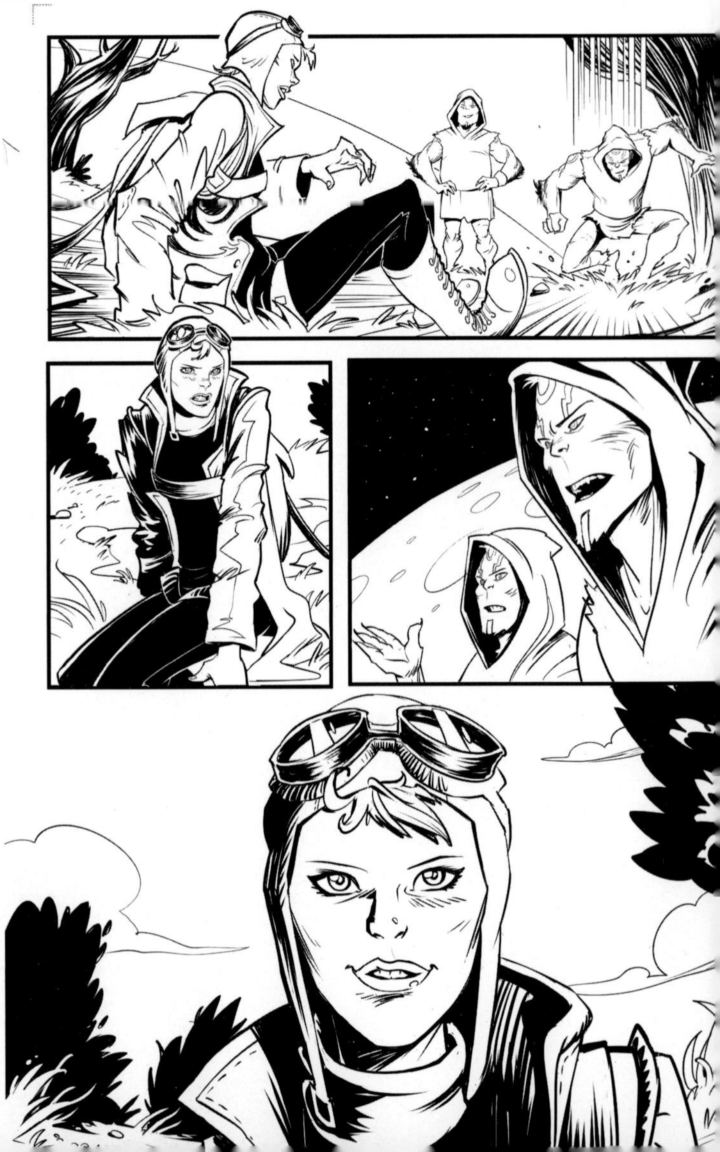

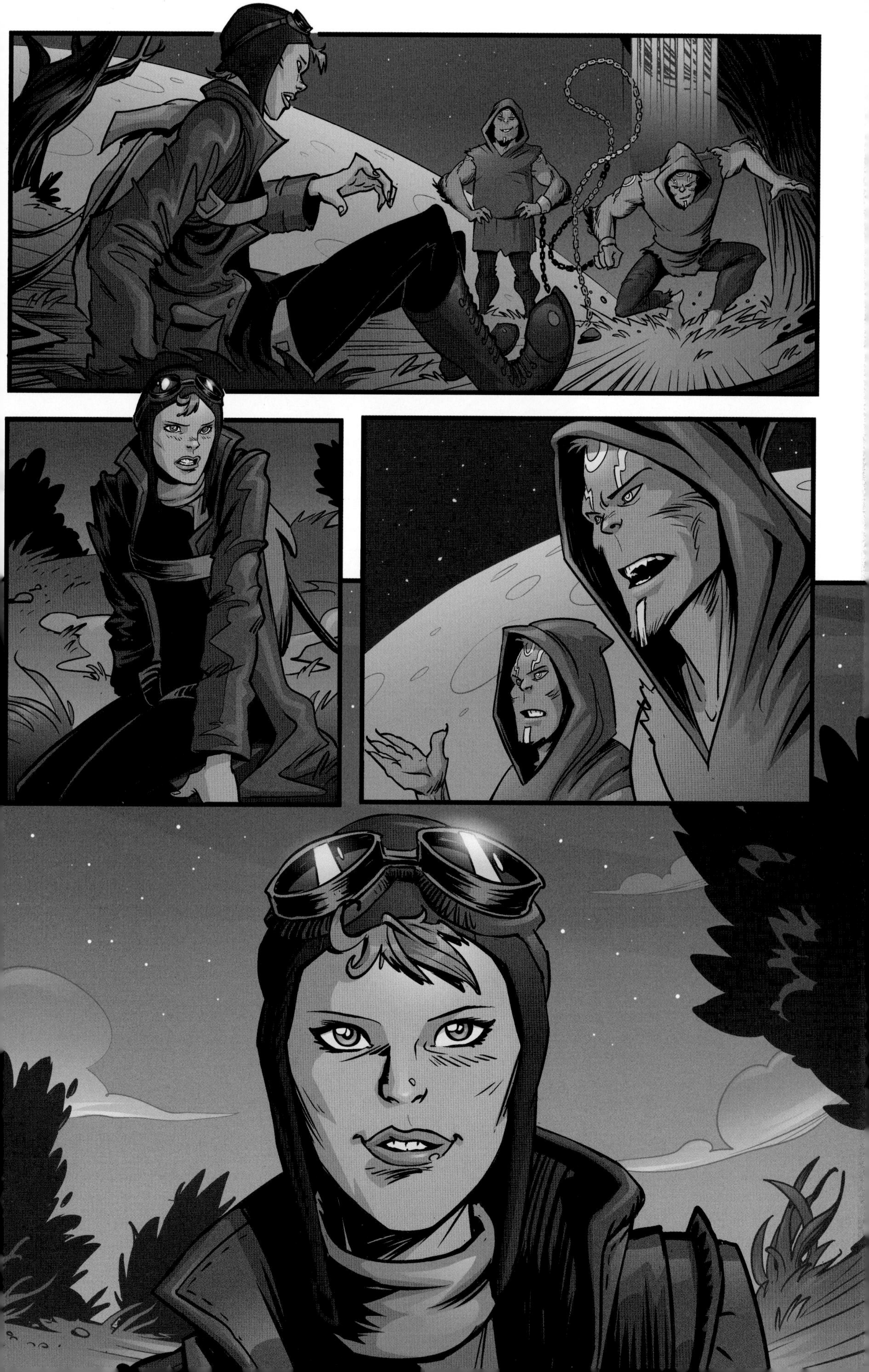

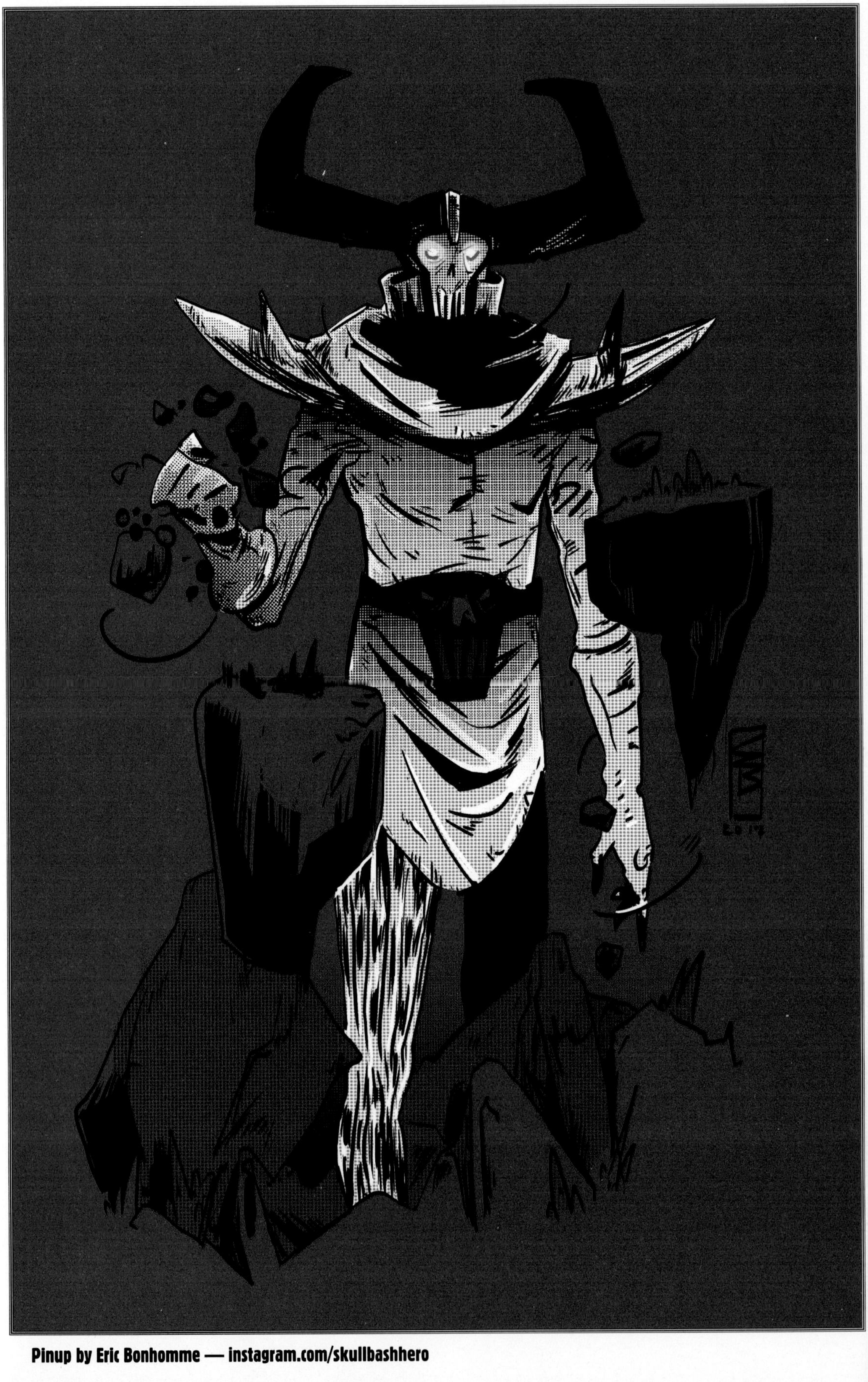

Pinup by Eric Bonhomme — instagram.com/skullbashhero

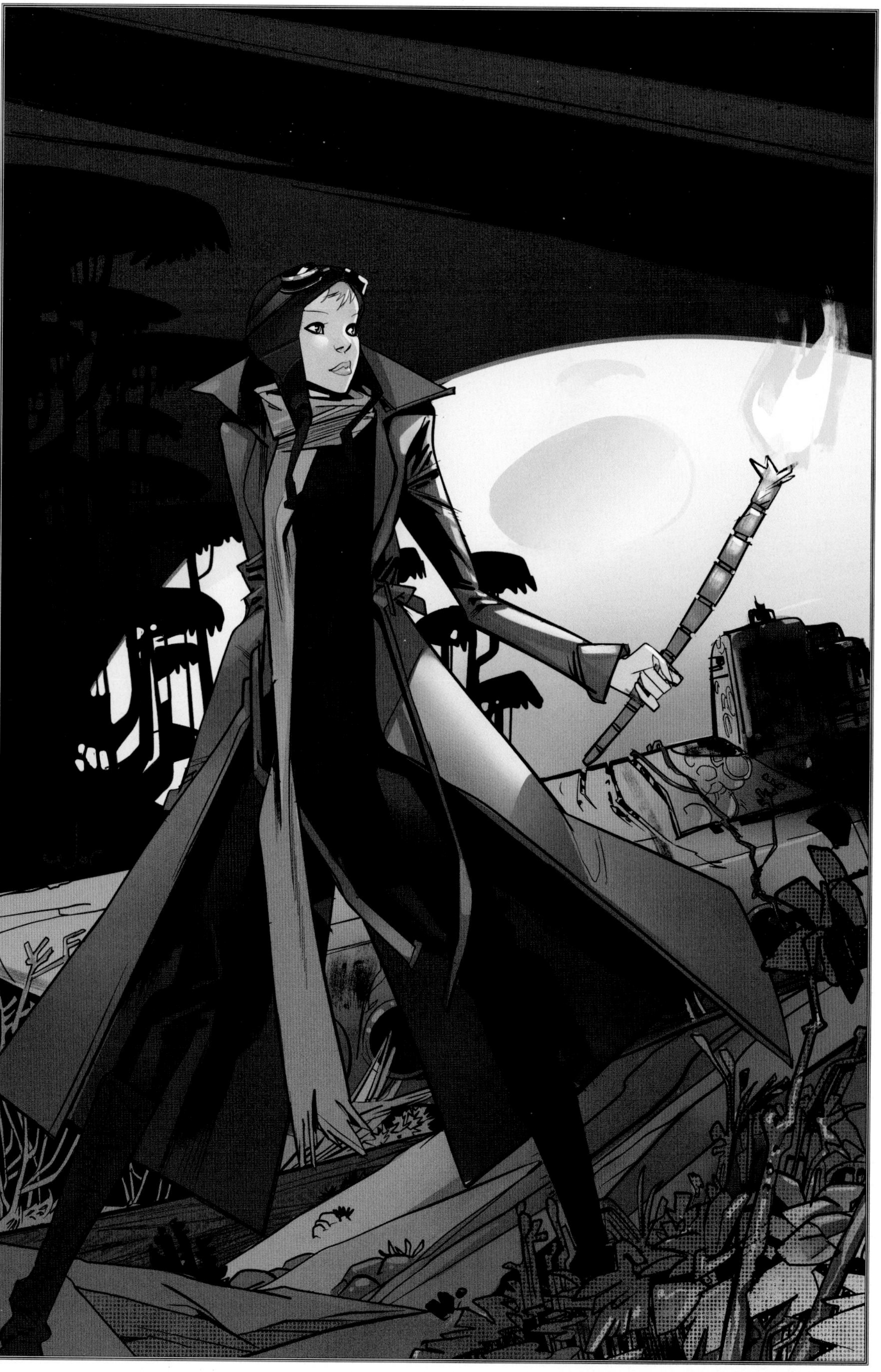

Pinup by Celor — instagram.com/celorart

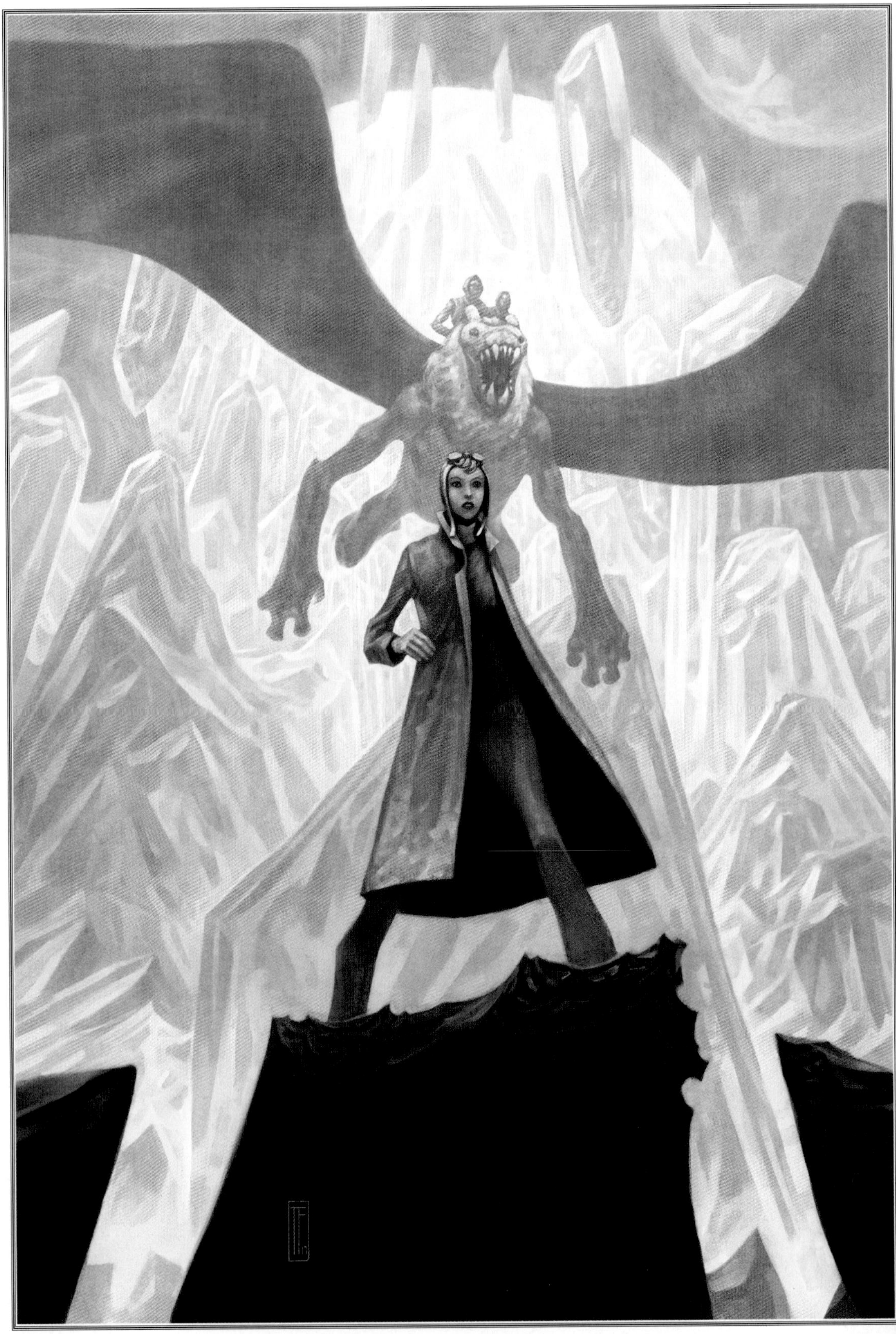

Pinup by Toni Fejzula — tonifejzula.blogspot.com

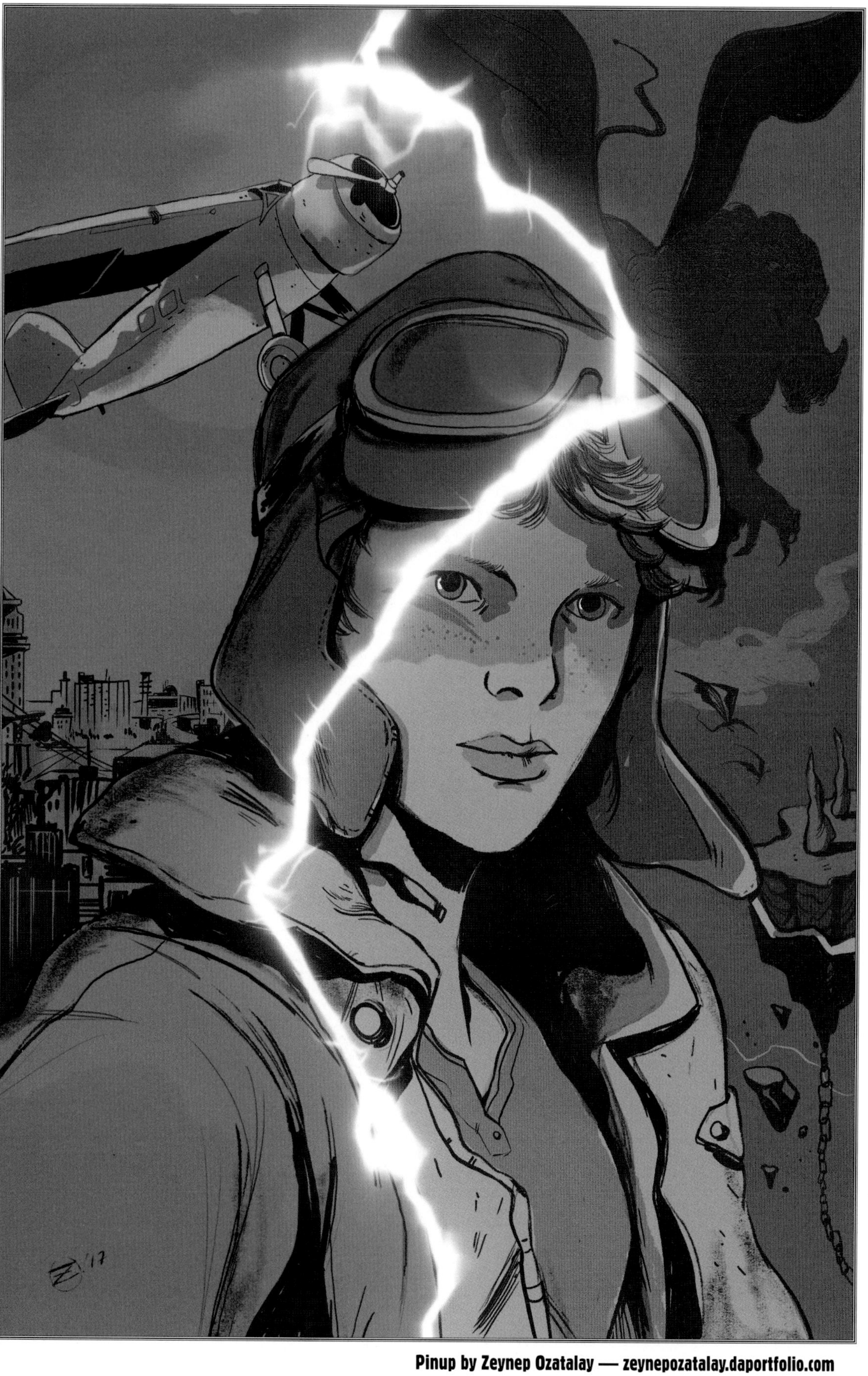

Pinup by Zeynep Ozatalay — zeynepozatalay.daportfolio.com

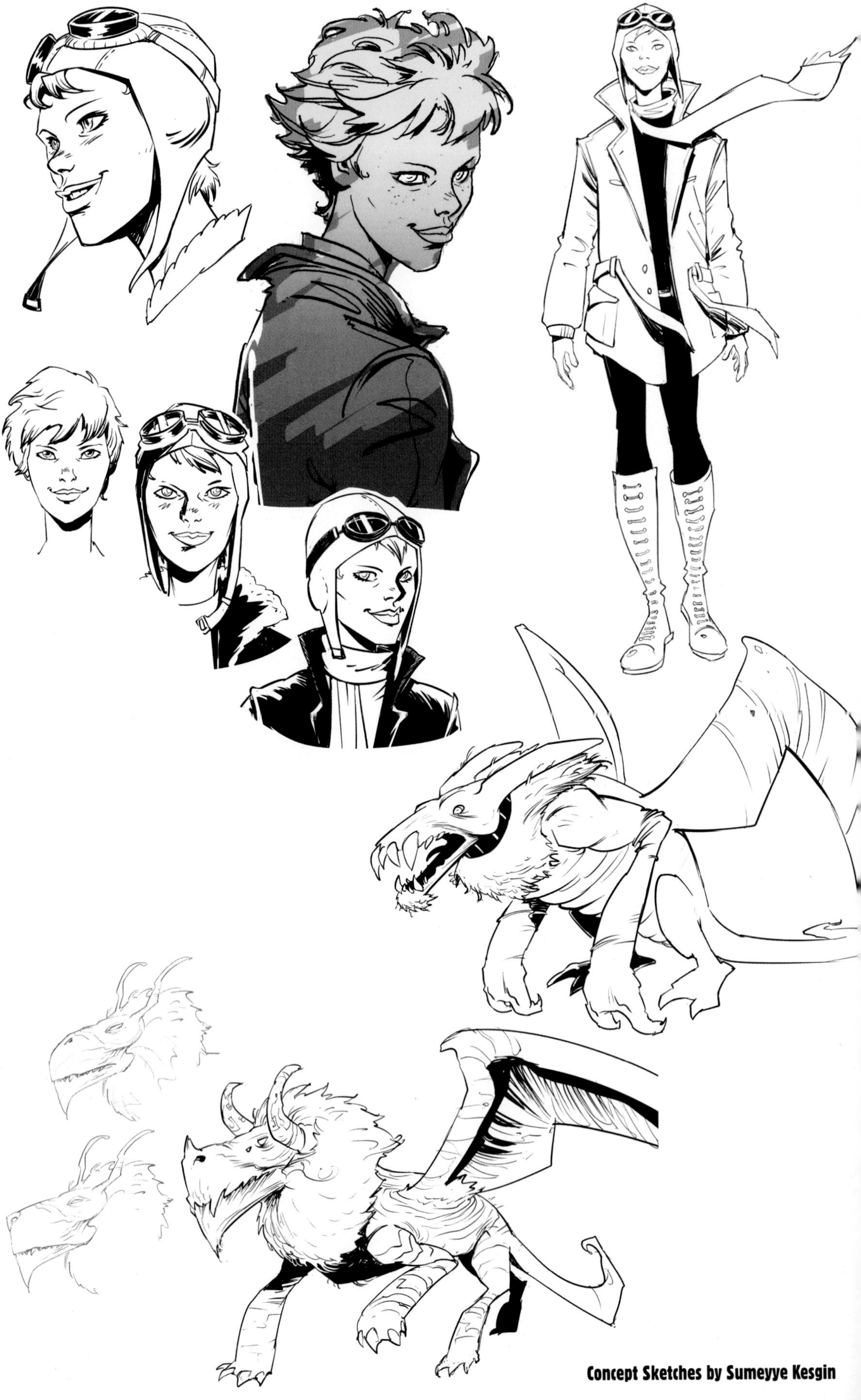

Concept Sketches by Sumeyye Kesgin

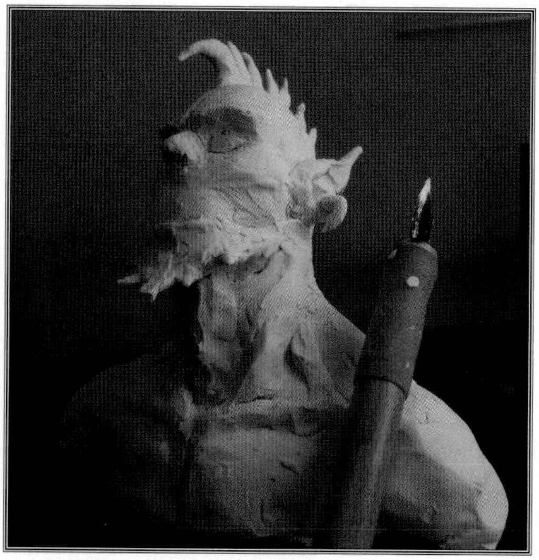

Sumeyye's clay model of Cort

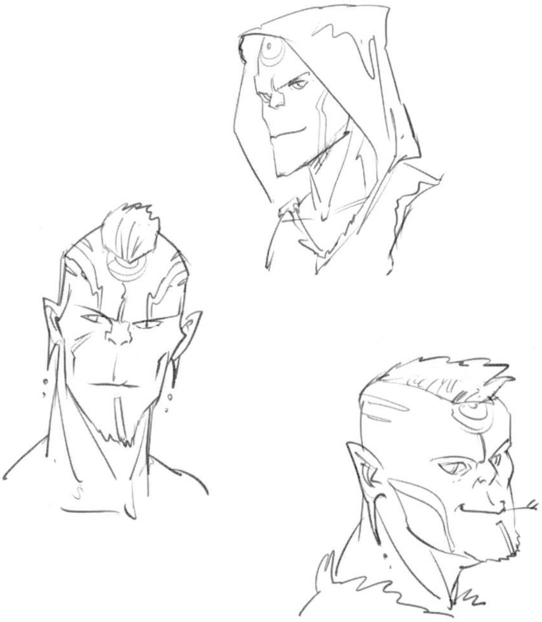

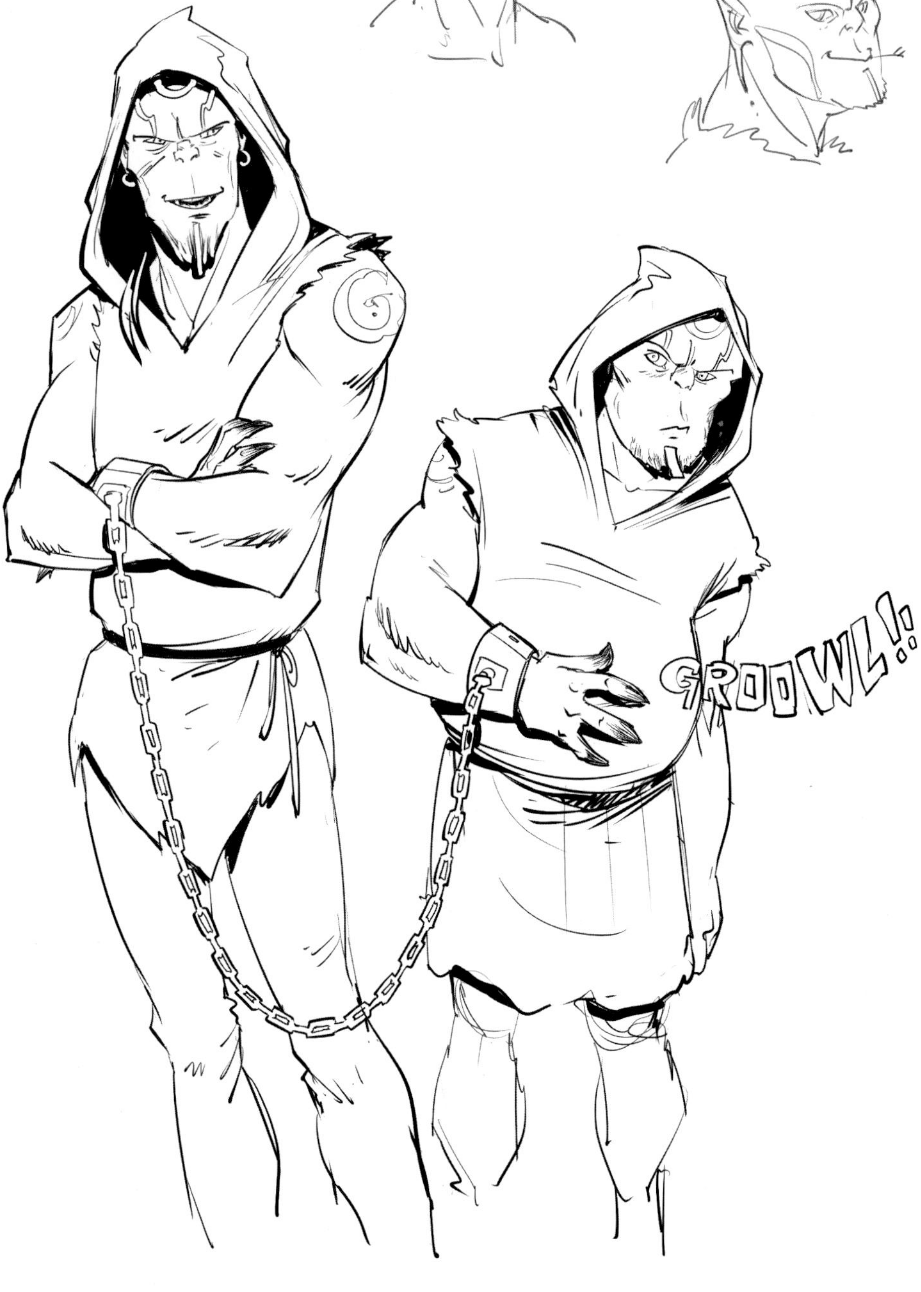
GROOWL!!

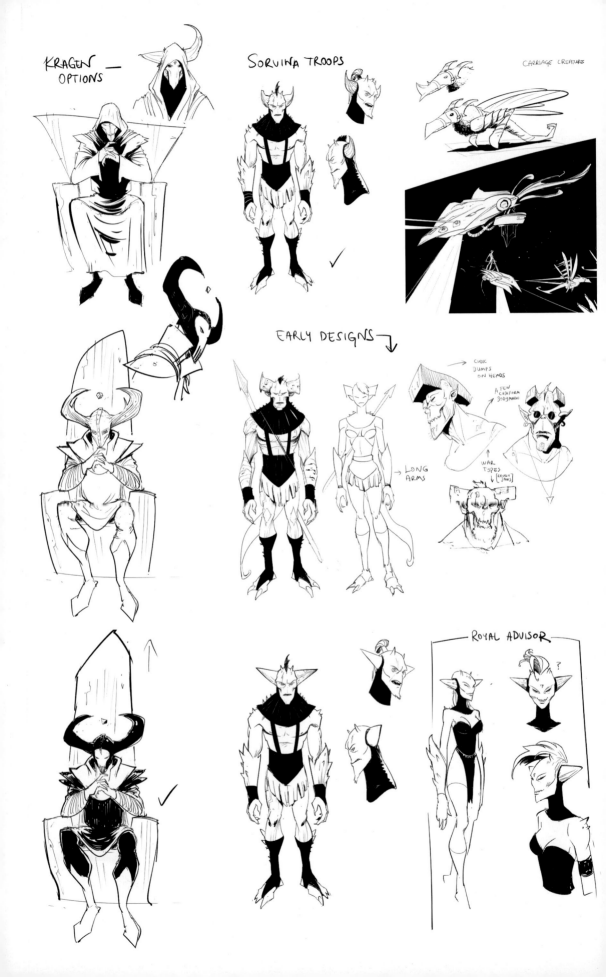

KRAGEN —
OPTIONS

SORVINA TROOPS

CARRIAGE CREATURE

EARLY DESIGNS

CUBIC
BUMPS
ON HEADS

A FEW
CUNIFORM
BODYMARKS

LONG
ARMS

WAR
TYPES
[ROUGH
JAWS]

ROYAL ADVISOR

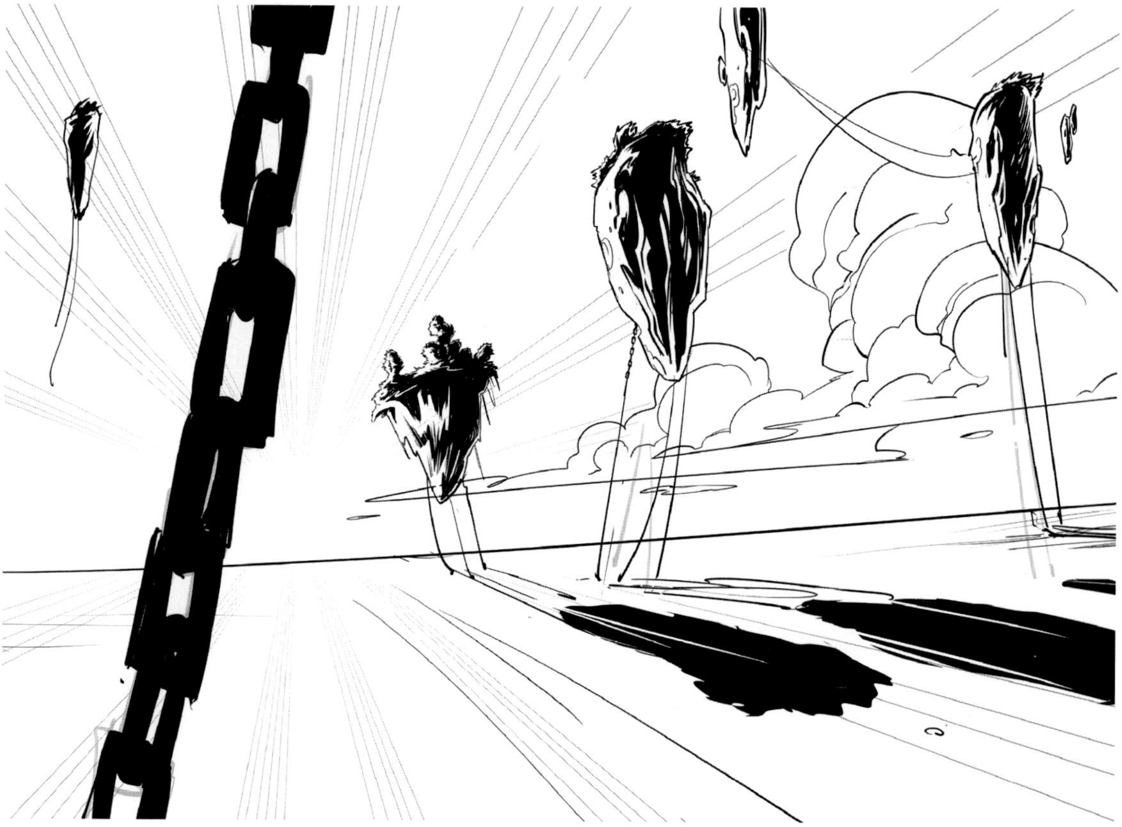

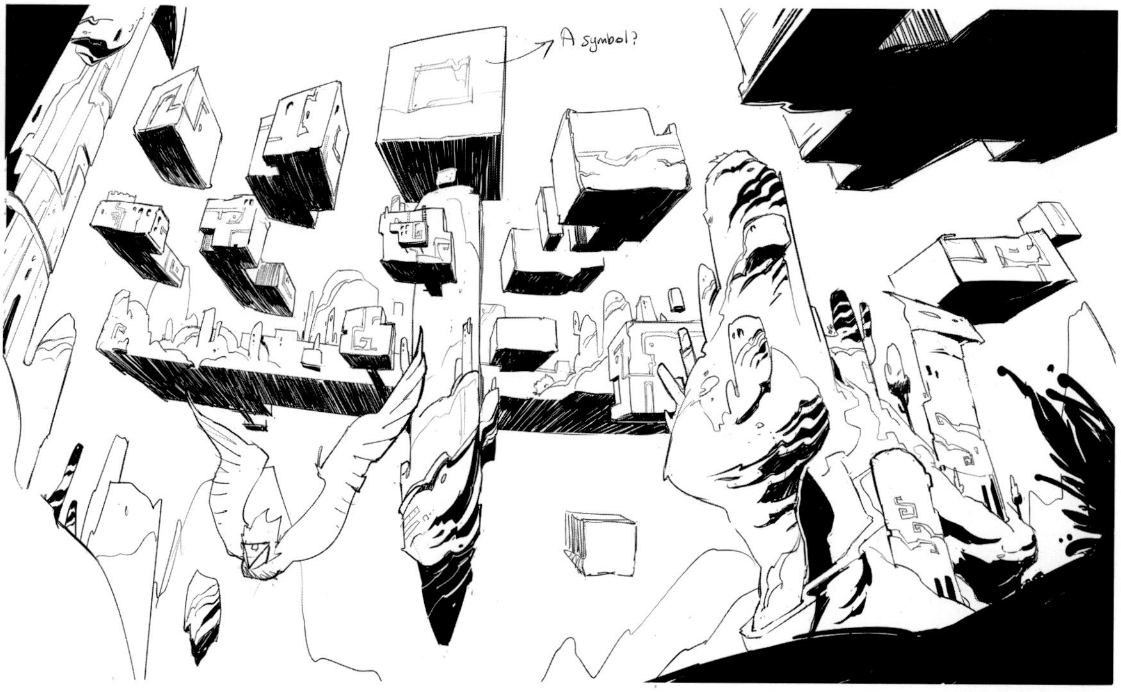
A symbol?

ABOUT THE CREATORS

Jay Faerber was born in Harvey's Lake, PA and got his start at Marvel and DC Comics in the late 1990s, where he worked on such series as THE TITANS, NEW WARRIORS, and GENERATION X. In 2001, he launched NOBLE CAUSES, his first creator-owned series, at Image Comics, which has gone on to garner much critical acclaim. Since then, Faerber has carved out a niche for himself, co-creating DYNAMO 5, NEAR DEATH, POINT OF IMPACT, SECRET IDENTITIES, GRAVEYARD SHIFT, ELSEWHERE, and COPPERHEAD. He also writes for television, most recently on the CBS series ZOO. He lives in Burbank, with his wife, son, dog, and cat. He really loves the Pacific Northwest and 80s television. You can follow him on Twitter @JayFaerber.

Sumeyye Kesgin is a freelance comic artist who lives in the chaotic city of Istanbul. She has worked on Turkey-based comics projects and Top Cow Productions' RISE OF THE MAGI and SEPTEMBER MOURNING. She loves cycling and has an army of stray cats. Her skills do not include writing her own bio. You can find her on Twitter @sumeyyekesgin1 and Instagram @kesgin1.

Ron Riley started off colouring Robert Kirkman's TECH JACKET (which is still kicking butt at Image Comics with an all new creative team), then soon after joined the creative team of Mr. Faerber's then-relaunched NOBLE CAUSES. Ron has been Jay's frequent colouring collaborator ever since, most recently on COPPERHEAD. Ron's also been the colour artist on numerous other titles, like ROB ZOMBIE'S SPOOKSHOW INTERNATIONAL, BOOM! Studio's HERO SQUARED and TALENT, among others. Don't follow him on Twitter @thatronriley...unless you're one hip cat.

Thomas Mauer has lent his lettering and design talent to Harvey and Eisner Award nominated and winning titles including Image's POPGUN anthologies and Dark Horse Comics' THE GUNS OF SHADOW VALLEY. Among his recent work are Black Mask Studios' 4 KIDS WALK INTO A BANK, Image Comics' ELSEWHERE, THE BEAUTY, and THE REALM, as well as Amazon Studios' NIKO AND THE SWORD OF LIGHT, and the World Food Programme's LIVING LEVEL-3 series. You can follow him on Twitter @thomasmauer.

Frank Pittarese has been in the comics industry for over 25 years. He's been an editor at DC and Marvel Comics, where he worked on such titles as SUPERBOY and GENERATION X (written at the time by Jay Faerber himself), and was also an editor and writer at *Nickelodeon Magazine*, overseeing the adventures of *SpongeBob SquarePants*. He's currently developing new projects for *Inner Station*, a soon-to-launch comic book publisher. Frank lives in Brooklyn, NY, with his husband and the latest in an ongoing series of hamsters.

COPPERHEAD writer **Jay Faerber** teams up with the stunning art team of **Sumeyye Kesgin** and **Ron Riley** to reveal the truth about what really happened to Amelia Earhart!

Mysteriously transported to a strange new world filled with flying beasts and alien civilizations, Amelia desperately struggles to return home. Along the way she forges alliances and makes enemies, as she goes from aviator to freedom fighter in a rebellion against a merciless warlord!

> "Get lost in this other world and you'll be in the best company."
> —Kieron Gillen (*The Wicked + The Divine*)

> "...a nice hybrid of *Tarzan* and *John Carter* with a lot of potential adventure hooks and a legitimately jaw-dropping final moment."
> —Major Spoilers

Collects issues #1–4

IMAGECOMICS.COM

$9.99 USD

ISBN: 978-1-5343-0469-7
Action/Fantasy

50999

9 781534 304697

RATED **T** / TEEN